Valda Marshall is a former journalist and TV writer who has worked in Sydney, Toronto (Canada), and New York. Her television writing credits include *Neighbours*, *Sons and Daughters*, *Richmond Hill*, and *Home Sweet Home* (ABC).

While with *Neighbours* she co-authored two books based on the Ramsay Street families: *The Ramsays: A Family Divided* and *The Robinsons: A Family in Crisis*.

Valda was born in Adelaide and now lives in Sydney. She is a committed republican and voted *Yes* in the 1999 referendum.

The First President

Presidet

An Australian story of love and politics

VALDA MARSHALL

The First President

By Valda Marshall

Published by JoJo Publishing

'Yarra's Edge'
2203/80 Lorimer Street
Docklands VIC 3008
Australia

Email: jo-media@bigpond.net.au or visit www.jojopublishing.com

National Library of Australia
Cataloguing-in-Publication data
            Marshall, Valda
            The First President

        ISBN 9780980556438 (pbk.)

    A823.3

Designer / typesetter: Rob Ryan @ Z Design Media
Printed in China by Everbest Printing

Author acknowledgments

I would like to acknowledge the following publications as helpful to my research for *The First President*:

The Diaries of Lord Louis Mountbatten 1920–1922, ed. Philip Ziegler, 1987, William Collins, London.

Letters from a Prince: Edward, Prince of Wales to Mrs Freda Dudley Ward, March 1918–January 1921, ed. Ruper Godfrey, Little Brown and Company, London.

King Edward VIII, Philip Ziegler, 1990, William Collins, London.

A King's Story: The Memoirs of the Duke of Windsor, 1998, Prion Books Ltd, London.

The Reluctant Republic, Malcolm Turnbull, 1993, William Heinemann, Melbourne.

Fighting for the Republic, Malcolm Turnbull, 1999, Hardie Grant Books, South Yarra (Vic.)

The Advertiser archives, State Library of South Australia

Edward Prince of Wales was a renowned playboy and lover of beautiful women.

Although most names and official events concerning the 1920 Royal visit to Adelaide are historically correct, Lily's story is a work of fiction.

Noelene Jones and other characters in her story are not based on any real persons, living or dead.

THE HOUSE OF WINDSOR

1840 Victoria, Queen of England marries her cousin Albert

1840 birth of Victoria (Vicky). Marries Frederick, Crown Prince of Germany

1841 birth of Albert Edward, Prince of Wales

1863 Albert marries Alexandra of Denmark

1864 birth of Albert Victor, Duke of Clarence

1865 birth of George, Duke of York

1892 death of Duke of Clarence

1893 Prince George marries Princess May of Teck

1894 birth of Edward, Prince of Wales

1895 birth of Albert, Duke of York

1901 Queen Victoria dies. Albert, Prince of Wales succeeds to the throne as Edward II

1910 Edward VII dies. Prince George succeeds to the throne as George V

1923 Duke of York marries Elizabeth Bowes-Lyon

1926 birth of daughter Elizabeth

1936 George V dies. Prince of Wales succeeds to the throne as Edward VIII

1936 Edward VIII abdicates. Becomes Duke of Windsor. Duke of York succeeds to the throne as George VI.

1947 Elizabeth marries Philip Mountbatten (Duke of Edinburgh)

1948 birth of Charles, Prince of Wales

1952 George VI dies. Elizabeth II succeeds to the throne.

1972 Duke of Windsor dies in Paris

THE HOUSE OF JONES

1866   birth of Jackson Aloysius Jones

1868   birth of Ethel May Smith

1891   Jackson marries Ethel

1892   birth of Samuel

1893   birth of Horace (Horrie)

1895   birth of Arthur

1899   birth of Thomas

1900   birth of Lily

1912   Lily leaves school to care for her sick mother Ethel

1914   Ethel dies

1921   a son (Jack Jones) is born to Lily, father unknown

1923   Lily dies

1924   birth of Charles Barrington (later knighted)

1926   birth of Valmai to Bruce and Sheila Evans

1930   Jackson dies, age 64

1951   Jack Jones marries Valmai Evans

1952   birth of Kevin (stillborn)

1954   birth of Rodney (accidentally drowns in childhood)

1960   birth of Noelene

1977   Jack Jones dies, age 56

1980   Noelene marries Sir Charles Barrington

2001   Sir Charles dies, age 77

2014   Valmai dies, age 88

2016   Noelene retires from career as opera singer

1

2016

The Lodge, Canberra

The Prime Minister was a man of cunning. Rat cunning. It was a skill he'd perfected over long years of public life. So when the subject of Australia becoming a republic came up once again on the public agenda, he decided to tread very carefully.

To be honest, he couldn't give a stuff which way the country went. Royal junkets (you could hardly call them tours) were a goddamn nuisance and cost the country too much time and money. So far as he was concerned, it didn't matter who made the speeches or shook the hands or presented the gongs for service to the nation. It was all window dressing. On the other hand, he was slightly worried that if a popularly elected president replaced the monarch, it might undermine his political authority.

Of course, there was no guarantee a referendum on the republic would be carried. One didn't have to be a rocket scientist to know it would all hinge on how the question was put to the people – the main reason why the last referendum had sunk without a trace 17 years ago.

Decisions. Decisions. As usual when the PM had a major policy to resolve, he consulted his breakfast cabinet.

'So what's the problem?' asked the PM's wife, spreading her buttered toast with Oxford marmalade (she held no truck with this 'Buy Australian' nonsense). She glanced at her watch. 'I can give you exactly five minutes before I leave for the office.'

The PM prided himself on being a New Age Man, sensitive to the needs of today's working wife. He believed in sharing domestic chores, and when the Lodge housekeeper was off duty, did his bit by pushing all the right buttons on the dishwasher. He'd only got it wrong once.

Both were lawyers and had met in a courtroom on opposite sides of an industrial conflict, a tricky case involving guard dogs and maritime workers. She now had a successful practice in Canberra specialising in marital and property disputes ... a lucrative field in a city where personal relationships broke up faster than snow under sunshine.

She was in her prime as a woman – mid-forties, elegant, good looking, with a mind as sharp as a tack ('the brains of a man' as the PM put it). In a good year, or even an ordinary one, she earned more than he did. He liked to think of them as Canberra's power couple.

'I'm trying to decide the right wording for the referendum,' he said.

'You mean, you don't want it buggered up again.'

She was right, of course. Spot on, as usual.

It was just before he'd entered politics, but he remembered it well. The 1999 referendum had been a botched affair with a question no one understood, a preamble no one wanted, and a republican movement that had shot itself in the foot because its members couldn't agree on how to choose a president.

When his party had won power, one of the planks of his platform was a promise to hold a plebiscite on Australia becoming a republic, followed by a referendum. As a politician he prided himself on being forward looking, moving with the times, sensitive to social change, and at the same time 'not neglecting the traditional core values which have served us so well in the past'.

It was a phrase he was fond of using. It was a fine line to follow, keeping a finger on the pulse of the mums and dads. Not always easy, this political balancing act of trying to sit on two chairs at the same time. But there was no one better equipped to do it.

There was another reason to dip a toe in the waters of public opinion and test it. If Australians decided they no longer wanted a monarchy (and all the public opinion polls seem to be pointing in that direction) he would go down in history as the man who made it possible. He liked the idea of wide-eyed little children being questioned by teachers in classrooms ('Hands up who knows the name of the Prime Minister responsible for Australia becoming a republic. Yes, little Johnny in the back row?'). It was an enticing thought. An exciting one. It would be the pinnacle of a brilliant career.

So a plebiscite had been held asking the Australian people to approve a change to the Constitution. It had been carefully designed to achieve the right result. No mention of the Queen. Not a word about the monarchy. Nothing that could offend the mums and dads. It was a masterpiece of manipulation. And the overwhelming answer (78% across all States and Territories) had been 'Yes'. Now, as promised, it was to be followed by a referendum.

'The question is,' said the Prime Minister in his most measured statesmanlike tone, 'What should be the question?'

'Keep it simple. Republic: yes or no?'

'Thank you,' said the Prime Minister. 'Good suggestion. Excellent thinking. I'll bear that in mind. The problem is that there are certain words the public doesn't respond well to, and "republic" is one of them – although it's hard to see how to entirely avoid it. And "president", that's another tricky one. No matter what way you say it, somehow it tends to sound a bit authoritarian. People think of a president as some kind of dictator ...' quickly adding, '... with all due respect, of course, to our good friend and partner the United States'.

The PM's wife looked at her watch again.

'So?'

'What I'm after is something that will combine the concept of Australia as an independent, democratic and self-governing nation free of the traditional constraints of the monarchy, able to control its own destiny, a nation that gives equal rights and opportunity to all its citizens regardless of sex, race or religion, to aspire to the highest role in the country, at the same time paying due tribute to the rich tapestry of our British heritage and history and a system that has served us faithfully and well over the years.' The PM was at his longwinded best.

'How about: Are you in favour of an Australian as Head of State?'

It was like a vote for motherhood.

'Perfect.'

On the same day the Prime Minister was deciding on the wording of the referendum, the internationally acclaimed Australian opera star, Noelene Jones, was sitting in her Sydney apartment, planning her future.

She had been advised early in her career to change her name to something Italian with an 'a' or an 'o' at the end of it. 'Jones' was a bit, well, *ordinary*, they'd said. And 'Noelene', like its close cousins Charlene, Raeleen, and Joylene, was too ocker … all right for a TV soapie star but not for a prima donna. But she'd refused, saying Noelene Jones was the name she'd been born with, and she was sticking to it.

She was 55 (turning 56 on Christmas Day), and had decided it was time to retire gracefully. Her farewell concert was to be staged outdoors in the Barossa valley of South Australia. It had been a good life, a long and successful career, which had seen her celebrated around the world. At another time in another country she'd have been made a Dame. But she was a modest woman, not given to pomp and ceremony, and was more than happy with the Australian honours that had been heaped upon her.

Making the decision to retire hadn't been an easy one. She loved singing, it was her whole life, and she was still at the peak of her musical abilities. But she didn't want to be another Nellie Melba, lingering on with a string of farewells. She'd seen too many who'd kept on singing long after their voices had given out. She remembered an American who'd been booed off the stage when it was clear she could no longer hit the high notes – a humiliating experience and one she didn't wish to follow. Unlike conductors who could go well into their seventies, singers had a limited shelf life. Noelene didn't want to be forced out. She wanted to do it at a time of her own choosing. And the right time was now.

So here she was, relaxed and comfortable in an armchair, working out what she'd do once that last concert was over. There'd be the occasional appearance for charity, of course.

Volunteer work. Teaching. She liked the idea of discovering new talent; guiding some young person to aspire to greater things in the same way she'd once been encouraged.

She had in mind establishing a singing scholarship. She was a wealthy woman, partly by her own success and also from an inheritance left by her late businessman husband. She'd done all the overseas travelling she wanted. Expensive jewellery didn't interest her. She lived on her own, simply and without extravagance. Her plan now was to use her money to try and repay what her singing career had given her over the years. She felt she owed music a giant debt.

Noelene took out a piece of paper and began to write down a few of the ideas she had that might help young people struggling to achieve musical success. It didn't have to be limited to singers. Budding composers could be encouraged. Librettists. Instrumentalists.

She would be generous with her financial support, as she had no one else to leave it to. Maybe she would name it the Jack Jones Foundation, in memory of her father?

The concept was dazzling, the possibilities endless. Little did Noelene know, as she plotted and dreamed and made notes of her future plans, that her life was about to move in a very unexpected direction.

2

1920

Lily was in the front garden weeding around the rose bushes when the call came. It was delivered by a boy on a bicycle – a note from one of her employers, Mrs Lyle Cavendish, who lived in the House on the Hill. The note was brief: *Dear Lily. Can you come and see me as soon as possible? The matter is extremely urgent.*

If the House on the Hill had another name, Lily had long forgotten it. An imposing brick and bluestone mansion in the Adelaide Hills, surrounded by English-style formal gardens, it was one of the private homes where Lily would regularly be summoned to help out when there were house guests or an important dinner party. Lily's domestic services were highly prized, as she had a reputation for being honest, hardworking and discreet.

As she climbed the hill to the house, Lily wondered idly about the urgency of the note. It didn't take long to find out. Almost as soon as she was ushered into the drawing room with its antiques, red velvet drapes, and family portraits, Mrs Cavendish asked an astonishing question.

'Lily, my dear,' she said. 'How would you like to work for the Prince of Wales?'

Lily was stunned. The Prince of Wales? To her, the Prince was a remote, boyish figure seen occasionally in the newspapers, the eldest son of King George and Queen Mary, someone so inaccessible and beyond her small world as to be akin to a god. And yet here was Mrs Cavendish asking if she'd like to work for him!

As she stood there, unsure how to respond, twisting her hands together with nervousness, Mrs Cavendish explained. The Prince was about to start the South Australian leg of his royal tour, and would be arriving in three days to stay at Government House as the guest of Sir Archibald and Lady Weigall. Sir Archibald (popularly known as 'Archie') was the recently appointed Governor, and his Aide-de-Camp, Captain Hewitt, was married to a sister of Mrs Cavendish.

Apparently something had gone wrong at the last minute with arrangements for additional domestic staff to cover the Prince's visit. Mrs Cavendish wasn't sure what – she thought it might have been illness – but it meant a housemaid was needed in a hurry. Her sister had mentioned it to Mrs Cavendish, who had immediately thought of Lily. It went without saying that any staff hired must have impeccable references and be completely trustworthy. No gossiping in the butler's pantry, no frivolous behaviour, and the work hours could be long depending on the Prince's official program.

A uniform would be supplied, and she would be under the personal supervision of the vice-regal housekeeper. If Lily took the job she would, of course, be required to live in. But it would be a great honour, an opportunity of a lifetime. So what did Lily think?

Lily didn't hesitate. 'Thank you, ma'am,' she said. 'If you think I'm good enough, I'd be happy to take the job. Thank you very much for recommending me. I promise I won't let you down.' She paused a moment. 'Of course I'd have to get my father's permission. But I'm sure he won't mind.'

Mrs Cavendish was well aware Lily had been looking after her father and four brothers since her mother died six years ago. When her mother took sick, Lily had left school at the age of twelve and had willingly taken on the cooking and cleaning and other household chores.

Her brothers all worked in the district, but her father's health had deteriorated since his wife's death and he now spent most of his days at home. Still, Mrs Cavendish was sure they could cope without Lily for such a short time.

'I'll speak to your father if there are any problems,' she offered. 'If he has no objection – and I can't see why he would – pack your things and be here at seven in the morning. James is driving to the city to pick up some parcels for me, and can take you as a passenger. That'll save you the expense of taking the train. He'll drop you off at Government House with a note to Captain Hewitt.'

Lily was expecting to be dismissed and shown off the premises by one of the domestics. But Mrs Cavendish unexpectedly walked her to the front door, just as though she were a guest and not a servant.

'Don't forget to curtsy if you meet the Prince. Not too low so you'll overbalance – just a bend of the knee is fine. Keep your head down and remember, never speak to royalty until you're spoken to. Always keep in mind he's the King's son. But I'm sure they'll give you the proper instructions when you get there.'

She smiled warmly and held out a hand. 'Good luck, Lily,' she said. 'I know you'll do us all credit.'

Her father raised no objection. To be asked by one of the landed gentry, the Cavendish family, to go into service at Government House, was an honour beyond his wildest imagination. It was like a royal summons direct from Buckingham Palace.

Jack Jones had been born in l866 when Queen Victoria had already been on the Throne for 29 years, and he'd lived through the reigns of two more monarchs, King Edward VII and now George V.

When war broke out in l914, his two eldest sons, Samuel and Horace, had both answered the call for young Australians to volunteer in the service of the Empire. Sam, to his bitter disappointment, had been turned down because of poor eyesight. But Horrie had sailed away in his thick, rough khaki uniform, and acquitted himself well in the stinking mud and trenches of the Western Front.

He'd copped some Hun shrapnel in one leg, been awarded a medal for gallantry, and eventually been shipped home. After he came back he was reluctant to talk of his experiences, beyond a few jokes about 'mademoiselle from Armentieres' and 'inky pinky par-lay voo.' On the serious things he was strangely quiet, saying it was all best forgotten. But a brass shell fashioned into an ashtray, sitting on the mantelpiece over the open fireplace, was a permanent and silent reminder.

Lily's father Jack was a simple man. Not stupid, but clear and uncluttered in his basic beliefs. God, King and Country were the guiding principles on which he had built his life. He regarded whoever was on the throne as there by divine right, and to question such things was close to blasphemy.

In the Jones household grace was said before every meal, they all went to church on Sundays, and the front page of a large leather-bound Bible, given to Jack and his wife Ethel as a wedding gift, recorded the family's births and deaths.

So when Lily told her father of Mrs Cavendish's request, his only reaction was one of enormous pride. 'Of course you must go,' he said. 'Your brothers and I can manage without you. It will be a wonderful experience, and your first visit to the city. I only wish your dear mother could be here to see it.' He cast his eyes heavenward. 'But I know she'll be looking after you.'

What to pack? Lily's wardrobe was minimal, mostly dresses and pinafores she wore around the house, some stout walking shoes, black patent leather for church, and two hats: one for everyday and one for Sunday best. But would they be up to the standard of what was required at Government House? Mrs Cavendish had mentioned a uniform, so that solved the problem of what to wear while at work. But there would be off duty periods, and she didn't want to look like a country bumpkin in front of the other domestic staff.

In the end she decided to take the blue silk she wore on Sundays, a pair of work shoes, the patent leather, and a flowered cotton dress. She was a good sewer, and with her mother's old treadle machine made all her own clothes, right down to her underwear.

Lily packed everything into the one battered suitcase the family owned, then went to the kitchen to prepare dinner. Her four brothers were already sitting around the wooden dining table with its kerosene lamp. And it was soon clear her father had passed on the news.

'So … you're leaving us for a bunch of nobs,' said Sam. 'Watch your step, girl. I've heard a few stories about them upper-class Poms.'

'I'm sure Lily can look after herself,' said Horrie. 'Anyway, she'll be too busy for any larking around. Good on you, sis.' The two younger brothers, Arthur and Thomas, didn't say anything. But she could tell by the looks on their faces that they were pleased with the news.

'I want one of you to walk Lily to the Hill tomorrow morning and carry her case for her,' said Lily's father. 'Six-thirty sharp. Which one of you's it going to be?'

'I'll go,' said Thomas. 'It's on my way to work.' He was fifteen months older than Lily and had a job in a local market garden. As well as in age, Lily felt the closest to him of all her brothers. They'd been only one class apart at school, and he'd once punched up an older boy who'd dared to make a pass at Lily.

Even as a young girl she'd been the reigning beauty of the one teacher school they both attended; a magnet for all the young lads pushing puberty and flexing male hormones. And now as an adult her looks were even more remarkable. 'Stunning' was the word for Lily.

Raven black hair worn long over the shoulders when other young women were cutting theirs into the fashionable flapper short bob; green-blue eyes, a flawless complexion, and a waist so tiny a man could fit his two hands around it. She was like a china doll, no more than five feet tall, but as her father was fond of saying: 'Good things come in small parcels, love'.

When Lily walked down the street, heads turned. But she kept to herself, discouraged any romantic overtures, and had never shown the slightest interest in anyone of the opposite sex. Her entire world was her home and family, and she loved her father and brothers as passionately as they were devoted to her.

Dinner that night was unusually subdued. Her father broke the silence once to ask Lily if she needed some ready cash to take with her to the city. When she told him what she had, he took out his wallet and pressed a one pound note into her hand, 'Just in case'. Sam asked what she'd say if the Prince of Wales spoke to her, and Lily said that would depend on what he said. And yes, she'd remember to curtsy. Beyond that there wasn't much conversation other than 'Pass the butter' and 'Does anyone want another slice of bread?'

Meal times for the Jones family weren't regarded as social occasions. It was more a case of serve, eat, and clear the table. Lily would then wash the dishes and pots while the five men sat around the fireplace and talked or read.

The lean-to back verandah, with its fuel stove, served as the kitchen. It had a scrubbed pine table with a large metal pan used for everything from washing dishes to plucking chickens or gutting rabbits. According to family lore, it was the same pan used to bathe Lily as a small child.

There was a cool safe for storing butter and milk, its sides hung with damp hessian; a small cupboard for dry goods, and a bench for sharpening and polishing knives. At the door leading into the dining room was a bucket of water and a towel. When the boys came in from work they were expected to take off their boots, scrape off the mud, and wash their hands. If they forgot, Lily, small as she was, would hustle them back outside and ask where they thought they'd been brought up, in a tent? She was exactly like her mother.

Now, as she washed and dried the dishes, she wondered who would look after the domestic chores while she was away. Would it be Tom, the youngest of the boys? Or would they all take turns, like they did in the last stages of her mother's illness, just before she went to the hospital and died. Well, it would only be for a short time. What had Mrs Cavendish said? The Prince would be arriving on Monday and leaving the following Friday. They could manage without her for a week.

Lily looked up at the stars and for some reason thought of her mother. What was it her father had said? 'She'll be looking after you.' A strange thing for him to say, as he rarely mentioned her these days. After all, it had been six years since she'd gone. But he'd kept all her toiletries on the dressing table exactly as she'd left them: the jar of cream she used to smooth and massage into her face before going to bed; the sweet scent of lavender water; the petit point set of hand mirror, comb and brush. If you looked close enough, there was even a strand of her mother's chestnut brown hair still caught in the prongs of the comb.

Just before she went to sleep, her father came in to say goodnight. He leaned down and kissed her gently on the forehead, and she caught that old familiar smell of tweed, sweat and tobacco. 'You're a good girl, Lily,' he said. 'God bless and look after you.'

3

As the Prime Minister was setting up the machinery for the referendum, Noelene was at home in Sydney arranging red roses in a vase. There was a buzz from the security entrance, and a pleasant male voice announced himself.

'Sorry I'm a bit late,' said the voice. 'Engine trouble. Broke down on the freeway.'

With a quick glance at her watch Noelene realised this must be the freelance producer who'd been commissioned to make a TV documentary on her life. She'd almost forgotten the appointment.

'Come on up,' she said. 'First to the right when you step out of the elevator.' Moments later she was opening the door to Mike Warner.

Between handshakes they sized each other up. She saw a solidly built, bearded man in a black turtleneck skivvy, corduroy trousers so well worn they were almost shiny, and a pair of slightly grubby sneakers. A crumpled face that was halfway between handsome and ugly. Piercing blue eyes and a small white mark like a fencing scar on the right cheek. Age? At a guess, mid-forties, she thought. He saw a tall, statuesque, handsome woman with reddish-brown hair, pale, creamy skin, and a figure that was amazingly slim considering her big voice.

Well prima donnas now had to look like supermodels, didn't they? The days of waiting for the fat lady to sing were long gone. 'Please come in,' she said. 'Make yourself at home.' Her voice was deep and husky, almost seductive.

The 90-minute program, commissioned by Friends of the Opera with some financial assistance from the government, was to be a tribute to her long and distinguished career. Its working title, Mike told her as he set up his tape recorder and notebook on a coffee table, was *Noelene Jones: a Life of Song*. He caught her look and quickly added, 'A bit banal, I know. Don't worry, it'll probably change a few times before we finally go to air.'

'So where do we start?'

'Let's start from the beginning. Parents?'

'Jack and Valmai. Dad was named after his grandfather, Jackson Aloysius Jones.' She pulled a face. 'Bit of a mouthful, isn't it? Jackson's an old family name, it goes back generations, but I haven't a clue where they got Aloysius.'

'Jones. Does that suggest a Welsh background?'

'Possibly. Dad never mentioned it.'

'Only child?'

'There was another. Two, actually. A boy, Kevin, was stillborn the year after my parents married. Two years later they had Rodney, but he died in a drowning accident while still a toddler. They never talked about it. I guess there were too many sad memories. I think they'd just about given up when I arrived.'

She smiled. 'Third time lucky.'

It was time to switch direction.

'Were your parents musical?'

'God no. Tone deaf, both of them. Couldn't hold a tune to save herself, my mother used to say. Dad was a bank clerk, and they met when he was transferred to the country. First week there, he landed in hospital with appendicitis. Mum was his nurse ... love among the bedpans.'

She's got a sense of humour, Mike told himself, as he adjusted the recorder and scribbled down some notes. That's going to make things easier.

'So if they weren't musical, how did you get into singing?'

'Eleanor Redshaw. My school teacher in Year Six. She told my parents she thought I should have singing lessons. Even offered to pay for them, that's the kind of person she was.

'I'd starred in a couple of school concerts, and to be honest I was a bit of a show-off. I could sing louder than anyone else, so they always put me in the front row. Also, I had perfect pitch and could sing anything once it'd been played to me.

'Anyway, Miss Redshaw thought my voice was worth training, so one day when my mother was picking me up from school, she talked to her about it. I started lessons with a Russian woman by the name of Madam Vladinov. Very imposing, a bit intimidating, especially for me as an 11-year-old, but she knew all about the human voice and how it worked, and that's what I needed. I think if I'd gone on singing the way I was, belting it out with no idea what I was doing, my voice would been have ruined in a few years. So she probably saved it.'

'What happened then?'

'Madam started putting me into singing competitions and eisteddfods. Her theory was it was the best way to test young singers – throw them into some tough competition and let them sink or swim. I was pretty nervous at first, but it taught me a lot about presentation and confidence. Singing before a critical audience ... well, a bit more critical than my parents or a roomful of classmates.'

'So you swam?'

Noelene smiled at the question.

'I swam. Third in the first competition I entered. Then runner-up. Runner-up again, tied with another soprano, Alexandra Dunhill. You've heard of her? She's now in New York with the Met. And finally the one that really got me started, first and gold medal in the Young Australian Singers competition, plus a chance to audition for an opera company. I was just eighteen at the time, and over the moon. The sad thing was Dad had died the year before, and wasn't around to help us celebrate.'

'Tell me a bit more about your father.'

'There's not much to tell. Country boy, born in South Australia. Orphaned when he was a child, and brought up by his mother's family. Moved to Sydney in his late teens.'

'Marriage,' said Mike consulting his notes. 'You were married very young – at 20. To Sir Charles Barrington.' He paused, uncertain how to phrase the next question. 'I understand he was quite a bit older?' If Mike thought that would throw Noelene, he was wrong.

'Don't pussyfoot around trying to be tactful. It doesn't bother me. Anyway, it's all on public record. Charlie was 56 when we got married, old enough to be my father. It shocked a lot of people.'

'Why?' But he already knew the answer to that one.

'It's obvious, isn't it? Young ambitious singer marries wealthy businessman to further her career. Well that's what everybody thought at the time. And they were wrong. I loved Charlie ... adored him. Being married to him was the happiest time of my life.'

She paused and closed her eyes, and Mike had the feeling he'd lost her to some other time, somewhere way back in the past. Then she opened her eyes and spoke again.

'Would you like to know how we met? Charlie was a widower. His wife had died of cancer, no children. I was in the opera chorus, and he was one of the company's sponsors. He used to come to the rehearsals, and we bumped into each other as I was on my way back to the dressing room. Literally. We were both in a hurry, he knocked me off my feet, and I went crashing to the ground. He helped me up, of course, apologised ... and then asked me out to dinner. Charlie always said our meeting like that was fate.'

Still Mike persevered. 'But it must've helped your career ... marrying all that money?'

'Of course it did. For one thing, I didn't have to work my guts out taking casual jobs to keep going. Goodbye to cleaning other people's houses. Goodbye to waitressing. I could finally concentrate on my singing.'

There was that smile again. It was as though someone had turned on a switch to light up the room.

'I was a rotten waitress, anyway. Always spilling things into people's laps. It's a wonder I wasn't fired. First thing Charlie did after our marriage was buy my mother her own home. He was very generous. He bought her a cottage in the small town where she'd grown up. A couple of chooks, a veggie garden. It's all she wanted. She lived there until she died a couple of years ago at 88.'

'Nice man.'

'Nice isn't the word for him. Charlie was wonderful. Kind, thoughtful, the most unselfish person I've ever known. I was heartbroken when he died.'

'Which was ...?' Again he knew the answer, but wanted to hear it from Noelene.

'Fifteen years ago. I was singing in Paris at the time, but

cancelled and came back immediately.'

Mike could still remember the headlines: DEATH OF HIGH PROFILE BUSINESSMAN. OPERA STAR WIFE FLIES HOME. It had been front page news at the time. He made a mental note to research the newspaper files and see if he could pick up anything else. He had a vague memory that the death of Sir Charles, with Noelene as sole beneficiary, had made her the second richest woman in Australia.

'I was really sorry Dad wasn't around long enough to get to know Charlie. They'd have got on well together. They both liked a good argument.'

'About what?'

'Politicians. Ripping people off. The injustices of the social system. Remember, they grew up during the Depression years of the Thirties. Dad told me once he'd never forget seeing men going from door to door selling pencils, begging in the streets, so they could feed their children.

'One of his uncles took him to Adelaide when he was a schoolboy, and he saw families living in tents alongside the river because they had nowhere else to go. Tent City, they called it.

'He felt everyone had a right to work and shouldn't have to fall back on the government for handouts. People queuing up at the butcher and the grocer with their ration books, just to stay alive. Dad felt it was shameful, degrading … an insult to human dignity. He'd get upset, just talking about it.'

Mike was doing some fast mental arithmetic. 'So he was here in Sydney when war broke out. Did it affect him?'

'Meaning, did he join up? Well, he tried. But he had a problem with his feet. One leg was a bit shorter than the other. Not much, but enough to be turned down.

'Anyway, the bank was happy, especially when they started

losing a lot of their staff. It gave Dad a head start – he was promoted to teller at 20.

'Dad stayed with the bank up to the time he died. He
would've been better off if he'd changed jobs, especially after
the war when there was some money around. My mother was
always urging him to do something else. Try your luck, Jack,
she'd say. Give it a go. Don't get stuck in a rut. But he never
wanted to work for anyone else. Some might call it lack of am-
bition. Dad called it loyalty.'

'Sounds like a nice guy.' Mike looked up from his notebook.
'Mind if I fill in with a few bits of trivia?'

'Be my guest.'

'Favourite food?'

'Pasta. Anything Italian.'

'Favourite flower?'

'Red rose.'

'Should've guessed that one,' said Mike with a glance at the
vase on the side table.

'I'm sentimental … they say it's the symbol of love.'

Mike looked up from his notes.

'And is it?'

'Love? Well Charlie never missed making sure there were a
dozen red roses in my dressing room before every concert … so
make what you like of it.'

'Moving on. Favourite piece of music.'

Danny Boy. She caught his look. 'Does that surprise you?'

'It does a bit. I thought you'd pick something from opera.
One of the classics.'

Danny Boy's a classic.' She looked at her watch. 'Look,
I don't want to seem rude, but can we cut this short for now?
I've got a farewell concert coming up, and need a bit of time

to prepare for it.'

'The one in the Barossa?'

'That's the one. I'm looking forward to it.'

'Mind if I come along and film it?'

'Not at all. Check with the organisers so they allot you some space. Here's the phone number.' She scribbled it down on a piece of paper and gave it to him. 'And come backstage afterwards. Let me know what you think of it.'

'I'm sure it'll be wonderful.'

'I hope so.' She paused. 'I'll let you in on a secret. I'm actually feeling nervous. Funny, isn't it? After all these years, you'd think I'd have nerves of steel. But this is my last public performance, and I don't want to let people down.'

Mike packed away his notes and his tape recorder and they shook hands again. He noted her fingers were completely bare of jewellery, not even a wedding ring. They were unusual hands, strong and square and workmanlike, the nails cut short, a strange contrast to the slim elegance of the rest of her. They looked like the hands of someone who wasn't afraid of getting dirty.

And the concert sounded promising. He could think of worse ways to spend a summer evening than among the vineyards, listening to the country's greatest living singer. What was it someone once called her? A national treasure.

As he was getting into his car, an odd thought came to him. Noelene said her great-grandfather's name was Jones. But shouldn't it have been something else when her father was born? Like the name of *his* father? Back in the twenties of the last century it would have been unusual if a woman hung on to the family name once she'd found a husband and married. Curious, that. He made a note to ask her about it next time they met.

When Mike had gone Noelene started to pour herself a glass of wine, then thought better of it. She should be checking her music, exercising her voice, making sure everything was in place for the final appearance. But she felt vaguely restless and disturbed.

Mike's questions had unsettled her, bringing back memories she'd been trying to forget. It was like turning over a rock, exposing its dark underbelly to sun and light, and seeing a myriad of insects scurrying out.

She should be thinking of tomorrow; instead her yesterdays now seemed to be crowding in on her. What was it she'd read somewhere, a quotation from Leonardo Da Vinci?

Men do wrong to lament the flight of time, complaining that it passes too quickly and failing to perceive that its period is sufficiently long; but a good memory, with which nature has endowed us, causes everything that is long past to appear to us to be present.

So was time only relative, no past, present or future, just a continuing stream of consciousness? An interesting thought. And if so, where did Noelene Jones fit into the overall scheme of things?

Charlie would have had an answer, or if not, at least a theory. She missed his guidance, his wisdom, his sensible down-to-earth approach to life.

It was at times like this that the pain of his loss was almost physical, cutting into her with the sharpness of a knife. But Charlie was long gone. Charlie was dead and buried and she was the one still living. Whatever the future held, whatever critical decisions she would have to make, the good and bad calls, the errors, the misjudgements, she was now totally on her own.

It was a lonely thought.

4

Mrs Cavendish's driver let Lily off at the corner of North Terrace and King William Road, where she could see the white building of Government House behind a thick stone fence. There was a uniformed policeman standing guard at the iron gates of the entrance.

'Don't know which way you go in, Lily,' the driver said. 'Better ask the copper there. D'you want a hand with that case?'

Lily said she was fine, she could manage, and walked slowly towards the front. As soon as she drew level with the policeman he stopped Lily and asked her business. She produced the letter Mrs Cavendish had written to Captain Hewitt, and explained she was to be employed as domestic staff.

'That way,' said the policeman, pointing her in another direction. 'You'll see a sign marked DELIVERIES. Ask at the gate, and they'll direct you.'

Lily thanked him and walked around the block until she found the gate at a side entrance. Like the front, it was also guarded by a policeman. Lily explained her mission, and after a phone call to someone inside Government

House, she was ushered through and told to go to the door marked STAFF ENTRANCE. Here she was met by a young man who introduced himself as Sinclair.

He took the letter from Lily, saying Captain Hewitt would be advised she'd arrived, and took her along a corridor to a door marked HOUSEKEEPER. Here he left her, after telling Lily to knock and introduce herself.

'The name's Mrs Druitt,' he said, just before he disappeared.

Mrs Druitt turned out to be an imposing woman in her forties, very large, wearing a striped apron over a black cambric dress. She gave the impression that the last thing she wanted to deal with right now was a nervous servant girl thrust upon her. But her appearance proved to be deceptive. When she spoke, it was in a warm, kindly tone aimed at putting the young woman at ease.

'So you're Lily,' she said. 'Welcome to Government House. We're very happy to have you. As you can imagine, things are a bit hectic at the moment. His Royal Highness is due on Monday, and there's still a lot to do. While he's here, you will be required to work as a housemaid, making sure all the guest rooms are clean, the linen changed daily, and attend to anything else that's needed.

'You will be under my overall supervision, of course. But for everyday duties you will be working with our senior housemaid, Miss Patchett. I'll introduce you to her later, when you're settled in your room. You may also be required to help out at dinner parties. I understand from Captain Hewitt you're experienced in that area?'

Lily agreed that yes, she'd helped out at some of the local homes since she'd left school, adding modestly she wasn't sure if she would be up to the standards required for a vice-regal residence.

'Don't worry,' said Mrs Druitt. 'You'll be shown what to do. I'm told Captain Hewitt's sister-in-law thinks very highly of you, so I'm sure you'll be fine.' She rang a bell and a young girl about Lily's age appeared.

'Sarah, this is Lily,' she said. 'She'll be with us for the duration of the Royal visit. Would you show Lily her room – she'll be sharing with Emma. When she's unpacked, take her along to Miss Patchett.'

'Yes, ma'am,' said Sarah, bobbing her head and bending a knee. Did one curtsy to housekeepers as well as princes? Lily wondered. Mrs Druitt put out a hand to Lily. 'I hope you'll be happy with us,' she said. 'Come and see me if there's any problem.' Then turning back to her desk and taking up a pen to write in a large leather-bound book, she abruptly dismissed the two.

Lily followed Sarah along what seemed like endless corridors, and up and down flights of stairs, to the wing that housed the domestic staff. She opened a door and ushered Lily into the room that would be hers for the next week.

It was small and sparsely furnished, two single iron beds, a wooden wardrobe, and a wash stand with a door concealing a chamber pot. One lonely vase, empty of flowers. There were no pictures or ornaments. Nothing personal, not even a family snapshot to help build up a picture of what the unknown Emma might be like. But the curtains were pretty, in a rose-patterned cretonne. And through the window Lily caught a glimpse of green trees and gardens outside. It was somehow strangely comforting, reminding her of the country landscape she'd left.

'Miss Patchett'll fit you out with a uniform,' said Sarah. She eyed Lily critically. 'Not very big, are you? Oh well, they say good things come in small parcels.' Her father's familiar remark brought a pang of homesickness. But it passed just as quickly, as she put all thoughts of her family out of her mind. There was a job to do, and she was determined to justify Mrs Cavendish's faith in her.

Lily opened her suitcase, and under Sarah's watchful eyes began to unpack the few things she'd brought.

5

The date of the referendum was set for March 30. As soon as it was announced, both republicans and monarchists went gangbusters. The catchcry of the monarchists was the same as it had been for the plebiscite: 'If it ain't broke, don't fix it.' It was beginning to sound like a cracked record. The rally cry of the republicans was 'It's time!', a slogan used successfully 44 years earlier by another prime minister, Gough Whitlam.

Both sides used tactics that could only be described as underhand bordering on sneaky. The monarchists carefully avoided any references to the Queen or her successor-in-waiting, the 68-year-old Prince Charles. The word 'monarchy' was nowhere in their vocabulary; it was as though the word had never existed. The republicans focussed on phrases like 'a strong and independent nation', and 'cutting the umbilical cord' (market research showing that last one to be particularly appealing to women).

Naturally all this campaigning didn't come cheaply. Both sides hired spin doctors to push their product, as well as pouring massive amounts of money into advertising. Posters appeared on telegraph poles; cars carried 'yes' and 'no' stickers; T-shirts with printed slogans sold like hot cakes in the shopping

malls. And talk shows, which often had to scratch around for
decent guests were suddenly flooded with celebrities, all anxious to explain why they would vote one way or the other.

Of course the newspapers swung into action immediately. This was a sales bonanza, and they made the most of it.
Hardly a day went past without an editorial, an informed comment, an in-depth analysis, an opinion piece, or a look behind
the scenes. There was even an article by a religious writer an-
alysing the Divine right of monarchs to rule ('which way would
God vote?').

Social and political commentators had a field day, expen-
sively sought after for their views. Cities and suburbs and country towns were road-tested to work out how the referendum
would go. Market researchers divided voters into groups and
categories (male/female, old/young, rich/poor, married/sin-
gle, tertiary educated/high school dropout) to try and decide
which demographic to focus on. But like most market research,
the results were inconclusive.

It was finally accepted that the result would be one of those
'unpredictables', to be decided on the day depending on the
weather, a reading of the stars, and whether one had rolled out
of bed on the right or wrong side that morning. The smart money was on a win for 'yes'.

Noelene Jones was among those invited to appear on the
popular TV talk show *Talkfest*. She'd already been named by
media commentators as one of a handful of high profile Australians who could be in the running for president, and was the
only woman on the list.

The show was hosted by Daniel (Danno) Littleworth, given to
him as a consolation prize for missing out on the job of prime
time newsreader. The show was sandwiched in between car-

toons and the midday movie and to everyone's surprise, most of all the network chiefs, was proving a cash cow.

Danno was 45 going on 30. And over the Christmas break an amazing transformation had taken place. The bags under his eyes had disappeared, his capped teeth gleamed like two rows of white tombstones, and contact lens replaced spectacles. Danno's once greying hair was now a wondrous thatch of henna red, and his clothes were trendy and cutting edge. He wore a gold chain around his neck, another on one wrist, and his shirt was unbuttoned just low enough to reveal the hair on his chest. The old Danno had been reborn.

Noelene had been phoned by the studio's PR person and asked if she'd mind being interviewed. 'You've been mentioned as a possible first president,' said the PR woman. She had a name that sounded like Holy Shit, but turned out to be Holly Shipp.

'The referendum has stirred up a lot of interest. We thought it would be interesting to get the female perspective.' But Noelene's kneejerk reaction was to refuse. Essentially a private person, she was reluctant to get embroiled in such a hot potato issue. Pushed, she finally said she'd like some time to think about it, promising to give her answer first thing tomorrow.

When Mike phoned to make an appointment for the next interview, she told him about the invitation. To her surprise, he strongly advised against it.

'I know that show and I know Danno,' he said. 'He's a bastard. He'll use you just to get good ratings. I wouldn't trust him as far as I could throw him. Don't do it.'

But Noelene had already made up her mind. She'd slept on it and decided if it would help the republican cause she'd accept the offer. She explained her reasons to a still sceptical Mike.

'Y'know, Australia becoming a republic was one of the

things Charlie and I used to talk about,' she said. 'It was after the 1999 referendum, the one that was lost. The result made him so angry. He felt the whole thing had been handled badly. If that question had been worded differently … well, that's what he believed. He felt the public had been conned.

'He felt even stronger about it than I did, which is funny considering he'd been brought up from childhood to believe in the monarchy. He told me his parents always had a photo of the King and Queen … well it was George V and Mary when he was born … hanging in their living room. He remembered it clearly.

'They were both English and came out as ten pound Poms, so I suppose it was natural for them to believe in King and Empire and all that kind of stuff. A reminder of home … you can't blame them for it. But Charlie felt differently. Charlie felt that as Australians we should stand on our own feet. Get rid of the monarchy and have an Australian as Head of State. And I feel the same way.

'So I thought it through and decided maybe it'd be a good thing if I went on the show. It would give me … what do they call it? A window of opportunity – to explain why we should change. And yes, I know the only reason they've asked me is because I'm a public figure. But that's a good thing too. People know me. Maybe they'll listen to me and take notice. So I've decided to do it. Call it a PR exercise for a good cause. At least it can't do any harm.'

She paused, waiting for Mike's reaction at the other end of the phone. It was a few moments coming. Then …

'Put like that, I agree,' he said. 'And good luck.'

–#–

As soon as she walked into the studio she knew she'd walked into a trap. The one-on-one interview had been turned into a debate, with the well-known monarchist Lindsay Fitzroy (he was something big in the CBD) pushing the case for 'no'. Noelene knew him by name and reputation, but had never met him before. A florid-faced man in his sixties, he prided himself on his noble ancestry, claiming direct descent from an English duke.

Wasn't Fitz the name given to the bastard sons of kings?

He'd lost the plebiscite and lost the plot, but was still in there fighting.

'We thought our viewers would like to hear both sides of the argument,' explained Holly. 'To present a more balanced viewpoint. Sorry I didn't have time to let you know. I hope you don't mind.'

Lindsay greeted Noelene with a great show of courtesy, calling her 'madam' and kissing her hand. He had bad breath and a curious way of talking in short staccato phrases rapped out like machine gun bullets.

'An honour,' he said, 'to finally meet you. Very chuffed. My wife and I are great admirers. Been to all your concerts.'

They were given chairs facing each other. Danno explained he would talk to each in turn, asking them their views and why they supported their particular cause. There would be an opportunity for questions from the studio audience, and then one minute allowed for a brief summing up.

I hate this, thought Noelene. *Black mark for bad judgment.*

The first questions Danno put to Noelene were about her retirement, and how she felt coming to the end of 'such a distinguished musical career'. Then he went straight for the jugular.

'You've been named in the papers as a possible president if Australia decides to become a republic,' he said. 'What's your reaction to this?'

Noelene answered the question very carefully. 'Honoured, of course, but I'm not really interested. I'm sure there are far better candidates than me. However, I do believe it's time we had an Australian as Head of State. So I'll be voting "yes" on March 30.'

Before Danno could ask his next question Lindsay jumped in, all guns firing.

'We already have an Australian as Head of State,' he said. 'The Governor-General.' He sat back, looking pleased with himself.

'That's news to me,' said Noelene. 'I think it will also be news to Her Majesty Queen Elizabeth. If you look up her website, you will see it lists Head of State of Australia as one of her titles.'

'A technicality,' said Lindsay. 'For all practical purposes, the Governor-General carries out the function.'

Don't let him get to me. Don't let him get away with it. He's wrong, wrong, wrong.

'Then tell me this. What happens when the Queen visits Australia? You can't have two Heads of State at the same time. Who takes precedence?'

'Now you're splitting hairs,' said Lindsay, sensing defeat but unwilling to concede.

'As a matter of interest, what d'you have against the Queen?' Danno asked Noelene.

'Absolutely nothing,' she said. 'She does a magnificent job. What other woman of 90 is still working full-time?'

She paused, choosing her words carefully. 'But she's not one of us. We're Australian, not English. When we visit her country, we line up in the queue for foreigners. When the Queen goes abroad to promote trade, it's British business she's promoting, not ours.'

Lindsay cut in. 'The monarchy represents stability, decency, and family values. It's above politics. When Charles comes to the throne, I'm sure he'll carry on the fine work done by his mother.'

'Hold on,' said Noelene, starting to get irritated. 'How do we know all this? D'you have you some kind of crystal ball? I grant the Prince of Wales seems like a reasonably decent human being, and as King will probably make a good fist of it. But who's to say what the royal line is going to throw up in the future? What if one day we're stuck with a loony, a drug addict, or a womaniser? I think you'll find history shows there've been a few of those in the past.

'Charles the second had 14 illegitimate children. And they were just the ones he owned up to'. A ripple of laughter. 'George the third was declared insane.' She'd done her homework.

Lindsay jumped to his feet in protest, but Noelene calmly continued.

'Unlikely to happen again, I know. But not impossible. And under our present system, whoever's on the British throne, good or bad, automatically becomes King or Queen of Australia.'

This brought a reaction and some handclaps from the studio audience. Lindsay looked thunderous.

'Let's take some questions,' said Danno.

A middle-aged woman put up her hand. 'How about State governors?' she asked. 'If we become a republic, what happens to them?'

'Good question,' said Danno. He looked over at Noelene for an answer.

'I don't know,' said Noelene. 'I'm not an expert on constitutional law. But I can't see how you could have a State governor representing the Queen, while at the same time abolishing the role of Governor-General. It'd be chaos.' As soon as the words were out of her mouth, she regretted them.

'Aha, that's it,' said Lindsay. 'That's my whole point. Chaos and anarchy. The destruction of decent society. For a start, we'll be tossed out of the Commonwealth.'

Noelene surprised herself by the sharpness in her voice. 'Absolute rubbish. India became a republic in 1947 and it's never been thrown out. It's still a member.'

There were a few more questions, then a minute each for the summing up. Noelene's was brief and pithy.

'My parents once told me that when they'd go to the movies, a picture of Queen Elizabeth would be flashed up on the screen and the entire audience would stand up while *God Save the Queen* was played. It sounds strange to us today, but that's the way it was then.

'We don't stand up any more in the movies. *God Save the Queen* is no longer our national anthem. The Privy Council is no longer our highest court of appeal. New citizens who once swore allegiance to the Crown now swear allegiance to Australia.

'Times change, we move on. It doesn't mean a loss of respect for the British monarchy. But it does mean respect for ourselves as a free and independent nation.'

Noelene sat down to rapturous applause from the audience. Lindsay's summing up was rambling and repetitive and he was gonged twice by Danno for going over his time.

But in the end it was impossible to tell who'd won the day.

As Noelene was leaving the studio an elderly woman approached, thrusting a piece of paper and pen at her. 'Would you mind?' she said. 'It's for my granddaughter. She's a big fan of yours.' Noelene smiled warmly, and signed.

She was moving away, heading for the waiting limousine, when the woman tugged at her sleeve and spoke again.

'I heard what you said in there, but did you really mean it? It's a big honour. Wouldn't you like to be president?'

But the wounds from the television encounter were still too bruising and raw.

'Not in a thousand years', she said.

6

It was a twilight concert in the Barossa valley, timed so concertgoers could have a picnic meal sitting out under a sky that was slowly turning from blue to pink to deep crimson.

'Gonna be a hot one tomorrow,' locals had said earlier. 'Gonna be a stinker.' And it was. A hot sizzling stinker. In the nearby city of Adelaide, you could have fried the proverbial egg on the pavement.

Noelene had arrived by plane and was resting in her hotel room. She'd had a call from Mike to let her know he'd secured a place in the press scrum. 'Good luck,' he'd said.

She invited him to come backstage after the concert for a celebratory glass of champagne.

'I'll be there,' Mike promised.

They were now beginning to build into some kind of relationship. She liked him as a person, and admired the quiet professionalism with which he went about his job. Here was a man who knew exactly what he was about and how to achieve it. She'd also done some background checking, and was impressed with what she'd found.

An Honours graduate of Charles Sturt University, majoring in the electronic media. Twice nominated for AFI awards.

A string of investigative projects, including one on the assimilation into Australian society of asylum seekers. There'd been a follow-up piece into government corruption in the granting of visas. It had been dismissed by the minister concerned as 'a media beat up', but in the end it had cost the polly his job.

As the sky slowly darkened and the stars began to appear, the crowd settled in for the performance. There were banners and signs all over the place: FAREWELL NOELENE! GOOD LUCK! AU REVOIR!!! A rash of exclamation marks as a reminder that this would be her last public performance as a singer.

Members of the orchestra slowly began to drift on to the stage, the white tie and tails and long gowns contrasting with the casualness of the outdoor setting. Instruments were tuned. Sound equipment was tested. A low buzz of excitement rippled through the audience.

Every television channel had a news team to cover Noelene's last concert. World rights had been sold. Music critics were sharpening their adjectives in anticipation. Noelene was still in superlative form as a singer, but there was always that question mark hovering. Would she still be able to hit those high notes as effortlessly as she had 30 years ago? Had she lost some of her edge?

But so far there were no signs of the voice failing. When her retirement was announced, some writers pointed out Melba had been the ripe old age of 65 when she made her final appearance at Covent Garden. Noelene was 10 years younger.

Mike took his place among the media contingent, and readied his camera. Watches were being checked. One minute to go. All eyes were now focussed on the side curtain through which the conductor and star would soon emerge.

The conductor was a grey-haired, distinguished-looking

man in his late sixties. The program notes listed his musical background, including 10 years with the Chicago Philharmonic and two more teaching at music institutions in Germany. He was now back in his hometown and had been commissioned to compose a piece of music in celebration of the 180th year of the State's foundation.

He walked briskly on stage, leading Noelene by the hand. She was wearing a simple red satin gown with something sparkly at the neck and in her hair. She smiled, and it seemed as though the entire audience smiled back at her. This woman has charisma, thought Mike. In spades.

Then Noelene announced her first number and the conductor raised his baton. The crowd quietened, as that glorious voice rang out.

She had made her choice carefully: Bellini's *Norma*, then arias from *Manon*, *Madame Butterfly*, and *Carmen*. Some lieder, and an English folk song. With each number the reaction grew more and more rapturous, people standing on their feet, shouting 'Bravo! bravo!' until it seemed there could be no more breath left in them. Once or twice Noelene had to lift her hand, asking them to stop so she could continue with the program. It was a love affair between artist and audience.

For her final number she sang the same one both Melba and Sutherland had chosen to finish their singing careers – an achingly beautiful rendition of *Home Sweet Home*. It brought down the house.

After the bows, the kisses, the speeches and the floral tributes, Noelene finally left the stage. She made one brief reappearance, called back when it seemed as though the crowd would never stop applauding. And then the lights on the stage dimmed, the musicians began to pick up their instruments and slowly file out, and Noelene was in her dressing room.

It was there Mike found her, shoes kicked off, looking exhausted and sipping a glass of champagne. She lifted the glass.

'Cheers. Glad you could make it. So how d'you think it went?'

'Fantastic.'

Noelene smiled. 'I wasn't fishing for compliments.'

'I know you weren't.'

They chatted for a while, and then a woman standing in the background looked over and tapped her watch. Noelene responded with a nod. It was a clear signal to Mike that some appointment was looming. Probably an after concert reception. Meeting the local VIPs and sponsors. He made a move to leave.

'Before you go,' said Noelene. 'What are you doing first thing tomorrow morning?'

'Nothing. I'm catching a plane back to Sydney at noon.'

'Is eight too early for you?'

'No. Why?'

'There's something I want to show you. I think you'll find it interesting.'

Noelene collected Mike from his hotel in a hire car, and they drove through the outer suburbs of the city to head up the winding road to the Hills. They were too low to be called mountains – more gentle hummocks rounded like a woman's breasts, slashed here and there with the black of past bushfires.

They went through small townships; now and then they passed the ruins of houses where the only thing still standing was a brick chimney. The landscape on each side of the road was brown and parched. There hadn't been any rain for more than a month. Drought weather.

Finally they reached a sign that said: 'Bisley'. 'This is it,' said Noelene, taking a road off the main highway. They went past a couple of shops, a gas station, a few more houses, and came to an old church and cemetery, long abandoned. Headstones tilted crazily, or had fallen to the ground. Glass jam jars that once held flowers now stood empty. The stained glass windows of the stone church had been boarded up to protect them. The heavy timber door was padlocked, with a sign directing visitors to the nearest church and minister.

Next door, with not even a fence separating them, was a small cottage. Like the church, it no longer showed any signs of human existence. It was a forlorn wreck of a place with a front door sagging on rusted hinges, and a garden that was a jungle of out-of-control weeds and vines. Noelene brought the car to a halt in front of it, and waved a hand towards the derelict building.

'My father's old home.' she said. 'I've just bought it.'

7

Lily found Miss Patchett more intimidating than Mrs Druitt, although in the domestic hierarchy she was several levels below the housekeeper. Like many people given a small amount of authority, she revelled in it, making it clear to the junior staff that she was in charge and they'd better not forget it.

'She's a bitch,' Sarah had whispered just before she'd presented Lily for inspection. 'A dried up prune of an old maid. Don't take any notice of her.'

But Lily, used to the kindness and courtesy of Mrs Cavendish and others she'd worked for, was terrified. What if she didn't come up to Government House standards? What if she forgot her place? It was all so bewildering.

Although the Hills houses she'd worked for had employed staff, it had never been more than two or three, and mostly locals she knew. She'd felt on an equal level to them, they'd all been honest working class. But here it was clear there was much more to it.

'Not very big, are you?' said Miss Patchett, echoing Sarah. 'Well we'll have to manage the best we can for a uniform.' She took out a tape measure from a pocket and ran it up and down Lily, her frown showed the results weren't pleasing to her. She went to a cupboard and brought out a folded pile of clothes and a white cap.

'You'd better take up the hem, or you'll be tripping over yourself. Sarah'll show you the sewing room. Hand stitch it – we'll need to take it down again when you've gone. Report back to me in an hour in your uniform, and I'll give you your instructions.' She frowned, examining Lily critically. 'And make sure none of that hair's showing. It's unhygienic, girl, to have it all hanging loose like that.'

'Told you,' said Sarah, as soon as they were out of earshot. 'Fancies herself, thinks she's a cut above everyone else just because she was personally hired by Lady Weigall. Everyone hates her. But be careful. She can make your life a misery if you get on the wrong side of her.'

They walked along another corridor and up some stairs to a room that housed two treadle sewing machines, an ironing board, and a table at which a young girl of about eighteen was repairing the hem of what looked like a linen tablecloth. Sarah nodded briefly at the girl, but made no attempt at an introduction. From a cupboard she produced a sewing kit of needle, thread and scissors, and handed them to Lily.

'Do it in your room if you like,' she said. 'There's a mirror behind the wardrobe door, it'll make it easier for you to measure. Think you can find your way back to Miss Patchett when you're done? I'd come back for you, but I can't spare the time.'

She lowered her voice, as if what she was about to say was a capital offence for which she could be executed. 'Everyone's going crazy about getting ready for his royal nibs. Bowing and scraping and working their ruddy guts out. Or working ours out, more to the point. You'd think the world was coming to an end. I'll be glad when he's gone and it's all over.' She pronounced 'he' with a capital H.

A uniformed Lily, her unhygienic hair now hidden under a white cap, was inspected and approved by Miss Patchett. She was then given a list of her duties, starting at six next morning. It was mostly making sure all the bedrooms were kept immaculate with fresh flowers and bed linen, the fireplaces cleaned and set again with fresh coal, the wash basin jug filled with clean water, mirrors polished, furniture dusted, plus attending to any personal requests the vice-regal guests might have.

A kitchen servant was responsible for the cup of tea and slice of thin buttered bread brought on a silver tray first thing in the morning, while ladies' maids and gentlemen's valets looked after the more important of the guests.

The most important guest, of course, was HRH the Prince of Wales who would be arriving from Western Australia by train the next day. Sir Archibald and Lady Weigall had given up their suite in the east wing for the duration of his visit, and moved to temporary rooms nearby.

A room next to His Royal Highness had been reserved for his young cousin, 20-year-old Lord Louis Mountbatten. The two were related through one of Queen Victoria's granddaughters who had married a Louis of Battenberg. Lord Louis, known as 'Dickie', was officially on the tour as a serving naval officer and unofficially as the Prince's confidant and companion.

Lily was excused from duties for her first day, and Sarah volunteered to show her around the grounds when she'd finished work. The gardens were immaculate, laid out in the English style. Lawns smooth and clipped as a croquet green, winding walks, beds and borders glowing in a riot of colour. With the Royal visit in mind, the gardeners had been given instructions early in the year to prepare plantings so that the gardens would look their best by July. Buckingham Palace had also been consulted on what flowers the Prince preferred ('His Royal Highness enjoys all forms of floral art, but is especially fond of roses.').

While walking through the gardens Lily discovered that Sarah, like herself, was a country girl. Her family had lived in a small town in western New South Wales, but moved to Adelaide when Sarah was twelve. She'd been working at Government House for the past year. Lily also found out that the sick chambermaid whose place she'd taken was Sarah's best friend Agnes.

'Measles,' explained Sarah. 'Poor Aggie, she looked a sight, all covered with spots. They sent her home to her parents. There was a real panic, I can tell you. Imagine getting something like that just when the Prince is about to arrive. Mind you, he's probably had 'em. But best to be on the safe side.'

At tea in the servants' dining room that night (cuts of cold mutton and salad) Lily met her roommate Emma, a plumpish cheerful-looking girl of eighteen. As they were undressing for bed, Emma confided she had a boyfriend, also in service at Government House.

'Eddie,' she said. 'He's a junior footman. Course, they're

not keen on any of the staff courting, so we've got to keep things a bit quiet. But when we've saved up enough money, we're getting married. You got someone special you're sweet on?'

Lily confessed she had no one, which surprised Emma. 'Good looker like you, I'd have thought all the young blokes'd be after you. You've never had a boyfriend?' Lily said no, she was too busy looking after her father and four brothers. Emma shrugged, clearly earmarking Lily as a romantic failure.

'Keep your eyes open for Simmons,' she said. 'He's in charge of the wine cellars. Never let him get you down there, or you'll be sorry. Wicked man.' Lily didn't ask why she'd be sorry or what made Simmons so wicked, but she got the message. She thanked Emma for her advice, and climbed into bed.

She was awake for a long time, thinking about her family, wondering how they were managing without her. In her mind's eye she could see her father sitting in his old rocking chair, dozing off in the warmth of the fire. And then there were her brothers smoking their pipes, reading the newspaper or playing cards. Did they spare a thought for their little sister?

'I miss you,' she whispered. 'I miss you all, my darlings'. It was the first night she'd ever spent away from her family. In the next bed Emma was gently snoring, a smile on her face. Dreaming of her Eddie, no doubt. Moments later, cheeks damp with tears, Lily was also fast asleep.

8

It's a sad house, Mike thought, as he followed Noelene up the front pathway. Sad and unloved, waiting for someone to bring it to life again. As if reading his thoughts, Noelene took a faded snapshot from her handbag. It showed a cottage with an arch of trailing roses over the doorway and a smiling young woman standing outside, a baby in her arms.

'See, same house,' she said. 'That's Dad and my grandmother Lily. I found it among his things when he died, but I thought the place would've been pulled down by now. Not many of these old ones survive these days. Then on my last visit a friend took me out driving, and there it was. I recognised it straight away. Tracked down the owner and made an offer. I gather there'd once been tenants, but it hadn't been lived in for years. He was about to bring in the bulldozers, said it was costing him too much money. He was glad to get rid of it. So now it's mine.'

'That's a nice story,' said Mike.

'My great-grandparents Jack and Ethel moved here when they married. They're buried somewhere next door in that old cemetery, but so far I haven't been able to find their graves. I'm not sure if they built the house, or if it was already there, but I'm told it dates back to the 1890s. I've found an architect who's an expert at restoring places like this, and he's going to draw up some plans and find a builder.

'Once it's done, it'll be my personal bolthole. A nice change from always staying in hotels. Like to look inside? But watch your step. I warn you – it's a total wreck.' She took out a key and opened the front door. 'I don't know why I bother to keep it locked,' she said. 'There's nothing to steal. But I suppose it keeps out vandals.'

It was like a dolls house inside, a shabby faded dolls house of four rooms and a back verandah that looked as though it had been tacked on as an afterthought. Through a broken rear window Mike caught a glimpse of an outdoor dunny covered in vines, an open space where a wooden door had once provided privacy.

And Noelene was right, it was a wreck. Peeling wallpaper, cracks in the ceiling and walls, rotting timber, flaking paint, rat droppings. And everywhere the overpowering odour of mould and decay. It smelt like death.

'This is my favourite,' said Noelene. 'The front parlour. It's the one they'd keep nice and tidy ready for company. I like to imagine Jack and Ethel sitting here, entertaining the vicar at afternoon tea.'

There was an open fireplace surrounded by cream and blue tiles. Once there had been a timber mantelpiece, but the only signs of it now were the rusted hinges embedded in the wall. The grouting of the bricks above the mantelpiece had crumbled away, leaving a few dangerously loose. Noelene touched one lightly.

'There's a lot of work to be done,' she said. 'I suppose you think I'm mad to take on something like this. But it'll be worth it.'

They did a quick tour through the rest of the house, with Noelene pointing out where she planned to add a kitchen and bathroom. They were the only modern additions she was making, as she wanted to keep it as close to its original character as possible. Two of the original rooms would be used as bedrooms, with the fourth as a study to house her books and CD collection.

'When does all this happen?' asked Mike.

Noelene shrugged. 'Who knows? I'm not rushing it. The first thing is to get together with the architect and work out some plans. These things take time. But I wouldn't mind being here by Christmas'. She smiled. 'My birthday.'

'So that's where the name Noelene came from. I was wondering.'

'My parents said I was their surprise Christmas package. I guess I *was* a bit of a surprise after six years of trying to have a family. They'd just about given up hope.'

It seemed like a good time to jump in with the question that had been on his mind. 'So your great-grandparents were Jack and Ethel Jones?'

'That's right.'

'I'm curious. Why do you still call yourself Jones after all these years? I assume you were born with your father's surname.'

'I was.'

'So what was *his* name?'

Noelene waited a long time before she answered. Mike had the feeling he'd strayed into forbidden territory.

'Look, it's all a bit complicated. I knew you'd eventually get around to asking me … in a way, I've been waiting for it. I can fill you in on some of the detail, but I can't tell you the whole story. It's one of those things my parents never talked about.'

'Sounds interesting,' said Mike. 'Tell me more.'

'The truth is my father was born out of wedlock, to use an old-fashioned expression. He wasn't ashamed of it. It just never bothered him, he was that kind of person. It seems some boyfriend of Lily got her pregnant, then panicked and shot through when he found out. She was very young at the time and it must've been terrible for her in a small country place like this. You know how people gossip.

'The good part is that apparently her family stood by her, she had the baby, and gave him her father's name: Jack Jones. That's all I know.'

'Well it happens in the best of families,' smiled Mike. 'I'm glad you told me.'

Mike leaned down and picked up a coin lying among the dust and debris. It had the head of King George V on one side. 'A 1931 penny,' he said, handing it to Noelene. 'Family heirloom. Keep it for luck.' She tucked it into her pocket.

As they walked towards the parked car the sun came out from behind clouds, catching the glass of the front panes. It was as though someone inside had just put a match to the old fireplace, causing the house to suddenly glow and come to life.

As she looked back Noelene had the strangest feeling there was a face at the window peering out at them. Man or woman? She couldn't be sure. Then just as quickly she dismissed it as an optical illusion, a trick of the imagination, and followed Mike into the car.

The sun retreated behind clouds, the glow was gone, and the cottage was an empty tumbledown wreck again.

9

Clarence House, London

Charles, Prince of Wales, was on the phone to his mother, Queen Elizabeth II. He hung up, looking vaguely irritated.

'Anything wrong? asked Camilla, Duchess of Cornwall, knowing something had set her husband on edge. After long years of togetherness she could read him like the proverbial book.

'Those bloody dogs again,' said the Prince. 'Gave one of the footmen a nasty nip on the leg. Mummy says it'll need stitches.'

The Lodge, Canberra

The Prime Minister had just been told by his Treasurer that he had made a slight miscalculation and the country was now in deficit, not surplus. The solution was to cut jobs or raise taxes.

It was one of those days.

—#—

The breakfast cabinet noticed the frown on the PM's face as he put down the phone. But she was more concerned with her fried eggs, which hadn't been cooked to her personal satisfaction.

'I've told Lin a dozen times I like them soft in the middle with brown crispy bits around the edges. She still doesn't get the message. Mind you, it could be a language thing. Maybe there's no word for "crispy" where she comes from.' She sighed. 'I've half a mind to replace her but I can see the headlines: PM'S WIFE FIRES CHINESE MIGRANT. I'll be accused of being racist, which is unfair, because some of my best clients are Asian.'

'She's not, y'know,' said the PM absentmindedly fiddling with his muesli.

'Not what?'

'Chinese. She's Korean.'

The breakfast cabinet frowned and attacked her eggs again. 'Whatever.'

The Prime Minister, his mind still on the country's financial catastrophe, was wondering how many public servants could be retrenched without too much fuss and bother. That would save a few million without upsetting the mums and dads.

Increasing taxes would be an unpopular option. Anything that hit the hip pocket was a no-no. The government might also look at cutting subsidies and grants to some of the more arty farty organisations. That wouldn't cause much of an uproar, and there were too many of them anyway.

Finally the PM decided to put the whole messy business on the back burner and concentrate on problems closer to hand, such as what to do if the result of the referendum was 'yes'.

'It's a tricky business,' he said to his wife.

'What ... cooking eggs with little crispy bits?'

'Choosing a president. It needs a cool head, mature political judgment, and a finger on the pulse of the people. Fortunate-ly for the country I happen to have an abundance of all three.'

'So who d'you have in mind?'

To tell the truth, he didn't have anyone in mind. The name and face of a future Australian Head of State was still a complete blank. But he felt it unwise to reveal this to his breakfast cabinet. 'Obviously the aim is to pick someone who's uncontroversial and won't rock the boat. We don't want any nasties crawling out of the woodwork after he's appointed.'

'Or she,' snapped his wife, using a sharp knife to spear her bacon. He decided to ignore the remark.

'Actually, I do have a plan of sorts,' He looked at his wife, but she was now busy turning her toast into little soldiers. 'I'm drawing up a vice-regal gene pool.'

She looked up in surprise. 'A *what*?'

'A gene pool.'

'I thought that's what you said. What's a gene pool?'

The PM pulled a piece of paper from his pocket.

'It's all here, written down. It came to me last night just before I went to sleep.'

'So that's why you were making all those strange snuffly noises. I thought it was hay fever.'

The PM decided to ignore the remark and push on.

'My theory is that if I have a clear view of the past, then I can better plan for the future.' He waited for his wife's praise, but she was too busy dipping her little soldiers into the runny yolk.

'I asked myself one simple question. Where did our Governors-General come from? Other than Pommyland, and it goes without saying we don't want any more of those. Obviously GGs don't fall out of the sky or come floating down on umbrellas like Mary Poppins. 'So if I can identify the sources, then it follows I'm halfway to finding the answers.' He consulted his piece of paper again.

'A gene pool will tell me where I should look to find an Australian Head of State ... based on previous experience.'

'So?'

'I've made up a rough list. Well it's not a complete list, but it'll give you an idea. Bill McKell, politics. Lord Casey, politics. Hasluck, politics again. Sir John Kerr ... well maybe we'll skip over that one. Ninian Stephen, law. Bill Hayden, politics. William Deane, law. Hollingworth, the Church. Jeffrey, the Army. So what d'you make of it so far?'

'There seem to be a lot of politicians.'

The PM sighed. 'Point taken. And that's the tricky bit ... that's the rub. It's been a handy supply source in the past and I wouldn't mind using it again, but I know the public won't wear it. Can't trust politicians, they keep saying. Can't trust politicians, on and on like a bloody cracked record. It's a pity, as a certain someone has been hinting for a job ever since he lost his seat and I owe him one. Well too bad. He'll just have to get on a few boards like the rest of them.

'But you see my point, can't you? There's a pool of presidents out there just waiting to be tapped. Take the armed services, for instance. You can always depend on a military man to stick to the rules of engagement and not try to do his own thing.'

He saw the frown starting to form on his wife's face and decided on pre-emptive action. '... Or *her*, as the case may be. The academic world's worth a look. A professor or a vice-chancellor could be useful, provided they're not one of those trendy radicals who write books.

'The diplomatic service ... there must be a few spare ambassadors floating around. Who've we broken off relations with recently? Community leaders. The arts. The sciences. Scouts. Salvos. RSL. Rotary.' The PM paused for breath, still thinking through his magnificent idea.

'To put the whole thing in a nutshell, it's got to be someone who'll be accepted without reservation. Someone with an impeccable background, good credentials, a bit of political nous, not too young and not too old, able to pick up the baton and run with it. Yes, my dear, I'm more than confident I can get on top of it all and pick the right man.'

'Or woman.'

It was infuriating how his wife always managed to have the last word.

10

Lily's roommate Emma was awake early, almost jumping out of her skin with excitement. 'Just think,' she said, 'today's the day the Prince arrives. Did you see his photo in the paper? A bit on the skinny side. Personally I like a man with more meat on him, if you know what I mean. But so handsome!' She poured water into the basin and began to wash her face. Lily followed suit, but slower. She was feeling the lack of sleep and still missing her family.

Mornings at Bisley were a regular routine she'd followed for years, ever since the death of her mother. Start the fuel stove. Bring in coal and wood to light the fireplace and make sure the old iron kettle hung over it by a chain had enough water to heat. Prepare the porridge, set the table, lay out the bread, butter and milk. Meantime her brothers would be shaving and dressing, getting ready for the day's work, while her father sat at the head of the table reading the newspaper and waiting for his breakfast.

If she'd been at home she'd have seen that the paper he was reading was a bit different from usual. Among the advertisements on the front page, the city department store, Miller Anderson, announced it would be closed today 'in honour of the visit of His Royal Highness the Prince of Wales'.

On an inside page a large headline read: ADELAIDE WELCOMES THE PRINCE, with pictures of the Prince of Wales, King George and Queen Mary, the Governor Sir Archibald Weigall and Lady Weigall. Queen Mary, regal and unsmiling, wore a tiara with a choker of pearls and diamonds around her throat. The Prince of Wales was in the uniform of an Army officer, military baton tucked under one arm, nervously staring into the lens as though not quite sure what to expect from this remote antipodean colony he was about to visit.

But Lily saw none of this. She was too busy getting into her uniform; too anxious about doing well in her new job. 'Do I look all right?' she asked Emma. Her roommate eyed her critically.

'Tuck in a bit more of your hair,' she said. 'Old Patchett goes off her rocker if any's showing. She's got a thing about it.'

It was still dark as the two made their beds and tidied the room, then went to the staff kitchen for breakfast. There Lily met Emma's Eddie, a gangling lanky 20-year-old with red hair, freckles and a wide friendly smile that exposed crooked teeth. He and Emma exchanged sly glances across the table, but Lily noticed they were careful not to speak directly to each other.

Sitting next to Eddie was a fair-haired young man with bold blue eyes and the faint beginnings of a ginger moustache above his upper lip. He seemed very loud and talkative, and told some slightly risque stories that brought a blush to Lily's cheeks and a stern rebuke from the senior butler:

'That'll be enough, Nifty. Ladies present. Get on with your meal.'

Nifty, not the least bit abashed by the reprimand, looked over at Lily and gave her a broad wink as if she were in on some secret conspiracy known only to the two of them. Lily, uncertain what to do, looked down at her lap and fiddled nervously with her table napkin.

Emma, noting Lily's embarrassment, leaned over and whispered: 'That's Eddie's friend. Don't take any notice of him.'

But Nifty wasn't so easily dismissed. When breakfast was finished he came over to Emma, and again with his eyes fixed firmly on Lily asked: 'How's about an introduction to your lady friend?'

Lily could again feel the blood rising to her cheeks. What was it about him that bothered her? He seemed open and friendly, and shook her hand politely as Emma made the introductions. But when he lingered and started to ask Lily personal questions, Emma told him they had no time for idle conversation. They had work to do, adding (tartly) she assumed he had too.

Nifty took the rebuff in good humour with a 'Right you are, luv', giving them a wide grin as they walked away. But Lily had the feeling she hadn't seen the last of him.

'Why's he called Nifty?' she asked Emma when they were both out of earshot.

'His real name's Peregrine', explained Emma. 'Bit of a mouthful, isn't it? So everyone calls him Nifty because he fancies himself as a snappy dresser. Spends all his money on clothes, according to Eddie. Reckons it gets in the girls.'

Shortly after breakfast they were called to a staff

meeting and addressed by someone she hadn't seen before, a stern-looking man called Wainwright, who seemed to be the person in charge of vice-regal household affairs. He reminded them that the Prince and his entourage were due at Government House around noon. This would follow his arrival by train at Adelaide railway station and a drive through the streets so the public could greet him.

The Governor, Sir Archibald Weigall, would board the Royal train at Smithfield. The program for today included a dinner party at Government House followed by an official reception.

Wainwright emphasised that on no account were any of the staff to talk to the Prince unless he first spoke to them, and to remember to curtsy or bow on meeting him. The Prince had his own personal servants travelling with him, but if Government House staff were required for royal duties they should address the Prince in the first instance as 'Your Royal Highness', and then as 'Sir'.

The royal apartments, of course, were out of bounds unless a staff member was assigned for specific duties. Any breach of these instructions, added Wainwright with a stern look, would mean instant dismissal.

After laying down the law, Wainwright permitted himself a smile so thin it seemed his face would crack in two. 'I now take pleasure in announcing that the Prince has graciously expressed a wish to meet members of the vice-regal staff. Therefore I would like everyone, whether assigned for duty or not, to assemble in the ballroom at three forty-five precisely for presentation at four to His Royal Highness. Mrs Druitt and Mr McDonald will give you further instructions.

'I expect you all to do your utmost to uphold the high standards of this establishment.' And with that frosty smile again, he was gone.

Lily looked at Sarah, who shrugged her shoulders and whispered: 'Bet old Patchett's first in line to shake his hand. Trust her.' Lily glanced at Miss Patchett, who was in earnest conversation with Mrs Druitt.

As a newcomer, Lily had been assigned to help Sarah check the bedrooms and make sure everything was ready for the extra guests. Rooms aired, bed linen tucked in, coverlets hanging smooth and straight, and fresh flowers from Government House gardens.

Later still she worked in the linen room, where her job was to check, iron, fold, and put away sheets, pillowcases and tablecloths from the laundry. A large book kept a record of every item that came in and went out, and Lily was shown how to initial it.

One thing she took pride in was her fine copperplate writing. At school she'd practised her hooks and circles to such perfection that she'd been given a class prize. As she signed the book, Lily's neat and elegant 'L.J.' stood out against the crosses and carelessly scrawled signatures. It could almost be the signature of a lady.

At noon, a buzz of excitement swept through the building. 'He's *here*!' hissed Sarah, as she met Lily in a corridor. They peered through a window and saw three gleaming Crossleys parked at the entrance. As a uniformed driver held open the door of the first one, a slight, fair-haired man in uniform emerged.

'Not very tall, is he?' said Emma, who'd joined them. 'My Eddie'd give him a good six inches or more.' Lily was more interested in the way everyone was bowing and curtsying, heads bobbing up and down like corks in water.

The Prince seemed relaxed and smiling, but she couldn't help thinking it must be a pain to have to shake the hands of so many strangers and look happy doing it. But then again, it was probably something he'd been trained for since birth.

And of course there were royal perks, like being waited on hand and foot and never having to lift a finger to do anything for oneself. Always another person to open doors and run the bathwater and lay out the clothes to wear and make sure you were on time for everything. It was like being a puppet, really, with someone else pulling the strings.

'Careful, or we'll be caught,' warned Sarah, as she heard footsteps coming, and just in time they ducked out of sight and back to the servants quarters. An instruction had been posted on the staff noticeboard reminding staff to assemble for presentation to the Prince.

The rumour factory was now in full swing. A form of vice-regal bush telegraph had passed along the news that the Prince had been escorted to his suite, accompanied by his cousin, Lord Louis. Both were highly eligible bachelors … a good catch for some nice well-bred Australian girl if one could be lucky enough to attract their interest.

There would be an afternoon rest period for the Prince, with no official commitments until the dinner party and reception. One rumour (relayed through Lady Weigall's personal maid and passed on through one of the junior butlers) had it there might also be a small informal party after the official functions, as the Prince was said to be fond of dancing. All staff had been told to remain on duty, whatever the hour, until otherwise instructed.

At three forty-five Lily joined the others in the ballroom. On Mrs Druitt's instructions they lined up in order of rank and length of service, with Lily bringing up the rear. She was amused to see that Miss Patchett hadn't managed to win herself a place in the front row, but was somewhere in the middle. Sarah had also noted it, and the two shared a smile. Wainwright walked up and down the lines like an officer inspecting his troops, checking shoes were polished, uniforms spotless, ties straight, and hair pushed under caps. Satisfied, he then took his place at the head, ready for the royal summons.

When it came, it was so low key to be almost an anti-climax. The golden-haired man Lily had seen through the window walked into the room, followed by an aide-de-camp and Sir Archibald and Lady Weigall. Close up she could see Emma was right – he was a small man, not more than five and a half feet tall.

He had a slim boyish frame and a smooth unlined face, hair neatly combed to one side. He was 26 but could easily have passed for years younger. He looked as though he had barely started to shave.

Wainwright was the first to be presented to him. The Prince then walked along the rows, shaking hands as each one was introduced. When they finally got to Lily, Wainwright looked puzzled, unable to connect her face with a name. Mrs Druitt, following close behind, came to his rescue.

The Prince smiled at her. He had the saddest eyes she'd ever seen.

'Lily. A lovely name,' he said, in his clipped English

accent. 'My grandfather's favourite. Did you ever hear of the Jersey Lily?'

Was it her imagination or did he hold her hand a fraction longer than was necessary? And then a wondrous thing happened, so unexpected that afterwards she was scarcely able to believe it.

For the first time in her life, Lily fell deeply, passionately, in love.

11

Newspaper polls were starting to edge towards a clear victory for the republic. *The Australian* claimed 55% of voters supported an Australian as Head of State, with 32% against and 13% undecided. The *Sydney Morning Herald* went even further, with all its political pundits predicting a landslide win for a 'yes' vote.

Someone had written a song for the republican cause, and it was being sung all over the country at public rallies:

We are Aussies,
We are free;
We don't want
The Monarch-EE.

It wasn't good. It was downright corny. But it caught the public imagination.

12

In the end it wasn't even a contest. Every State and Territory voted for Australia to become a republic, with NSW registering an overwhelming 78% for 'yes'. Champagne corks popped across the nation, and Her Majesty the Queen was duly informed she was out of a job.

'It's what one expected,' she told the Duke when he woke from his post-prandial nap. 'One is only surprised they didn't do it years ago.' The Duke didn't register any emotion one way or the other at the news. But the Queen had found that at his advanced age it wasn't always easy to know what her husband was thinking. Or indeed, whether he was thinking at all.

As soon as the result was known, the Prime Minister swung into Action Man mode. The question that had been deliberately left out in the wording of the referendum (the same question that had split the republican movement in 1999) was how the new president would be chosen. The PM needed to come up with an answer – and fast.

First up was to check what had actually happened 17 years

ago. All he knew was that there'd been bitter arguments, in some cases almost leading to punch-ups. It had been a very controversial question. So the PM went to the source of all wisdom – the Parliamentary library – and checked through the records.

Some republicans had favoured a direct election (for that read 'people's choice'); others had wanted a bipartisan approach with the Head of State chosen by a two-thirds majority of Parliament. But what was overwhelmingly clear was that nobody felt it should be the personal choice of the Prime Minister – the old system used to select a Governor-General. That had long since been consigned to the mothballs of history.

But how to sit on two chairs at the same time? How to keep everyone happy?

Neatly sidestepping his breakfast cabinet, the PM retreated to his study with a couple of well-sharpened pencils, a ruled pad, and a bottle of the finest scotch from The Lodge cellars. He then drew up a set of options, scoring each one out of a possible ten.

OPTIONS FOR CHOOSING A PRESIDENT

Option 1: bite the bullet and make the choice myself.

Pros: shows strong leadership. Fast and efficient. No mucking around. Eliminates the need for time-wasting consultation with the Opposition. Handy way to repay past favours. Has worked well in the past, so can't see why it shouldn't work just as well for a president. Like the monarchists keep on saying, if it ain't broke, don't fix it.

Cons: if the president turns out a dud, I'll cop the blame. Unlikely to have the support of those who keep saying they don't trust politicians.

Marks: 2 out of 10.

Option 2: choose the president, but make sure of bipartisan support before any public announcement is made. Delude the Opposition into believing they've had a say in it.

Pros: gives an appearance of political unity.

Cons: I'll still be blamed if the president turns out to be a dud.

Marks: 4 out of 10.

Option 3: set up a Royal Commission.

Pros: the public and press like Royal Commissions (and they're always good for a headline).

Cons: expensive. Time wasting. Dangerous. Who was it that said never set one up unless you know what the outcome's going to be? Anyway, the word 'Royal' is a turnoff. Defeats the whole purpose of the exercise.

Marks: 5 out of 10.

Option 4: Declare it a people's president and let the public choose whoever they damn well like.

Pros: the perfect answer to all those who say they don't trust politicians.

Cons: we could finish up with a pop star or a cricketer as president.

Marks: 6 out of 10.

The Prime Minister sat for a long time looking at all the options, chewing the end of his pencil and drinking his tax-funded whisky. He was well into his third glass and beginning to nod off when the inspiration came to him. And it was so devilishly brilliant and foolproof he wondered why he'd taken so long to think of it.

He carefully wrote it all down on the pad before he could fall asleep and forget it, giving himself ten points and an elephant stamp. Then he locked it all safely away in a drawer.

The Prime Minister retired for the night, satisfied that Option 5 was a stroke of genius.

'Why are you smiling like that?' his wife asked from her half of the marital bed. 'Found a way to stab someone in the back? Discovered how to halve the national debt? Worked out some more perks for the Prime Ministerial pension fund?'

'Better than all that,' said the PM. 'I've just ensured myself a permanent place in the history books of this country.'

Two days later the announcement appeared in all the papers:

FROM THE GOVERNMENT OF AUSTRALIA
TO THE PEOPLE OF AUSTRALIA

Following a majority 'yes' vote to the question of whether Australia should become a republic, the criteria for selection of a new Head of State will be as follows:

All Australian citizens between the ages of 45 and 75 years, including State Governors and Governors-General past and present, will be eligible for the office, with the following exceptions:

(a) persons holding a dual allegiance to another country

(b) persons with a criminal record

(c) serving politicians and anyone who has held political office within the past five years.

The mode of address to be 'His/Her Excellency the President of the Republic of Australia'.

Yarralumla will be retained as the official residence in the Australian Capital Territory, as well as Admiralty House in Sydney.

The term of office will be five years, to be extended at the government's discretion. There will be a limit of two terms. The appointment can be terminated only by an executive decision of Cabinet after open debate in Parliament, with reasons for the termination fully disclosed to the public. Transparency of process to be paramount.

In the event of a president dying during the term of office, the most senior State official will fill his/her place until a new Head of State can be appointed.

The announcement was followed by a press conference at which the Prime Minister unveiled his plan for choosing the country's first Australian Head of State.

The governments of each of the States and Territories would be invited to nominate a candidate for president. An additional two would be chosen by the public on the basis of one vote per person. Ballot boxes for the public to nominate would be set up in all post offices across the country.

The final list of names would be voted on in a national election on June 30. The three candidates scoring the most votes would be submitted in a short list to the Prime Minister for a final choice. He looked around with a smile on his face, awaiting approval.

'Sounds a bit complicated. Who's going to supervise all this and make sure it works?'

The Prime Minister had been expecting the question and had his answer ready. A Presidential Selection Committee would oversee the selection of candidates. A second one, The Constitutional Reform Committee 'would be charged with overseeing the mechanics of this country becoming a republic, and recommending appropriate changes to the Constitution, currency, postage, nomenclature, and other related matters within its jurisdiction'.

It was another way of saying things would never be the same again. But like those in public service, prime ministers had a special language of their own.

The PM glanced around the room at the assembled press.

'Any other questions?'

A man in the back row put up his hand.

'What's the word from Buck House?'

The PM frowned; he didn't approve flip talk from journos

when it came to royalty. Republic or not, there was a certain standard and protocol to maintain.

'Naturally as a matter of courtesy we've kept Her Majesty fully informed at all times. I am also pleased to announce that as the soon-to-be former monarch of this country, she has been invited by my government to attend the inauguration of the new president. In view of her age it is by no means certain she will be able to attend, but I am assured that if not, there will be a senior member of the royal family there to represent her.'

There were a few more questions such as a possible date for the inauguration ('a bit premature, that will be decided further down the track') and what were the PM's personal views on the type of president he'd like to have ('I have no personal views. It's entirely a matter for my fellow Australians to decide'). And then the conference was declared closed.

Action Man had read his public accurately. The method of choosing the first president was greeted with almost universal approval, one newspaper going so far as to praise it as 'a statesman-like plan that elevates the choice of president above the level of party politics, and at the same time pays service to the rights and will of the common people. The Prime Minister is to be congratulated on his wisdom and foresight.'

'Pontificating pretentious pious piffle', said his wife when he read it out to her from the paper next morning. She was a whiz at alliteration.

'What d'you mean?' asked a somewhat miffed PM, who had been expecting praise from his breakfast cabinet.

'It's like wearing a belt with braces. A win-win situation. The people vote, but you choose the winner.'

The PM didn't quite understand what his wife was saying so decided to ignore it.

'Well you must admit it satisfies all the major requirements. No pollies involved – that'll go down well with the mums and dads. The States and Territories have the right to nominate, which will keep them onside. The public will be able to take part and nominate the president they want. That should keep everyone happy.'

'It seems to me,' said the PM's wife, neatly castrating her boiled egg, 'that the public's going to have two bites at the apple.'

'Two?'

'Well they're going to vote twice, aren't they? Once at the ballot boxes and then again at the election. You could still finish up with some dumbcluck as president. Have you thought of that?'

The PM hadn't, but didn't want to admit to faults in his plan.

'It's going to work,' he said. 'I can see it now on the day of the inauguration … the pomp, the glitter, the massed bands, the dignitaries. And me on the dais, making the opening speech.'

He cleared his throat and went into rehearsal.

'My fellow Australians, Your Royal Highness, honourable guests, Mister President …'

'Or Madam.'

The PM sighed. The plan for choosing the first president might be a win-win situation, but when it came to dealing with his breakfast cabinet it was lose-lose, all the way.

13

Lily was haunted by those eyes and the touch of the Prince's hand. It was as though she had been hit by a bolt of lightning. She went about her duties in a trance, scarcely taking in what her roommate was saying. Emma, who'd complained earlier of the extra work the royal visit would bring, was now an ardent fan.

'Isn't he *luvverly*? Did you notice his cuff links? They've got crowns engraved on them! Or it could've been the Prince of Wales feathers, I didn't get close enough to look. Just think ... he's going to be here five whole days. I don't think I'll be able to stand the excitement. Eddie says all the kitchen staff are in a tizz, getting ready for tonight's dinner party.'

Before Lily could respond they were both summoned by Miss Patchett. Emma was assigned to linen room duties, while Lily was told to stand by in case any of the houseguests needed some attention. Her orders were to remain with the senior chambermaid Sarah and follow her instructions.

It was clear there was a strict hierarchy among the domestic staff, and as a newly arrived substitute, Lily's place was the lowest of the low. She bobbed a curtsy, said

'Yes, Miss Patchett', and set out to look for Sarah. She found her sitting at a desk in a room with a row of bells marked with numbers that (she guessed) corresponded to various parts of the house.

She was right. When a bell marked '5' rang, Sarah said 'That's the Blue Room. Third to the left at the top of the stairs. Nobody important, just see what they want and come back and tell me.'

The nobody important turned out to be a middle-aged woman with a plummy English voice who handed Lily two blouses and asked her to have them laundered and ironed as soon as possible. Not a please or a thank you. Just do it. Lily took them back to Sarah, who directed her to deliver them to the laundry room.

'That's Mrs Gibson,' she said. 'Came out from England with the Governor and Lady Weigall. She's on their personal staff, but we've never been able to work it out exactly. I think she might've been a nanny or something who's been pensioned off. She likes to put on a few airs, but we've been instructed to look after her.'

Later still, Lily was asked to help out at the official dinner. Not to wait on the table – that job was given to the permanent Government House staff. But she was to be a runner between dining room and kitchen, stacking dishes, removing uneaten food from plates and placing it in rubbish bins, handing over the dirty crockery and cutlery to the scullery maids. The plates were Royal Doulton, but she wasn't nervous about handling them. Apart from the Government House crest embossed in gold, it wasn't much different from the crockery used in some of the Hills homes where she'd worked. Mrs Cavendish, for instance, always served the food on fine porcelain china, specially imported from England.

Each time the door to the dining room opened she strained to catch a glimpse of the Prince inside. Once she thought she saw him in dinner jacket with decorations. But it was only a fleeting glimpse. And it was so brief it could have been someone else.

At nine o'clock the women guests, led by Lady Weigall, left the table and adjourned to a private room. Half an hour later the men, after port and cigars and some after dinner jokes considered unsuitable for delicate female ears, also left the room to rejoin the ladies. Lily was busy in the kitchen and didn't see them go. The dining room was now empty, the last plates and glasses cleared away.

Although Lily's duties seemed as though they were at an end, she was instructed to remain on standby with the rest of the domestic staff, in case she was needed.

Following the dinner there was an official reception. At 10.30 pm a small group of hand-picked guests stayed on for an informal dance. By this time Lily had been excused from further work and was told she could retire. She was walking down the corridor to her room, when she unexpectedly ran into Nifty. She smiled and tried to pass him but he blocked her way with both arms.

'Whoa there,' he said. 'What a stroke of luck. I've been hoping I'd run into you.' He was so close she could smell his hair lotion, and noticed for the first time there was a gap between his front teeth.

'I've got Saturday off,' he said. 'How's about we walk out together, just the two of us. I'd like to get to know you better.'

He was very close now, breathing heavily and pressing against her. Lily tried to move away, but he blocked her at every turn.

'I'm sorry,' she said. 'I don't think my father would allow it.'

'Your father!' said Nifty. 'What's he ruddy well got to do with it? You're of age, aren't you? Surely you can make up your own mind whether it's "yes" or "no"?'

'Then it's "no",' said Lily. 'Please let me pass.'

But Nifty was stubborn, still blocking the way. Suddenly he leaned down and kissed her. His lips were wet and sloppy and made her stomach turn over, but the shock of it gave Lily a sudden courage. She pushed him away and ran down the corridor towards her room. He didn't try to follow.

She was still shaking as she undressed and fell wearily into the narrow iron bed. Far away in another part of Government House she could hear the throbbing rhythm of the specially hired band. It put thoughts of the encounter with Nifty out of her mind as she strained her ears, but couldn't recognise any of the music. Probably the latest dance fad from London – the Weigalls would have made sure of that.

She'd read somewhere the Prince was fond of dancing. So who was he partnering? Which lucky woman was fox-trotting around the ballroom in his arms, looking into those sad blue eyes?

She felt a sharp stab of pain at the thought, but didn't know enough about love to recognise it as jealousy. Her body ached with exhaustion, and she was still missing her family. Although the mattress was hard and unyielding, she sank into it as though it was made of featherdown. It had been a long day. Her eyes closed, and in seconds Lily was asleep.

Next morning the newspaper headline on the front page read THE PRINCE OF SUNSHINE ARRIVES. Rain had been forecast, but by some royal miracle the sun had come out just as the Prince's car drove through the streets. Emma relayed all the news of the night before. She'd finished at the same time as Lily, but had stayed up late so she could meet Eddie when he came off duty.

'He said you've never seen anything like it,' confided Emma. 'Course the reception was a bit stuffy. Lots of shaking hands and bowing and scraping, officers standing to attention and all that. Eddie doesn't know how his nibs can stand it. But when all the bigwigs had gone and the band started up, Eddie said it was just like a party. He said it was amazing how the Prince changed.'

'What d'you mean, "changed"?'

'Well he acted like he was one of us, and let his hair down. Good and proper. Anyway that's what Eddie said. The Prince got hold of some drums and started banging away at them. Not half-bad either. Then blow me down if Archie didn't pick up a pencil and pretend to be conducting the band.'

'Sir Archibald? The Governor?'

'One and the same. Eddie says it was a scream. Everyone laughed themselves silly. Course, none of the servants could let on they thought it was funny. They just had to stand around with poker faces, like nothing was happening. But Eddie says the Prince was amazing. Didn't seem to be tired at all, had a whale of a time, and the dance didn't finish until two this morning.'

'Did the Prince dance with anyone special?'

Emma gave her a sharp look. 'Why d'you want to know?'

Lily began to feel uncomfortable. 'Nothing. Just curious, that's all.'

'Well Eddie did mention there was one young lady the Prince seemed a bit keen on. Anyway, he danced with her more times than any other, if that's anything to go by. Eddie said she had flamin' red hair and a good figure.' She paused, frowning.

'On the other hand, it could've been the Prince's cousin who was dancing with the redhead. Whatsis name again? Lord Louis something-or-other?'

'Mountbatten.'

'That's it. You're better on the names of these toffs than I am.'

'I read it in the paper,' said Lily.

And that was all Emma could tell her of last night's activities. Lily, desperate to know more about her loved one, kept asking questions. Did Eddie overhear anything the Prince said? Was he smiling or laughing when he was dancing with the flamin' redhead? How many times did they dance together? How many other women managed to catch his eye? Were they all beautiful? Did the women have to curtsy when he asked them to dance? Who was his partner for supper? Was he bored? Was he tired? Did he seem happy?

'Blimey', said Emma. 'You want to know a lot, don'tcher?' She looked closely at Lily. 'Not stuck on him, are you?'

'Course not,' said Lily. She could feel a blush starting to rise up and redden her cheeks.

'Cos if you are, you can forget it. Princes don't give a stuff for common servants like us. They stick to their own class. He's the King's son, don't forget. You'd have to have "Lady" in front of your name for him to even look twice at you.

'By the way, Eddie reckons Nifty's a bit keen on you. Don't be put off by the way he carried on at breakfast, he's really not a bad sort of a bloke when you get to know him. So ... what d'you think of him?'

Lily tossed over in her mind whether or not to tell Emma about last night's incident in the corridor, then decided against it. She'd be going home in a few days so there was no point to it. Aloud she said: 'Sorry, Em, but he's not my type.'

'So what's your type, Lily?' teased Emma as she poured water into the china washbasin.

Lily shrugged. 'Don't know,' she said, hoping Emma would drop the subject. Fortunately she did and began washing her face, her mind now on tomorrow's activities.

'Well here goes. Another day of toil and trouble. Just hope old Patchett doesn't work us as hard as she did yesterday. I was fair whacked out, and you should've heard Eddie going on. Reckons he finished up a cot case.'

So Lily gave in to commonsense and decided to put the Prince out of her mind. She'd been brought here to do a job, and she was determined to do it to the utmost of her ability. When it was all over she'd return to her family and the comfortable familiarity of old times. She would entertain her father and brothers with anecdotes about life at Government House. To celebrate her return she would buy them gifts from the city shops. A wool scarf and a new pipe for her father. Tobacco and socks for her brothers. In less than a week it would all be over, and the royal party gone.

But one thing was still niggling away in her mind, and for the life of her she couldn't get rid of it. Something the Prince had said as he held her hand.

Who was the Jersey Lily?

14

By the third week of April the machinery had been put in place to choose the first president. A selection committee had been set up to oversee the procedure, and a former head of the Prime Minister's Department, Richard Carruthers (known around the Canberra traps as 'Slippery Dick') had been brought back from a Gold Coast retirement to chair it.

The names nominated for the committee were interesting. One was the well-known Aboriginal rights activist Mae Pindari; another was Dr Brawn-Davies, Dean of Law Studies at the University of Western Australia and author of the best-seller *Australia: Republic or Monarchy?* Written originally as her thesis for a doctorate in political science, it had earned a gold medal from the International Society for Historical Studies plus a string of literary awards. It had been extensively quoted by both sides during the run-up to both the plebiscite and the referendum.

Of the men, there was a churchman known for his outspoken views on social issues, a community leader, a migrant spokesman, a representative of the public service, and a prominent businessman. All in all a nice mix, the PM told his breakfast cabinet the next morning. No one likely to rock the boat or cause any problems.

'What problems?' snapped his wife, trying to decide between a muffin and a crumpet (the crumpet won). She was not in a good mood, still smouldering over a case involving an adulterous husband and some missing millions squirreled away in a Swiss bank account. Men, she'd long ago decided, were devious and untrustworthy bastards. Especially when their marriages broke up.

'They've got ten fingers, haven't they? All they have to do is add up numbers and tick voters' names off the list, for God's sake. A child could do it.'

Yes a child could probably do it, explained the PM patiently. But there was more to it than who had the most votes. Fine judgment was involved. Commonsense. Core values. Diplomacy. And the bottom line was the good of the country. At some stage the committee might need to do some adjustment and fine tuning to come up with a result.

'What you mean is ... cheat?'

The PM sighed. He hated it when his wife was in one of her hissy fits. 'I mean, it's vitally important we get the right person. Someone who will uphold the dignity of such a high office.'

'What dignity? The last one you appointed turned up blind drunk at a State dinner. If I remember it right, he had to be scraped off the floor.'

The PM winced. That was a nasty one. A bumper. He'd had to take him aside for a quiet word. Phrases like 'rest and recuperation', and 'Alcoholics Anonymous' had figured in the conversation. 'Retiring for health reasons' was also dropped into the mix. Fortunately the Queen's man had seen the error of his ways, and there had been no trouble since.

'I was let down by my department,' said the PM. 'They didn't do their research properly. Someone should have warned me he was a lush. How was I to know?' The PM was very skilled at passing the buck.

The boxes for public nominations were now in place at all post offices across the country. Painted in the national colours of green and yellow, and marked PRESIDENT: YOUR SAY, they were colourful, conspicuous, and had cost a packet (estimates were close to half a million dollars). As soon as each one was installed, the votes for first president started to flow in.

The letter drop of an information brochure was a bit slower, timed to tie in with a massive television, radio and print campaign. It had cost another packet, but the PM didn't give a toss. Printed on glossy paper with his personal signature, it was targeted at every Australian household.

FROM THE OFFICE OF THE PRIME MINISTER
My Fellow Australians –

On March 30 you indicated clearly by way of a referendum that you wish to replace the present monarchical system by a republic with an Australian as Head of State. In line with our great democratic system, your government is now pleased to put this change into effect.

All Australian citizens who are registered to vote are invited to submit the name of any Australian citizen between the ages of 45 and 75 years to be president. As announced, there are no restrictions as to sex, race, religion, or political affiliation, but please note that serving politicians and those with criminal records are excluded from consideration.

Nomination forms can be downloaded from the Australian Government website or collected at post offices around the country. All nomination forms must be placed in the clearly marked ballot boxes at Australian Post offices.

A presidential selection committee will supervise the counting of names submitted by the public. The two individuals with the most nominations will be added to those nominated by State and Territory governments. A short list will then be chosen, on which the public will be invited to vote. The final choice for President will be ratified by both Houses of Parliament on a non-party basis.

Every Australian citizen is entitled to submit one presidential nomination only. Any subsequent nominations will be discarded by the selection committee. The closing date for nominations is June 30, 2016.

I look forward to your personal participation in this major and historic event.

Noelene read hers and immediately tossed it in the bin.

In spite of the air of excitement at the country becoming a republic, the Prime Minister was still unsure whether he was reading the public mood correctly. Could the mums and dads be relied on to make the right choice for the two wild cards? Clearly some guidance was needed; it was time for a Mission Statement.

His press secretary advised that buying time on television would be the most effective way to get his message across. Readers of newspapers tended to skip pages with government announcements, and talkback shows were unpredictable. It was finally decided an informal chat, sandwiched in between news and current affairs, would be the answer.

The Prime Minister went to a lot of trouble with his TV appearance. He didn't want to look authoritarian; on the other hand an open-necked shirt seemed too informal … even allowing that a former PM (what was his name again?) had gotten away with it 48 years ago.

In the end he called in a wardrobe expert who suggested a charcoal grey suit worn with the tie that was presented to the PM by the National Press Club when he'd addressed one of its lunches. It was a nice navy blue tie covered in yellow squiggly bits. Its meaning had been explained to the PM at the time by the club president, although for the life of him he couldn't remember now what it was. It had been hanging on his tie rack for months, and this seemed as good a time as any to wear it.

It also might get the Canberra press gallery onside.

'Dear friends,' he said, leaning forward and looking directly into the camera as instructed by his media adviser ('think of it as talking to just one person in the privacy of their lounge room ...')

'Dear friends,' he repeated by way of emphasis. 'Some of you may be feeling concerned about the changes as a result of the referendum. Changes make us nervous. Nothing to be ashamed about. Perfectly understandable. We all feel more comfortable with the old and the familiar.

'As your Prime Minister, let me reassure you there is no cause for alarm. Even when we make the historic move from monarchy to republic, life will go on much as usual. Many of the changes will be superficial and barely noticed. There will be absolutely no disruption to the way you carry on your normal daily lives.

'I am delighted that we can offer you the chance to take part in this historic occasion by nominating your choice for Head of State. My government has deliberated long and carefully about the issue, and feel this is a unique opportunity for you to have a say in the future of this great country of ours.

'It is 115 years since we first united as a commonwealth. Now another milestone has been reached and the time has come for us to shed the trappings of the past and move calmly and confidently into the future.

'This then is my Mission Statement. I promise that my government will continue to serve you, the people, to the utmost of our ability. We will abide by your decision to become a republic. And I have the utmost faith that whoever is finally chosen to be our first president will be worthy of the role.

'God bless Australia. God bless you all!'

It was a classic text from Prime Ministerspeak: or How to Keep the Mums and Dads Happy.

Noelene had just returned from another visit to Adelaide. This one was part pleasure and part business. The business was conferring with members of the South Australian Arts and Music Trust about a new rehearsal hall that was to be named in her honour. It would be opened at the end of the year. The pleasure was talking to her architect about plans for her great-grandparents' cottage.

The architect was a busy man and warned he wouldn't be able to start work on the project for at least three months. But he was the best in the business, famed for his sympathetic restoration of nineteenth century houses, and so she'd decided to wait until he was ready. There was no point in rushing the work. In the meantime he'd done some preliminary research on materials.

There was no difficulty with replacing the timber and stonework, and the painting and decoration would be straightforward. But the bricks were a problem. The brickworks that had made them had gone out of business in the last century, and there was no one around with a similar product.

'I've got someone on my staff chasing it up,' he said. 'We may not find an exact match, but we'll try and get as close as possible. By the way, watch it if you're going through the place. I noticed there're a lot of holes in the floor, and some of the bricks around the fireplace have worked loose. I wouldn't want one landing on your foot; it could be painful. Just be careful.'

Noelene knew exactly what she wanted to do with the old cottage. New plumbing and wiring, of course – that went without saying. A brand new bathroom with an old-fashioned claw foot bath and a marble-topped wash basin set in mahogany. A kitchen with an old-fashioned potbelly stove. Copper pots and pans.

But it was the parlour with its open fireplace that excited her imagination the most. She pictured herself in a rocking chair in front of a glowing fire in winter, reading a book or listening to music. There would be a cat curled up at her feet, of course. A ginger one she'd call Marmalade.

There'd be framed prints on the wall. Old photographs. And if she was lucky, one of those foot pedal organs you could sometimes find in the old Lutheran churches and second-hand shops around the Barossa. No television, computers, or fax machines. This would be her own private space, her bolthole, where she could hide herself away when life became too hectic.

In the back garden there'd be a vegetable patch and some grape vines over a trellis. She'd lived most of her life in hotels and apartments and liked the idea of growing her own tomatoes and lettuce and herbs. She was still thinking about it when the phone rang. It was Mike.

'Where've you been?'

'Adelaide. Sorry, I suppose I should've told you.'

'That's okay. I'm not your keeper. Can I pop over? There's something I need to discuss.'

'Sure. Come for dinner, if you don't mind potluck. I brought back a very good red and it's sitting here, breathing its little heart out. Just give me time to unpack. Half an hour suit you?'

'Perfect.'

By the time Mike arrived the potluck had turned into spaghetti bolognaise and the table was set for two. Mike was carrying a bunch of flowers which he handed to Noelene. It was an unexpected gesture she hadn't expected. A bit out of character.

'Thanks, they're lovely. What's the occasion?'

'Nothing. Just happened to be passing a florist and thought you'd like them.'

She knew him better than that.

'Are you trying to soften me up for something?'

'In a way, yes. Let's talk about it over dinner.'

They sat down, and Mike got right to the point.

'I keep an ear on things, and your name keeps coming up as president. If you're nominated, I think you should run.'

'Run? You make it sound like an American election'.

'I'm saying at least consider it if it's offered to you.'

'What am I supposed to do – put my own name in a ballot box?'

'Of course not. But I think you'll find there're a lot of people who will. I'll be very surprised if you're not nominated by one of the States … and if not, there's still the people's vote. You're an Australian icon.'

'So are Bananas in Pyjamas.'

'Be serious.'

'I am. Look, I want to enjoy my retirement, not spend it pinning on medals and shaking hands. This might sound strange seeing the career I've had, but I'm really a very private person.

'Public life doesn't appeal to me any more. Anyway, if I'd had any thoughts of running, going on that TV show knocked it all out of me.'

'Remember what John Kennedy said: "Think not of what your country can do for you, but what you can do for your country." '

'Not fair. Now you're using emotional blackmail.'

'I'm appealing to your sense of patriotism.'

'I don't have any. No, that's not strictly true. I do love my country … and I'm sure whoever is finally chosen will do a fine job. But this business of ballot boxes is crazy. It's opening the floodgates for every crank and nutter around, and turning the thing into a popularity contest.'

But Mike wasn't giving up without a fight.

'Don't you want to see an Australian as Head of State?'

'Of course I do. It doesn't make sense to have one the other side of the world. I'm happy we're finally becoming a republic, but I don't want to be its first president. So don't try to talk me into it.'

'Okay, fair enough. I'll drop the subject; I respect your wishes. The only reason I brought it up was because it could make a difference to the documentary … affect its whole direction. I need to know these things if I'm to do a good job with it. So keep me informed … and if you change your mind, let me know.'

'You'll be the first. I promise.'

Later that evening, still thinking about Mike's words, Noelene went to bed, only to toss and turn until three in the morning. When she finally fell asleep it wasn't the presidency she dreamed about but her grandmother Lily.

There was that small smiling figure from the photo, framed by an arch of climbing roses, baby clasped in her arms. That baby who was her father. She was smiling at Noelene as if telling her something. What was it?

Noelene awoke with a feeling of intense grief and loss.

15

Noelene was right on one thing. The PM's decision to add a people's choice had opened the floodgates. Every wacko, ratbag and loony wanted a say. There were letters to the editor, calls to talkback radio, public rallies and demonstrations. Picking the president had turned into a national sport.

The green and yellow ballot boxes were an immediate hit. People queued up with their forms, anxious to be among the first to record their vote. Among the early nominees were Emma Chissit and Gert (by the Sea) ... quickly eliminated by the selection committee.

It was also proving a financial bonanza for shopping centres close to where the boxes were located. Shop owners reported a sharp upturn in sales and customers, although no one could explain why. A professor of sociology put forward the theory that the ballot boxes had become the new social centre, replacing the office water cooler or the old-time village square. Like many academic theories it couldn't be proved, but it seemed to make sense.

A few smart business operatives cashed in quickly on the new business opportunities. Tea towels, coffee mugs, jigsaw puzzles, school pencil sets. There was even a board game titled

PRESIDENT! with penalties for flying the Union Jack or singing *God Save the Queen,* and a square marked Head of State
as the final goal. A player unlucky enough to land on the one
marked 'monarchist' was shipped in irons back to England as
a convict, until freed by paying a fine.

Graffiti began to appear on walls: QUEEN LIZ APPLIES FOR
DOLE was one of the most popular. More names started to
crawl out of the woodwork and appear in the daily papers.
Where were they coming from? In an attempt to plug the leaks,
the selection committee issued a statement, denying any of its
members guilty. But the guessing game still went on.

Don Bradman, was clean bowled when someone pointed
out he'd long ago gone to that great cricket pitch in the sky. Ky-
lie Minogue, 48, was too busy raising a young family. Dame
Joan Sutherland surfaced briefly, but at 90, born the same year
as the Queen, was eliminated on grounds of age. Out for the
same reason was the wobbleboard king Sir Rolf Harris, 86.

The pop singer John Farnham, 63, was an early hot favourite. He qualified on all counts, and was still popular with the
public. An added bonus was that a touch of grey at the tem-
ples and a few extra kilos in weight now gave him the look of
a distinguished elder statesman. But there was some question
whether he'd be prepared to take on the job as he was about
to begin another farewell tour of the nation.

And Mike was right. Noelene's name was coming up more
and more frequently in the unofficial polls. In two weeks, she
had zoomed up in the popularity stakes to number four.

—*#*—

When the Presidential Selection Committee had its first meeting in Canberra, it faced a staggering 20,048 names from the yellow and green boxes. There were, of course, the public identities. But it was the unknowns who were proving a headache. Friends nominated friends, neighbours nominated neighbours, and favoured relatives were thrown into the mix. A Joe Papadopoulos had been nominated at least a dozen times. Why was he so popular? The local greengrocer giving away free fruit and vegetables? No one could come up with an answer.

'So how do we deal with all these names?' asked Brawn-Davies. 'What's the ruling from the chair?'

The ruling from Slippery Dick was that it would be left to a computer to sort it out. By the next meeting he hoped the numbers would be reduced to a more manageable size.

'Who's going to operate the computer?' asked Mae Pindari. No one put up a hand. But Slippery Dick said the prime minister's department had offered one of its staff for the duration of the sittings. Problem solved.

'Hope she's a good looker,' said the public service representative. Slippery Dick frowned. Although he had been renowned in his Canberra days as a pants man, he didn't approve of sexist talk.

The meeting was declared closed, and the committee adjourned to the Members Bar for drinks. On the way they passed the PM's press secretary in a corridor.

'How'd it go?' asked the secretary. 'Anything to report back to the old man?'

'Good consensus', said Slippery Dick. 'Fruitful discussions. A couple of minor queries on technical points, but nothing critical. Tell him everything's under control.'

And so the first step on the long bumpy road to choosing an Australian as Head of State began.

16

At breakfast in the servants' quarters, the conversation was almost exclusively on the Prince: what he'd done, the things he'd said, the clothes he'd worn, the food he'd eaten. Every bit of tittle-tattle, real or invented, was passed around the table, examined, commented on, and then handed to the next person. Those working close enough to him to be regarded as authorities were regarded with awe as they relayed their own personal 'what I saw' or 'what I heard' stories.

There was also some speculation, particularly among the younger women, on what royalty wore to bed at night. Was it true the Prince went to sleep in silk pyjamas with crowns embroidered in gold thread? One chambermaid swore she'd heard it from another who'd had it on good authority from HRH's personal valet.

The truth was that none of them had been closer to the Prince than filling his wine glass or removing a plate. The handful of staff assigned by Sir Archibald to look after the Prince's personal requirements were all senior staff, some of whom had been at Government House for more than 20 years. They were highly trained and knew their places,

which was to serve their superiors and keep a discreet
silence on what went on inside the four walls of the private
rooms. To breach this trust would mean instant dismissal.

They took pride in their work, and kept themselves
aloof from the rest of the servants. They ate their meals
separately, waited on by the junior staff. Lily was pleased
to note that the dreaded Miss Patchett was not one of the
privileged few.

Nifty was again at the table, sitting next to his best
friend Eddie. But he'd either got the message that Lily
wasn't interested or he now had his eye on someone else.
Either way he didn't once look in her direction, and after
breakfast disappeared without a word.

When Lily reported for duty she was put to work
checking the guest accommodation. Although it was
winter, sun streamed in through the windows. Looking
out as she adjusted the curtains, she thought she glimpsed
the Prince walking past the rose beds with a companion.
She felt strangely pleased his walking partner was not a
woman. When the Prince turned to talk he looked up to
the taller man, and Lily caught a glimpse of his face.

It was just a glimpse, but it was enough for a shiver of
excitement to run through her. Just as quickly, she put such
feelings firmly aside and moved back from the window.
Emma was right. They were worlds apart, and to think he
would even look at someone of her class was absurd. And
yet she still couldn't forget the touch of his hand, and the
way he'd spoken. 'Lily ... a lovely name ...' His words were
burned into her memory.

She didn't catch any more glimpses of the Prince, and
domestic staff had been forbidden to go anywhere near

the royal suite unless instructed. But snippets of news filtered back through Emma and the ever-faithful Eddie. In the morning the Prince had been driven to Jubilee Oval for a rally of Boy Scouts. Later still, he'd gone to Austral Gardens to meet returned servicemen and nurses.

All this had been relayed through one of Eddie's mates on the Government House staff, a brother (or was it a cousin?) of the chauffeur assigned to the royal limousine for the day.

The Prince wouldn't be back until well into the afternoon, Emma told Lily, as he was going to the races. It would be a busy day, as after the races there was to be a levee at Government House, followed in the evening by a State banquet.

After cleaning and tidying the guest rooms assigned to her, Lily had a brief break before her next duties. Her mind had been so full of the Prince that she'd almost forgotten about her family. Were they missing her? Who was cooking the meals, making sure her father's slippers were in place each night alongside the rocking chair by the fire, setting the stove, scrubbing the floors, doing all the hundred and one things she'd looked after for the past six years? She searched in a drawer, and found some paper and envelopes, probably left there by Emma's former roommate.

As Lily sat down to write her family a letter, she found it unexpectedly difficult. She'd been top of her class in grammar and composition, so there was no problem in composing a sentence. In her last year of school she'd won high praise from her teacher for an essay on Arbour Day. But writing about trees was different from writing about oneself. The problem lay in trying to put into words exactly how she felt, digging down deep into her innermost emotions, especially as she wasn't sure what they were.

She'd never been away from home before, and had no idea what to say. Somehow her thoughts seemed too private, too personal, to commit to paper. In the end she wrote a few brief lines to say she had settled in nicely, and shaken hands with the Prince. After some pencil-chewing she added a P.S. 'Am looking forward to coming home', but then had second thoughts. Would that worry them? Would they think she was unhappy or badly treated? So she scratched it out, and wrote instead: 'The people here are very nice, and I am making new friends.'

Emma gave her a stamp and showed her a post box where she could mail the letter. The rest of the day was uneventful. Cars delivered people to the front door and went away again. The kitchen staff prepared food for the evening – a small family meal, as the Prince and his entourage would be at the Grand Central Hotel for the State banquet.

What with one thing and another and being kept busy with her housekeeping duties, Lily had almost put the Royal visitor out of her mind. Almost, but not quite. Because when she finished work and retired to her room to read the newspaper, there he was again all over the front page, still regally controlling the weather.

RAIN CLOUDS DISPELLED
ROYAL PROGRESS A PERSONAL TRIUMPH
A CITY OF LIGHT
WONDERFUL ILLUMINATIONS

Lily, impressed, showed the paper to her roommate. But Emma was too full of complaints of her own problems to be interested. She said Miss Patchett had made her polish a piece of brass twice because she'd left fingerprints on it. 'A coal scuttle,' said Emma, full of righteous indignation. 'Who's going to ruddy well see it?'

Emma said she'd been on the point of handing in her notice, but Eddie had talked her out of it. She could easily get work waitressing; a friend who owned a cafe in Rundle Street had promised her a job if she ever wanted it. More pay and far better hours than working at Government House, even if there was a bit of prestige attached to it. But Eddie said it wouldn't be right, letting down the Governor and his lady just as the Royal visit was starting. It would be unpatriotic.

Another thing, too. As it was known they were walking out together people might think he'd encouraged her to leave. Although Eddie had ambitions to one day move to the country and buy a small property, he couldn't afford to jeopardise his present job. He was doing well, and had been promised a promotion when the senior staff butler retired.

'So what with one thing and another I might as well stay on,' said Emma. 'But she's a pain, no two ways about it.'

Still disgruntled, Emma undressed and went to bed. Within minutes she was asleep and snoring with gentle snuffles, chest heaving and pink face almost buried under the sheets. But sleep didn't come so easily to Lily. She lay awake on her bed, fully dressed, staring at the ceiling. What were her father and brothers doing? Were they missing her?

Then her thoughts turned to the Prince. She imagined the cream of Adelaide society lining up to be presented to him. Beautiful women in elegant satin gowns and expensive jewellery, who would attract the royal eye and fascinate him with their brilliant wit. What could she say if she ever had the opportunity to talk to him? What do you say to a prince? 'Honoured to meet you, Sir'. 'I hope everything's to your satisfaction, Sir'. Or should it be 'Your Royal Highness'?

Close to midnight, still restless, Lily decided to slip quietly out and go for a walk in the gardens. It would help clear her head, and the fresh air might make her sleep. With Emma still gently snoring, Lily slipped out a door leading from the staff quarters. Although the mid-winter night air was crisp and chilly, her body felt warm and glowing as if lit by an inner fire.

She walked past the rose gardens, turned a corner, and then an incredible thing happened. Someone else was in the gardens and in the darkness they collided, throwing her off-balance so that she fell heavily to the ground. As she lay there, stunned but unhurt, she saw that the person she'd bumped into was no other than the Prince of Wales.

'I'm frightfully sorry,' he said in that unmistakeable clipped English voice. 'Didn't expect anyone else to be around at this hour of the night. You caught me by surprise.' He held out one hand and helped Lily to her feet. It was only then she noticed a second person watching from a short distance away. The Prince peered at Lily in the half darkness.

'It's Lily, isn't it? What on earth are you doing out here on your own at night?'

Lily explained how she couldn't sleep and had gone for a walk, and then realised he was still holding her hand. They were so close she could see the gold signet ring gleaming on one finger, and catch the scent of the cologne he was wearing. It had a clean, tangy smell, like freshly cut flowers.

'What an amazing stroke of luck,' said the Prince. 'It must be fate. I was hoping we'd run into each other again.'

'Come on, David.' The tall man ahead was gesturing impatiently, looking at his watch.

'That's Dickie,' said the Prince. 'My shadow. Always in a hurry. Likes to keep me on my toes.'

He looked at her again, and Lily felt herself trembling.

'Until next time,' he said. Then with a wave and a 'cheerio' he joined this companion and the two disappeared into the darkness.

Ten minutes later she was back in her room and in bed.

When she finally fell asleep, she had a dream in which she'd turned into a princess, and a golden-haired prince was climbing a castle turret to rescue her.

She woke to find the face of an alarmed Emma leaning over her. 'You all right, Lil?' she asked. 'You were acting kind of funny. I was worried. Did you have a bad dream?'

'It's nothing,' said Lily. 'Nothing at all. I'm sorry if I disturbed you. Go back to sleep.' It was only then she realised her nightgown was damp and her body drenched in perspiration.

17

A new player had entered the game. He was Harry Winston, born Henryk Waliezwsnki, a name changed within a year of migrating to Australia because no one could spell or pronounce it.

Harry had arrived with just fifty dollars in his pocket, but by hard work and a shrewd eye for opportunity, had built up a successful real estate business. His first purchase had been a run-down weatherboard cottage in an unfashionable area of Sydney. But the land on which the cottage sat, once a sewerage farm, had turned out to be a goldmine. Following Bob Hope's recipe for success ('buy on the outskirts of a growing city') his total holdings were now close to $2 billion.

Harry was balding, ugly, overweight, and suffered from peptic ulcers. He lived in a mansion on the Sydney waterfront, owned a yacht, a helicopter, and a private jet, and gave generously to all the major political parties. If the country hadn't long ago abandoned knighthoods, by now he'd have had 'Sir' in front of his name.

Harry's biggest asset was his wife Sapphire. She was Mrs Winston number two (the first had been shipped home to some obscure middle European country). Sapphire (he called her 'Saph') was 30 years younger and came from eastern suburbs aristocracy. He'd met her in Monte Carlo where he'd been checking out the tax benefits and she'd been bronzing herself on the beach.

It was love at first sight. She loved the size of his bank account and he loved the size of her breasts. His wedding gift was a week in Paris, where in one day Saph had clocked up $15,000 on his gold credit card. And that was just buying handbags and shoes. It was as though Jackie Onassis had been reborn.

Back in Sydney the Winstons quickly built up a reputation as social hosts. The Prime Minister and his wife had been frequent guests at their lavish dinners, and each December took delivery of Harry's personal Christmas gift – a case of the finest French champagne. So it was with a great deal of pleasure, as well as considerable surprise, that the PM noted Harry's name coming up as the people's choice.

Harry would make an excellent president, he told his wife that morning at breakfast. Perfect for the job. Well-regarded in the business community, and a shining example of how a near-penniless migrant could achieve success in multicultural Australia. And it went without saying Sapphire would be a decorative asset to Yarralumla. 'Liven the place up,' said the PM. 'Give it a bit of bloody style for a change.'

The PM's wife didn't share her husband's enthusiasm. 'What, that fat, pompous, vulgar foul-mouthed overbearing git?' were her precise words. She had a gift for language. 'The man can't even string two sentences together without tripping over his tongue. How come he's in the running?'

'Popular demand,' said the PM, although to tell the truth he was also puzzled at how Harry had made it.

'Popular demand, pig's arse. If Harry's on the list, there's only one reason. The bastard's bought it.'

As usual the PM's wife was dead right. Harry had bought his wife, he'd bought his waterfront mansion, and now he planned to buy the presidency. Not for nothing had he called himself Winston after the great World War II leader. To Harry, the name represented Doggedness, Determination and Power, all of which had propelled him to the top of the business ladder. He was particularly pleased after he'd become a true blue Aussie (and planted the gum tree given to him) to realise he shared the name with a former prime minister.

The Harry Winston Development Corporation had 208 offices spread right across Australia. So on the first day of the campaign to pick a people's president, Harry sent a newsletter to the manager of each branch.

His command of the language, as the PM's wife had pointed out, might be on the shaky side. But there was nothing wrong with his mathematics. With an average staff of 20 in each of the 208 offices, that represented 4160 potential votes.

The newsletter was carefully worded with the help of a spin doctor. Harry wasn't blatant enough to put himself forward as the next Head of State. But he did suggest to branch managers it could be in their interests to encourage staff to take up the government's invitation. There was also an offhand reference to bonuses. He added it was his personal opinion the job should go to someone with a high public profile and a proven track record in business.

Harry's philosophy, the way he explained it, was a simple one. If you thought of the Australian people as shareholders, then there was no difference between being chairman of a company and president of a country. The letter finished on an uplifting patriotic note: 'So let's all pull together for the good of this great nation, and ensure the right person is chosen for the job.' It wasn't hard to figure that the right person was Harry.

He looked at the letter before sending it, pleased with his work. *His Excellency the President of the Republic of Australia*. It had a nice ring to it. It would look particularly impressive on the gold-embossed personalised Christmas cards he and Saph sent out each year to friends and business colleagues. Mention of the festive season caused a curious back flip in Harry's mind, as he sat contemplating a rosy tomorrow. His thinking went something like this. There was no more prestigious job than Head of State, a role shortly to be vacated by HM the Queen. He would replace her as number one, with Saph as First Lady.

So wouldn't the boot be on the other foot, placing him above the Prime Minister in order of precedence? Would the PM now have to bow and scrape and defer, instead of the other way around? It was an enticing thought.

So Harry sat and plotted and pondered, gazing into the crystal ball of his bright new future. And the more he looked, the more he liked what he saw.

He made a note to cancel the next Christmas delivery to The Lodge.

Kelvin ('Big Kel') Brady, who was even richer than Harry, had a much simpler approach. He handed a blank cheque to the country's top lobbyist and said: 'You've got three weeks. Get me on that fucking short list.'

18

Jason Lazlo, soccer superstar, didn't have to spend one cent to get himself nominated as one of the wild cards in the people's choice. As soon as the ballot boxes were in place, his fans went into overdrive. They rallied by the thousands, determined to win their sporting hero the country's top job. In every city and State they were busy stuffing signed nomination forms into the green and yellow bins. By the end of the first week Lazlo's name was up there among the favourites.

At 45, Jason was the world's oldest soccer player. If chosen, he would be the world's youngest president. It was an interesting double that should ensure him a place in the Guinness Book of Records.

'What's a president supposed to do?' Jason asked his manager. It was the morning after a night spent with a spectacular blonde, and he was having trouble putting his mind to the presidential nomination. But he'd seen the newspapers and read the predictions, and felt he owed it to his fans to show some interest.

The manager hadn't any more of a clue than Jason, but offered to do some research and find out the details. Meantime he suggested it might be a good idea if Jason had his shoulder length locks cut shorter, and was seen now and then in a suit and tie.

'Bloody hell,' said Jason. 'I'll look like a bloody bank clerk.' But he made an appointment for the next day with his hair stylist.

Jason Lazlo had been top dog in the international soccer world for as long as anyone could remember. Born to Hungarian parents, he'd come to Australia as a baby. At thirteen, when playing school soccer, he'd been spotted by a talent scout and given a sports scholarship. At 18 he was the top scoring player in the country.

There'd been offers from overseas, of course. He'd done a couple of seasons with Manchester United and also an Italian club based in Milan. The money had been phenomenal. But he'd blown most of it on gambling and women, and as a result had found himself in a spot of trouble with the Italian tax authorities. There'd also been an episode involving the wife of a prominent government official. Nasty things had been threatened involving a body part he'd prefer to protect.

So when an opportunity to return to Australia came up, along with some lucrative deals in commercial endorsements and television, it was like a lifeline. Jason grabbed it with open arms and had been a national sports icon ever since.

The next day his manager reported back to him. 'The job's a pushover,' he said. 'Nothing to it. Piece of cake. From what I gather it's shaking hands and opening things and signing bits of paper.' He was proud of his research.

'You mean, like the Queen does?'

'Exactly. You could do it in your sleep.'

'What's it pay?'

'Ah, good question. I couldn't find the answer to that one. Apparently the government's still working it out. But bear in mind, sonny boy, you're just about at the end of your career. So don't knock it.

'By the way the job comes with two houses, including a nice piece of prime waterfront property. Harbour views, never be built out. Plenty of OS travel, of course. All expenses paid, that goes without saying. Limo and driver. Wall to wall servants. This could work into a handy little retirement package.'

The oldest soccer player in the world thought about it. His mental processes had slowed down over the years by too many balls being bounced on his head, but he was still sharp enough to know that his manager was right. His body was giving out on him, his feet weren't as fast as they used to be, and younger players were starting to breathe down his neck. He didn't have a lot of good playing time ahead of him. Six months, max.

'You've sold me, mate,' he said. 'What've I got to lose?'

And then there were the loonies. A young woman was arrested as she posed naked in front of Parliament House, Canberra. She claimed she was a symbol for 'the stripping away of old values.' It wasn't clear what values she was stripping away or which side she was on.

Dennis Jackson, University student, aged 19, set fire to a ballot box, destroying an estimated 107 entries. He said it was in protest against the government wasting its funds on a presidential campaign when the money could be better spent protecting the environment and saving endangered species. He was charged with arson and public mischief.

Arnold Arbuckle, aged 52, who'd had three tries for a Senate seat (running as candidate for the Health and Happiness Party), announced he'd quit politics and was nominating himself as the next Head of State. There was a lot of discussion by the selection committee on whether he was eligible, but it was finally decided there was nothing in the rules that said a political failure couldn't run for president. Then it was discovered he was a Kiwi and had never bothered to take out citizenship.

All the major political parties took out full-page advertisements in the daily papers, urging Australians to 'exercise your democratic right, but think carefully before you nominate'. Names and pictures were featured, with the favoured few split evenly between company CEOs, trade union officials, and community leaders.

To further help the public make up its mind, there were editorials, opinion pieces, profiles, columns, comments, surveys, polls, think tanks, brains trusts, and focus groups. Current affairs presenters explained nightly how the nominations process was progressing. Washington correspondents reassured viewers that unlike the United States, an Australian president would not have a red panic button to push.

Bookmakers were taking bets. Sky writers trailed 'VOTE FOR' signs as they circled in planes over the cities. Posters started to come out like a rash on telegraph poles and fences.

Booths were set up, with volunteers handing out brochures praising the virtues of one candidate or another. Experts commented on experts. Nobody could agree on anything.

Dinner parties became war zones. Spouse was pitted against spouse, child against parent. Punch-ups were common, along with insults, raised fists, shouting matches, street marches, public demonstrations, and threats of action for defamation. At least once the police had to use a water cannon to calm a riot.

There were core and non-core promises. One candidate pledged to give a copy of *The Magic Pudding* to every Australian child under the age of five. The country broke out in an epidemic of baby kissing. It was just like an election.

And the real one was still to come.

19

No date had been announced for the naming of the first president. Although the short list would be known soon after the election, the Prime Minister wanted to give the impression of taking his time before coming to such an important decision.

Decision-making came easy to the self-proclaimed Man of Action. Strong, resolute, finger on the pulse of the nation. Someone who could reach a statesman-like resolution when the situation called for it. Of course there were times when his mouth engaged before his brain, but it happened rarely. He was looking forward to the job of choosing the country's first president, as he told his wife that morning.

'It's a challenge, but fortunately I am well equipped to handle it,' he said. 'It's no harder than picking a Governor-General. Easier, when you think about it. All it needs is clear thinking, an ability to read character, and a keen professional judgment.'

'So how come you stuffed up the last one?'

The PM winced and decided to change the subject. He didn't like to be reminded of past mistakes, especially when eating breakfast.

'About the inauguration,' he said. 'It's fixed for November, but I'm still waiting to hear from the Palace. Personally I'm not optimistic about the Queen coming. I keep a close ear to these things, and the High Commissioner reports the royal doctors are concerned about the effects of a long air trip on someone her age.

'Mind you, it's not exactly flying cattle class, is it? They always stick them up the pointy end and bung a curtain around them. She's not going to be in one of those seats with knees up to your chin, having to stand every time someone wants to go to the loo. No chance of Her Majesty dropping dead from a thrombosis … she'd have plenty of room to give the old gams a workout.'

'Why do we need a royal anyway?' asked his wife. 'I thought the whole point of the exercise was to break free from the monarchy.'

'It's a matter of symbolism and tradition,' the PM explained. His wife could be difficult at times, and this was clearly one of them. 'Core values. It's about not forgetting those things that have stood us in good stead in the past. Remembering the strong links that have bound our two countries together. Reconciling the old with the new. Paying tribute to the rightful place of the British monarchy in the annals of our glorious history, while recognising there is a need for us to now be in charge of our own affairs and our own destiny.' He rolled the words around on his tongue like a throat lozenge, savouring them.

'You don't have to make a speech,' snapped his wife. 'I'm not one of your constituents.'

Meanwhile, as the list of popular nominations grew longer, the selection committee was busy trying to reduce it to a manageable size. Duplication of names had reduced the numbers, the largest coming from NSW and Victoria. The State with the smallest number of nominations was Queensland, where one wag had suggested The Big Pineapple. But then, as Slippery Dick commented, those bananalanders had always been different from the rest of us.

There was no difficulty in sorting out the rejects. These included Fatso the wombat (no animals) the Wiggles (no groups) and *Waltzing Matilda* (no songs). Sir William Deane and Sir Gustav Nossal, two popular early nominees, were ruled out as both had turned 85. The loonies were easy to eliminate; it was the ones still left that were the problem.

Some stayed on top like cream on a bottle of milk, while others moved slowly down into oblivion. Unfortunately for Harry, his was one of the names that had started to slide. Not far enough to put him out of the running, but enough to move him to number five.

'Should we keep him in?' Slippery Dick asked at the fourth meeting of the committee. 'I understand the Prime Minister's quite keen on him.'

'Bugger the PM,' said the public servant. 'If he hasn't the numbers, he's bloody well out.'

Noelene's name was slowly creeping up to the top of the list. Jason Lazlo was also a popular favourite. There was some spirited discussion on the relative merits of the two.

'My God,' said the community leader. 'Can you imagine it? Tossing that hair, flashing those teeth. Gold chains clanking everywhere.'

'But she's a very fine singer,' cut in another committee member.

'Not *her*', said the community leader, looking irritated. 'I'm talking about the soccer player.'

'Well I can tell you now,' said someone else, 'you can write off Noelene Jones. The PM won't go for a sheila.'

Slippery Dick didn't like the way the conversation was going. It was getting away from him, and he tapped his pen on the table for attention.

'Let me make it clear this is a serious mission we've been entrusted with. It's been given to the Australian people to make a choice, and it's not our job to approve or disapprove of their nominees. All we're required to do is submit a short list to the Prime Minister, and I for one have absolute faith in his good sense and judgment to make the right choice.'

There were some subdued mutterings and a couple of comments that sounded like 'what judgment?' and 'pigs might fly.' But the committee quickly settled down again to business and the counting continued.

20

The Prince had three more days of receptions, inspections, galas, lunches, dinners, banquets, balls, loyal demonstrations, speeches of welcome, salutes, marches, displays by school children, meetings with local dignitaries, bows, curtsies, and handshakes. His Royal Highness was not looking forward to it. Not one little bit. 'Papa hasn't the remotest idea what's involved in these tours.' he told his cousin Dickie on the first night. 'These Orstrylians have very hearty handshakes. My right arm feels as though it's about to drop off.'

After two days the press was already hailing the tour as an unqualified success, especially as the Prince still seemed to be controlling the Adelaide weather. It had been nothing but sunshine ever since he arrived. And the pattern was being repeated today. His speech at the State banquet had been described as 'brilliant'. In the eyes of his loyal subjects, the royal visitor could do no wrong.

Meantime, local business was still shamelessly cashing in on the royal visit. A soap manufacturer had bought space on the front page for this advertisement:
WELCOME TO THE PRINCE

BURFORD'S PRIZE NO. 1 SOAP
BURFORD'S CANDLES (B'S EXHIBITION CANDLES)
WELCOME IN EVERY HOME

Today's program was due to start at 10.30 am with a people's reception at the Exhibition Building, followed by a meeting with Army and Navy veterans. In the afternoon there was to be a march of naval men through the streets, followed by a visit to a local beach, Glenelg, and then dinner at Government House. At 9.00 pm the Lord Mayor was hosting a ball in the Adelaide Town Hall.

Lily was vaguely aware of comings and goings as she went about her duties, but was in a part of the house where she couldn't catch even a glimpse of the Prince. She was polishing silver when a message arrived to report to Miss Patchett. Not a complaint, Lily hoped, as she made her way to Miss Patchett's room. She cast her mind back, trying to remember what she'd done that would justify a black mark against her name. Maybe Miss Patchett had heard about the midnight walk in the garden, and was going to read her the riot act to remain at all times within the house? Well, she could always plead ignorance. She could say she was still learning the ropes, and promise to follow the rules in the future.

And then the most astonishing thing happened; so amazing she could hardly believe it. She was told to take a tray of tea to the Prince of Wales' suite. What's more, His Royal Highness had made a special request for her. Miss Patchett looked as though the words were being dragged unwillingly from her, making it clear she didn't approve of the Prince's action, royal or not.

'I can't imagine why he asked for you,' said Miss

Patchett, lips twisted as though she'd just sucked on a lemon. 'We have plenty of senior staff perfectly capable of looking after the needs of our royal guest. I must say that to use someone as young and inexperienced as yourself is highly irregular. But we must defer to His Royal Highness's wishes. After all, it's in the nature of a command.

'All I ask is that you show proper respect, curtsy when you enter, don't speak unless spoken to, and leave immediately once you've made your delivery. If you go to the kitchen, they'll supply you with what you need. I've already advised the housekeeper.'

She inspected Lily from top to toe with a critical eye.

'Too much hair showing, tuck it under your cap, girl. And put on a clean apron. You'll find one in Linen Supply. Just make sure when you take it to sign the book.'

With a peremptory gesture by Miss Patchett, still far from pleased by this unusual turn of events, Lily was dismissed. She made her way quickly to the kitchen, nerves tingling with excitement and apprehension. Why had the Prince asked for her? And what if she did something wrong?

Miss Patchett's order had clearly been quickly followed through in the kitchen as the tea tray was waiting for her, set with a fine bone china cup and saucer (Government House crest in gold), matching small plate with biscuits, milk jug and sugar bowl, and a neatly folded linen serviette. The teapot was warmed and at the ready, waiting only for the boiling water to be poured into it. The assistant housekeeper, Mrs Campbell, handed the tray to her with a smile and some kindly advice.

'Keep the tray steady, love,' she said. 'When you knock at the door and have to hold it with one hand, just make sure it doesn't tilt so everything slides to one side. Don't enter until His Royal Highness tells you. When he does, place the tray on the side table, the one nearest the window. Curtsy when you go in, and again as you leave. If His Royal Highness speaks to you, answer politely, but otherwise hold your tongue … although it's permissible to say 'Is there anything else, Sir?' before retiring. Any questions?'

Lily said she had no questions, took the tray, and escaped.

She climbed the staircase to the private rooms, making sure she was keeping the tray level. There was a man in a dark suit standing at the entrance to the upper landing, and she had the feeling he was some kind of security person keeping guard. But he made no attempt to stop her, apart from a brief look to check what was on the tea tray and to ask her name.

She stood outside the door of the Prince's room, and knocked. There was no answer. She knocked again, and this time the door was opened by the Prince himself.

'Hello there,' he said, smiling. 'Please come in.'

He was wearing a dark blue silk dressing gown over his day clothes, and the bed covers were rumpled, as though he'd been having a rest. Close up in daylight he looked even more handsome than she'd remembered, but she couldn't help noticing a network of fine lines around his eyes, strange in one so young. He looked somehow frail and vulnerable, like a small boy pretending to be a grown-up.

Although she was six years younger, Lily had an almost overwhelming urge to take him in her arms and protect him, to tell him not to worry, that everything would turn out all right. Why did she feel like this? It was ridiculous, really. What would a prince have to worry about? Instead she kept silent, carefully carrying the tray to where she'd been told, curtsied, then turned to leave.

As she did, the Prince reached out and caught Lily's hand to hold her back. She trembled, and he seemed to sense her nervousness.

'Don't worry, I won't bite. I just want to talk. Tell me about yourself. Who are you? Where do you come from? And do you often go wandering around the gardens at night?'

Lily, mindful of Miss Patchett's instructions not to linger and to keep any conversations with the Prince brief, didn't know what to do. She could hardly withdraw her hand, as that would seem disrespectful. But she felt distinctly uncomfortable.

'My name's Lily Jones,' she said. 'I live in the Adelaide Hills, and I've been employed as temporary staff for your Royal Highness's visit.'

'Ah, Jones – a good Welsh name. I'm particularly fond of that country and its people.' He was still holding her hand, examining the palm, as though trying to read the lines on it. 'Such a small hand,' he said, suddenly releasing it. 'Such a tiny person. How old are you, Lily?'

'Twenty, Sir.'

'Born in the reign of my great-grandmother. Very fitting.'

What was fitting about her being born at the turn of the century? Lily wasn't sure what he meant by the remark, but remained silent. There wasn't much she could do or say but she couldn't help wondering if Miss Patchett was keeping an eye on the clock, checking on how long she'd taken to deliver the tea tray to the Prince's room.

'Would you like me to pour the tea for you, Sir?'

'Never mind the tea. It can wait. Do you have a family, Lily?'

'Yes, Sir. I live with my father and four brothers. My mother's dead.'

'Four brothers? What an amazing coincidence. I, too, have four brothers.' He paused, with a slight frown. 'Or did have. My youngest brother died last year.'

'I'm very sorry, Sir,'

'No need to be. John was an epileptic, you see. Not much of a life for him, poor boy. Merciful release, if you ask me.' He spoke in short, clipped phrases in a voice that was light and high pitched. Posh, was the way her mother would have described it. That's the way posh people talk. Why did the Prince's voice bring back memories of her?

'Do you have a gentleman friend, Lily?' The question startled Lily from her reveries, it was so unexpected.

'Me, Sir?'

'I can't believe someone as lovely as you doesn't have an admirer. Tell me now, isn't there someone to whom you're attached? Someone who has a prior claim on your affections?'

'Oh no, Sir. There's no one. I've never even thought about it.'

Was it just her imagination, or did the Prince seem pleased with her reply? Lily was finding it hard to separate dream from reality. He was smiling at her now, like a small boy who had been unexpectedly given a special treat.

'Well all I can say is that the young men where you live must be totally blind. But their loss is my gain.'

What did he mean? She didn't dare think about it. Lily was caught between an overpowering feeling of physical attraction and an awareness of the class differences between them. It was like a chasm that could never be crossed. Prince and commoner. Master and servant. It was just the way she'd been brought up.

Lily edged closer to the door, looking for an escape.

'I'm sorry, Sir, I should get back to my duties. Is there anything else you require?'

The Prince was observing her with amusement coupled with genuine concern. 'I've alarmed you, haven't I? That's my trouble, sometimes I act before I think. If I have, then please forgive me. It's just that I'd like to know you better ... that is, if you'd allow me?'

Allow him? Lily was so much in love she'd have crawled on her hands and knees over red-hot coals if it would make him happy. But she was still puzzled.

'Why me, Sir?'

'Because I need someone to talk to, someone I can trust.'

A prince, lonely? Lily could hardly believe her ears. Here he was surrounded by people ready to act on his smallest request, a string of courtiers and officials all anxious to make his life as pleasant as possible. A prince cushioned by every luxury that money and privilege could buy. And what about Lord Louis Mountbatten? Surely as cousins the two must be close. She shyly ventured to say as much.

'Dickie? Nice enough chap, and we get along famously.' He smiled again. 'Truth is, young Dickie's got other things on his mind at the moment. He met this girl in Melbourne, and the poor fellow's lovesick.'

But still Lily hesitated.

'I'd be honoured to be of some service, Sir. But I still don't understand how.'

'Tonight,' he said. 'Meet me in the gardens after the ball.' Was it a request or a command? She countered with a question.

'How will I know when you're there?'

'You'll know. I'll send you a signal.'

But she was still undecided, torn between wanting to see him again and fearful of being found out and dismissed in disgrace. As if reading her mind his next words were; 'Don't be afraid. Please try and come.'

Then he said something so extraordinary Lily could hardly believe what she was hearing.

'My grandfather once loved an actress – Lily Langtry. They called her the Jersey Lily. She was very beautiful and he loved her until the day he died. He never forgot her.

'Do you believe in fate, Lily? That some things are meant to be?' He kissed her gently on the cheek. 'I do. And I have the strangest feeling history is about to repeat itself.'

21

A new republic. A new era. It called out for a new flag. But the old one was still flying over Parliament House. In all the euphoria following the referendum, one question was crying out for an answer: what do we do with the Union Jack?

There it was – red, white and blue in the top left hand corner. Children saluted it in school playgrounds. Flag bearers carried it at the head of processions. Every club and community centre had it hanging on a wall, alongside a picture of the Queen. It was hoisted to the top of the flagpole every time an Australian scored gold at the Olympics, creating confusion as to which country was the winner. But Australia had now cut its last link with the old country. Clearly it was time for that reminder of colonial days to go.

There had been many attempts over the years to design a new Australian flag, but so far they'd all come to nothing. There was still a lot of sentiment attached to the old emblem.

Servicemen's organisations claimed this was the flag thousands of Australians had fought and died under in wartime. Monarchists clung to it as the last visible symbol of a great Empire that once stretched, coloured pink, across the world. The Loyal League of Free Settlers, founded when Australia was still a colony, voted 'over our dead bodies' against its removal. (One wag commented that from what he'd seen of its members, most of them were half dead anyway.)

Even those who didn't particularly care one way or the other seemed strangely loath to discard the old flag, citing cost as a reason.

Advocates of change pointed out that Canada, still a monarchy, had long ago replaced the Union Jack with the maple leaf. Our close neighbour just across the Tasman, New Zealand, had recently done the same, with a large silver fern on a black background. The arguments made no difference. Things seemed at an impasse but it was obvious something had to be done, and quickly. The Prime Minister went into Action Man mode, pressed the buzzer, and called for the relevant file.

It was a thick one, going back at least 40 years. There had been a number of competitions to design a new flag, but so far none of the winners had fired the public imagination. A leading newspaper had even offered a prize of $50,000, inviting its readers to send in their ideas. But the judging committee had rejected all of them as unsuitable.

When the file arrived the PM spread it out on his desk and closely examined all the designs on offer. The first thing he noted was the large number of kangaroos. There was the boxing kangaroo, yellow on green, flown when Australia had won the America's Cup. But he quickly dismissed it as too kitsch and gimmicky. The flying kangaroo was vetoed on the grounds it was the commercial insignia of an airline. And some of the kangaroos seemed to be jumping backwards, not a good concept for a country looking to the future.

And there was another tricky question: should our national

flag feature an animal popular in restaurants as a low cholesterol meat?

Other native fauna were briefly considered. The koala was cute and cuddly, loved by children as a stuffed toy and by tourists as a photo opportunity. But as a national symbol, the PM felt there could be a problem with an animal that spent most of its time asleep. The wombat and platypus were also dismissed. Plants and flowers didn't seem to have what it took to be featured on the Australian flag. The yellow wattle wasn't bold enough; gum leaves ditto. The PM now turned his attention to some of the other ideas that had been put forward. And there was no shortage of them.

One that had kept coming up over the years was to replace the Union Jack with the Aboriginal flag, a striking design in red, gold and black. It was eye-catching and instantly recognisable. Its supporters made the point it would be a fitting recognition of the Indigenous community as the country's original inhabitants.

But opponents claimed that Aborigines were only one part of a multicultural society, and adopting the flag as a national emblem could be seen by some as divisive. How would Asian-born citizens feel about it, for instance? Or those from European or South American origins? They argued a new flag should be inclusive, something with which all Australians could identify.

Then there was the Bicentennial flag, a bold geometric design in green and yellow. But the PM felt there was nothing about it that was distinctively Australian, nothing that shouted to other countries 'this is us!'. On the other hand, a design featuring a map of Australia was strong on identity but low on aesthetics.

When the PM came to the Eureka flag he lingered a long time, trying to make up his mind. Now here was a design that might be worth considering. Featuring the five stars of the

Southern Cross in the form of a cross on a blue background, and flown by rebellious diggers at the Eureka Stockade, there was at least a sense of history to it. It had tradition and it had style. But above all it represented mateship.

Mateship was a word dear to the heart of the Prime Minister, and never mind that his wife claimed it was 'blokey'. To the PM it was a sacred symbol of national identity. He was fond of it, praising it publicly whenever he had the opportunity. Mateship, along with fair play, had even featured in his policy speech at the last election, and had gone down well with the mums and dads.

Mateship was footy and beer. It was not being a dobber, helping a pal when he was down and out, lending the odd fiver without asking for it back, shouting a round of drinks at the local pub, and never welshing on a friend. Mateship was what it meant to be an Australian.

So he spent more than a little time on the Eureka flag, pondering how his breakfast cabinet would react to it. But at the end of a long day it, too, went out the door.

One thing was certain – he had to come up with a solution, and fast. If the Union Jack was still centre stage at the inauguration of the country's first president in November, it would be a public relations disaster; those Fleet Street hacks would have a field day. And with the country already involved in an expensive poll, the last thing the PM wanted was another voting contest.

The Prime Minister was an egomaniac with delusions of grandeur, but even he knew the task was beyond him. He decided to fall back on a rule that had never let him down: when in doubt, form a committee. And so the Flag Committee was born.

After two days behind locked doors the Flag Committee

came up with a solution that was so easy, so blindingly obvious, the PM was annoyed he hadn't been the one to think of it. The Union Jack would be replaced with a large Commonwealth star, leaving the Southern Cross where it was. Minimal change, maximum impact.

The PM rewarded himself with a double scotch.

It was amazing how easily it all finally came together. There were no protests, no fuss, no riots in the streets, no bloodshed. Almost overnight the Union Jack disappeared into the dark recesses of colonial history.

The flag was approved by all political parties in a joint late night sitting of Parliament. Legislation to make it official was rushed through to give time for flag makers to gear up production before November. And wonder of wonders, most people seemed to like it.

Of course there were some objections from a few diehards; but the PM explained the new flag would be phased in gradually so there would be a minimum of disruption. He pointed out it would be similar to the changeover in 1966 from pound sterling to dollar and from imperial measurements to metric, when the two systems had existed side by side for a transition period to give the public time to get used to them.

Most of those resisting the change were the elderly, and the PM assured them there was no compulsion to adopt the new flag. This was a free country, and so far as he was concerned they could keep flying their Union Jacks as long as they liked. Even the Loyal League of Free Settlers finally gave it grudging approval, while reserving the right (as with matters of sex) to do as they wished in the privacy of their rooms.

The PM added one more concession. He announced that in recognition of the Indigenous population 'and its rightful place in our history', all government buildings would fly the Aboriginal flag alongside the new one on national holidays.

Some saw this as patronising, others as a stroke of political genius. But it was gestures like this that made it crystal clear why the PM was at the top of his career ladder.

For once even his breakfast cabinet couldn't fault it.

22

That night Lily retired to her room as usual, but long after Emma had changed into her night clothes and climbed into bed, Lily remained fully dressed in a chair, reading a book by the light of a lamp. It was hours before she could meet the Prince as he was still at the Lord Mayor's ball. But Lily knew she must stay awake. What if she fell asleep and missed the signal he said he'd send her? She wasn't sure what was ahead, but she was filled with a mixture of fear and excitement. Fear she'd be caught and sent home to her family. Excitement at seeing the man she loved so desperately.

At eleven she thought she heard something out in the gardens. But when she peered through the curtains, she saw it was just one of the staff emptying kitchen rubbish into a large bin. Eleven-thirty. Midnight. Just when she'd almost given up hope she heard the sound of someone whistling. Or was she imagining it? Maybe it was just the wind whistling through the trees. She listened again. This time the sound was low pitched but the tune unmistakeable. *Lily of Laguna*.

Lily rushed to the window and peered out. There were two men standing in the gardens, and she immediately recognised the shorter of them as the Prince of Wales. He was still in formal clothes, white tie and tails, while the other man (cousin Dickie?) wore the uniform of a naval officer.

The Prince saw her face at the window, and beckoned her to join him. Lily quickly put down her book and checked herself to make sure she was neat and tidy. She was wearing the simple flowered cotton dress she'd packed in her suitcase, her hair loose and flowing over her shoulders. Then she took off her shoes so she could leave quietly without disturbing Emma.

Too late. She was almost at the door, shoes in hand, when Emma stirred and opened her eyes. 'Where're you going?' she asked. 'Why're you all dolled up like that?'

Lily hesitated. All her life she'd been brought up to tell the truth. But on the other hand, how could she tell Emma she was going to meet the Prince of Wales? If she did, and Emma believed her, it would be all over Government House by tomorrow. She shuddered at the thought. Being hauled before the formidable Miss Patchett. Given a severe lecture on knowing her place, and then sent packing without a reference. And what would her father and four brothers say when she returned home? They'd be bitterly disappointed in her. She could see her father's face and hear him say: 'Lily my girl, I expected better of you.'

So she took the coward's way and told Emma she was slipping out to meet a friend. This was the only time they could meet, as he'd been on duty until midnight.

'A gentleman friend?' asked Emma, all excitement. 'You're a sly one, you are. Only here a few days, and already you've cottoned on to someone. What's his name?'

Lily, anxious not to keep the Prince waiting, said no,

he didn't work with Eddie, and she couldn't tell Emma anything more about him as they'd agreed to keep it secret. But the word 'secret' only inflamed Emma's curiosity more. She got out of bed and clutched at Emma's skirt, trying to hold her back.

'Come on,' she pleaded. 'You'n me are best friends. I won't tell anyone, honest! If it's Nifty then Eddie'll be pleased, as he says he's always going on about you.'

Lily gently disengaged Emma's hand and prepared to make her escape.

'I can't tell you,' she said. 'He's a bit shy; he doesn't want everyone to know about us. And it's not Nifty.'

Emma flopped back on the bed, clearly disappointed.

'I think you're mean,' she said. 'I tell you everything, but you won't even give me his name.'

'I'm sorry, Emma,' said Lily. 'But I promised I wouldn't say anything, and I can't go back on it. I might get him into trouble.'

'Get him into trouble!' exclaimed Emma. 'You, more likely Corblimey, if Patchett ever finds out, you're done for.'

'I know. Please don't say anything.'

'All right,' said Emma, still disgruntled but accepting the inevitable. 'I'll protect you, love.'

Lily quickly went through a side door, half afraid the Prince might have given up waiting for her. But there he was, standing in exactly the same spot where she'd first seen him from the window. Except that now his companion had moved away and was standing with his hands in his pockets, looking up at the sky.

'Ah, there you are,' said the Prince, with that crooked smile she was starting to know so well. 'I was beginning to think you'd changed your mind and weren't going to come.'

He went over to his companion and spoke to him briefly in a voice so low Lily couldn't hear what he was saying. But it could have been a request for privacy because the other man smiled and with a 'Right you are, David,' disappeared from sight.

As soon as he'd gone the Prince took Lily's hand and they began to stroll the paths together like a couple of young lovers.

She was worried someone would see them from the windows, but it was a dark part of the gardens with a lot of shrubs, and they were well hidden. The excitement of being so close to him felt like an electric charge through her body. But with the excitement there was also calmness and trust, a feeling that this was where she belonged – by his side.

'Tell me all about yourself,' said the Prince.

It was like uncorking a bottle. The words poured out as she told him about her early days growing up in the Adelaide Hills, the way she'd had to leave school at 12 when he mother took sick, how she'd looked after her father and four brothers since her mother's death, the grand homes where she'd worked, and how one of her employers, Mrs Cavendish, had recommended her for this job. It felt so natural talking to him like this, telling him all the things that had happened to her since childhood. It was like talking to an old and trusted friend. She finally paused, breathless. 'Well that's about it, Sir,' she said.

'Then tell me this,' said the Prince, and even in the darkness she could see he was smiling. 'When my lovely Lily goes to sleep at night, who does she dream about?'

For the second time that night Lily sought refuge in a lie.

'No one,' she said. 'I don't dream of anyone.'

It was a relief when the Prince began talking about himself. He mentioned once again the young brother who'd been diagnosed with epilepsy and sent off to the country to be cared for by a nurse. He told Lily he'd been with the Army in France when he'd been given news of John's death. 'Poor little blighter', he said. 'It wasn't much of a life.'

He spoke fondly of his sister Mary, eldest in the family, saying it was his hope she'd be allowed to marry a man of her own choice. 'I can't think of anything more ghastly than a marriage without love. Think of it, two people forced to live together for the rest of their lives. Hell on earth … one would be better off dead.'

Lily was startled by the intensity of the outburst. He stopped walking for a moment and looked at her.

'D'you realise how lucky you are … to be able to choose the one you want? To enjoy the blessing of a happy family life … all those things denied to someone like me?'

Lily was troubled. Was he being forced into a marriage he didn't want? She vaguely remembered reading stories about various European princesses tipped to become the future wife of the Prince of Wales. At the time she'd taken very little notice of them. It was a world away from hers, something as remote and unreal as reading about a being from outer space.

She'd had no interest in how brides were found for British royalty. But hearing the Prince talk like this filled her with a sudden pang of jealousy. What kind of woman would be considered suitable for a man who would one day sit on the throne? Was there already someone chosen, waiting for him on the other side of the world?

Lily knew she shouldn't ask questions of royalty, but her feelings got the better of her. She chose her words carefully.

'Sir,' she began.

'Please … David. That's what all my friends call me.'

But it was still too personal a step for her to take. 'Sir,' she began again, ignoring his frown. 'You said you didn't want your sister to marry someone she didn't love. But how about you? What if your parents insist on it?'

'They can insist all they like. I've three younger brothers all perfectly capable of producing heirs to the throne. It's not a national crisis if I don't marry.'

The man in the naval uniform suddenly came out of the darkness and approached them, looking at his watch.

'We should get back, David,' he said. 'Before they send out a search party.'

'My faithful bodyguard,' said the Prince. 'Always looking out for me.'

'One-thirty,' said the young naval officer, checking his watch again. 'It's another big day tomorrow. You'll need your sleep.'

'All right,' said the Prince, releasing Lily's hand. 'But let us escort you back.'

'Please don't,' said Lily, still alarmed she might be caught. 'I'll be all right, truly.'

He was about to walk away when he suddenly paused, picked a flower from a nearby bush, and handed it to her. She could smell its heady scent in the darkness.

The Prince leaned down and for the second time kissed her on the cheek, 'I must see you again,' he whispered.

'Tomorrow night.'

When he'd gone she looked at the flower in her hand. It was a red rose.

Lily waited for the two men to enter Government House, then made her way back to the side door near the scullery. Emma was asleep when she got back to their room.

She undressed quickly, then climbed into bed. But she couldn't sleep. She lay awake, thinking of everything she and the Prince had talked about. What did he want with her? Why had he sought her out? Just before dawn she fell into an uneasy doze, only to be woken an hour later by Emma demanding to know all the details of her secret midnight assignation.

'Come on,' she pleaded. 'Who is he? Are you going to see him again?'

But Lily refused to give any information, selfishly hugging to herself the memory of last night. Emma finally tired of asking questions with no answers, and clearly miffed, began washing her face and hands.

Lily was five minutes late when she reported to Miss Patchett, but luckily the senior housekeeper's mind was on organising fresh linen for the guest rooms. She barely glanced at Lily before sending her off to report to the housekeeper. Lily breathed a sigh of relief. So no one had seen her slipping out from Government House last night.

She worked hard all day, but it was mechanical; her mind wasn't on it. Around her she was vaguely aware of comings and goings, doors being shut and opened, the sound of engines as cars pulled up at the front door and then departed, whispered instructions, orders being given, murmurs of 'There he is!' and 'Did you see him?'

And there could be no doubt whom they were talking about. The golden haired Prince who had held her hand last night in the darkness, kissed her on the cheek and murmured that he must see her again. 'My lovely Lily,' he'd said, as if she belonged to him.

She had got away with her escapade last night. Should she risk everything for another meeting? Or would it be better to pretend it never happened, and just go on as usual? After all, the Prince and his entourage would be leaving Adelaide on Friday. Soon it would all be over. She would go back to her home, and her stay in Government House would be just a memory ... something to tell her children and grandchildren at another time, in another life. What had the Prince called it? The blessing of a happy family.

I won't decide now, she said to herself halfway through the morning when changing sheets on the guestroom beds. I'll think about it later. After all, the Prince might change his mind. There could be someone at the ball tonight, a bewitching beauty who'll make him forget I ever existed.

But she was deceiving herself, avoiding the truth out of fear it would hurt her. She was just a little country girl, but she had a heart just the same as the highest lady in the land. And that heart would be broken if the man she loved found somebody else.

23

There was a message from Mike on the answering machine when Noelene arrived home from a meeting with Friends of the Opera. The message was brief and intriguing. 'Call me,' it said. 'Important.'

'Seen the papers?' were his first words when she phoned him. 'Not yet,' said Noelene. 'I've just got in. Why?'

'Thought you might like to know you're still there on the people's choice for president.'

'So?'

'Just touching base to see if you've changed your mind.'

'Sorry, no,' said Noelene. Her resolve had been strengthened by the last visit to her great-grandparents' home and the image of cosy nights cocooned by the fire, away from public life for the first time since she was a young woman.

She had thought it all through. She'd spend six months in Sydney and the rest of the year in the Hills, combining it with some teaching and maybe an occasional appearance for charity. In between she'd start writing her memoirs. A publisher had approached her and now seemed the right time to do it.

'Can I come around anyway? I thought you might like a progress report.'

'On what?'

Mike laughed. 'The documentary. The Life and Times of Noelene Jones.'

It had gone completely out of her mind. Noelene glanced at her watch. 'Fine,' she said. 'Just give me an hour to organise myself and go through the mail.' For some reason she couldn't explain, she felt a warm glow at the prospect of seeing him again.

As she unpacked she thought through their relationship, examining it like a scientist studying a microbe under a microscope. There was nothing even remotely sexual about it, not even a hint of romance. Of that she was certain. Although she could see Mike could be attractive to women in a craggy-hunk kind of way, there was only room for one man in her life and Charlie was now gone.

But she also recognised that over the months this thing between them had become more than just friendship. It was something else … the feeling she could lean on him for help, a rock and support whenever she needed it, a shoulder to cry on. She was reluctant to admit it but she was beginning to depend on Mike. Question was, how long would he be there for her?

Charlie had been special, the kind of person who comes along only once in a woman's life. He had been husband, mentor, companion and lover all rolled into one. But since Charlie died there had been no one for her to confide in, no one to ask for advice. To be able to sit down with Mike and relax over a glass of wine, to talk about the things that were important to her, to swap jokes knowing they shared the same sense of humour, was an unexpected luxury. It was knowing that here was another human being she could trust totally.

There'd been plenty of acquaintances over the years, people she'd met in the course of her long musical career. There were the cards at Christmas, the notes, the phone calls, the 'Hi, how are you?' as someone she'd met in another part of the world passed through Sydney. But they were brief fleeting moments that never really amounted to anything. Just the flotsam and jetsam of life as a celebrity.

Mike's private life was still largely a mystery to her. He had never discussed it, so she had no idea whether he was emotionally committed or not. Was there a wife somewhere in the background? A partner? Children? Somehow he seemed like a loner, although she couldn't explain why she thought that. It was more a gut feeling than anything. Maybe it was the way he was always there at the other end of the phone whenever she rang him. But again, that could just be the nature of the business.

She knew one thing – she admired him for his honesty and professionalism. Even with her limited knowledge of how the television industry worked, she could see he was dedicated and hardworking. And he had never once pushed her, never applied pressure on her to do or say anything she didn't want.

It was nearly two hours before Mike arrived, apologetic, newspaper in hand. 'Sorry if I kept you waiting,' he said. 'I got caught up with some urgent calls and lost track of time. Look at this. You're now number three.' He handed the paper to her.

Noelene glanced at it, uninterested.

'Big deal,' she said. 'Number three to a soccer player and a pop singer.'

'But it shows people want you,' said Mike. 'That must count?'

Noelene shrugged.

'Maybe. I'm just not interested. Where do they get these

numbers from anyway? I thought they were supposed to be confidential?'

'Who knows? Pay enough money and you can buy anything,' said Mike. 'The whole thing's crazy. A madhouse. We'll finish up with the lunatics running the asylum.

'Anyway that's not the reason I came over to see you. It's about the documentary'.

'How's it going?'

'Good. Hopefully, it'll be finished next month. But I need some more information about your family, a few more talking heads. Do you have any relatives here in Sydney?'

'Not one. Dad was an only child and as far as I know all the South Australian connections are dead. There may be some distant cousins somewhere, but he never mentioned them. My mother had a sister and brother, but they won't be any use to you. Uncle Rodney was killed in World War II. Bomber pilot, shot down in Germany. Aunt Hazel married an American serviceman and went to live in Chicago.

'I looked her up once, and we had a nice visit together. But she's dead now, no family. I heard her husband remarried and moved to Texas, but I can't be sure.'

'What about school friends? They might be useful.'

'I can give you some names if you like. I don't see them that often, but there are one or two who still keep in touch. We have lunch now and then, that kind of thing. I'll look them up in my address book.'

'Ever been to a school reunion?'

'Only once. That was enough. Someone tracked us down from the school magazine.' She winced at the memory. 'It was a bit of a shock. We couldn't recognise each other … we'd all become fat and frumpy!'

Mike laughed. 'I can't imagine you fat and frumpy.'

'Figure of speech … you know what I mean. People change. They move on.'

'Anyway, I'd appreciate the names if you can give them to me. Could be very interesting. By the way, how's that house of yours coming on?'

'It's not. The architect's still working on it.'

'Let me know when you make your next trip over there. I'd like to come with you … film some footage.'

'Maybe next week. I'll call you.'

'Fine. I'll keep in touch.' Mike got to his feet, and his bulk seemed to dominate the room. He was solidly built, like a rugby player, and his body reflected his character – strong, tough, dependable. His handshake as he was leaving was warm and firm.

Noelene's mind had unaccountably shifted back to the presidential campaign. 'You said this business of people's choice is crazy. But won't it at least mean we'll finish up with the president we want?'

'It means we'll finish up with the president we deserve,' said Mike. Charlie couldn't have said it better.

A week later Noelene remembered Mike's words and called him. 'About that trip to Adelaide,' she said. 'I have to go back to see the architect. He's found some brick samples he wants me to look at. Want to come along?'

'Fine,' said Mike. They settled on Monday.

When they arrived, the house was smaller than she remembered. Do bricks and mortar, like old people, shrink with age? And someone had been using it as a rubbish dump, in spite of the warning signs BUILDING SITE: ENTER AT OWN RISK. Empty bottles and beer cans littered the front garden she'd so recently worked in.

Mike was nosing around, his camera at the ready. 'I'll start with a few establishing shots,' he said. 'Would you mind standing at the front door?' She posed, smiling, one hand on the door knocker.

This is where Lily stood. This is where she held my father in her arms.

Now Mike was wandering around taking exterior shots, every few minutes rapping out a brief command. 'A bit more to the left. Don't look at me, look at the front gate,' and finally: 'Just one more. Perfect. Now let's go inside.'

The front door almost came away on its hinges when Noelene turned the key in the lock and opened it. Inside was a mess. One of the panes in the front window was broken, with pieces of glass strewn over the uneven wooden floor. Nearby was a small rock the size of a cricket ball. Someone practising bowling skills, using the window as a wicket? Vandals? Maybe the same ones who had turned the front garden into their personal rubbish tip.

Mike was readying his equipment again. 'Stand just where you are, then walk slowly around the room inspecting everything. Forget I'm here, don't look at the camera. Keep it natural.'

Keep it natural. Easier said than done. Noelene had never felt comfortable posing for publicity pictures, and now she was being asked to become an actor. Years of performing roles on the opera stage had trained her to be other people; it was being herself that was the tricky bit. Still, she had confidence in Mike and knew he was only doing his job.

She posed at Mike's directions, remembering the architect's warning not to dislodge any of the loose bricks. Then she made a slow circuit of the room, lifting up torn wallpaper to see what was underneath, tapping walls, checking gaps in the floorboards, even picking up the stray rock and examining it with a puzzled frown as if to say: 'Where did this come from?' Not once did she look towards Mike and his camera, as he followed her around.

'Great. That's it,' Mike finally said. 'Now let's do the next room.'

They went through the rest of the house, Noelene explaining as they moved along what she planned to do once the builders had finished. The four-poster bed. The add-on bathroom. The kitchen with its copper pots and old-fashioned country feel. Coffee and conversation around a scrubbed pine table.

'Can we go back to the front room?' asked Mike. 'I'd like to get one more shot of you at the fireplace.'

Noelene stood, one hand touching the wall where the old wooden mantelpiece had once been. 'How's that?'

'Perfect.'

Noelene was about to walk away when she felt one of the bricks move. The brick next to it was also loose. She jiggled them hard and they came away in her hand, leaving a cavity in which was something metal. She reached in and pulled out a small tin box.

'What've you got there?' asked Mike, coming over to look at it.

The box was locked, but it was so old the rusty hinges gave way the first time she tried to open it. Noelene looked inside.

'Jewels? Family treasure?' asked Mike.

Noelene smiled. 'In your dreams.' She sniffed and pulled a face. 'It smells musty. Wonder how long it's been here?'

'Many years by the look of it. What's in it?'

Noelene peered into the box again. 'Just a few bits of rubbish.' She held up a piece of ribbon. 'Who'd want to save something like this? Maybe some children once used it as a hiding place. I'll go through it when I get home.' She put the tin box to one side and they went out to inspect the overgrown back garden.

It was her favourite place. She planned to bring it back to life once she moved in. It would be an English garden, of course. In the time of her great-grandparents everyone had an English garden. It was part of the colonial heritage. A sentimental link to the country they still thought of as Home.

There would be climbing roses over the front door, just like in Lily's photo. Red roses. Phlox and petunias and lavender and violets and daffodils and Sweet William. Hollyhocks standing in a row like sentinels. And sunflowers. She must have sunflowers.

'See those two trees?' said Noelene, as they explored the back of the cottage. 'I'm going to buy myself a hammock and hang it between them. All my life I've wanted to laze around in a hammock, but I've never been able to have one.'

'No time?'

'No trees. Charlie and I lived in hotels or apartments from the time we were married.'

'So … no pets either?'

'Not even a goldfish.' She smiled. 'Sad, isn't it?'

'I know how you feel. I'd love a dog, but they don't allow animals in my apartment block. Against the rules of the body corporate.'

It was the first time he'd made a reference to his personal life, and she noted he said 'my' not 'our'. So maybe she was right in guessing he was a loner.

She thought of telling him about Marmalade, the ginger cat that would sit purring at her feet in front of the fire, but decided against it. It might sound too whimsical. Finally they took a stroll through the fallen down gravestones next door.

'Cemeteries make me sad,' said Noelene. 'All these people that were once loved. All these lives, gone and forgotten.' She paused, straining to read a faded inscription on one.

> *Emily Grace Hardcastle*
>
> *Born April 23, 1895*
>
> *Died November 4, 1897*
>
> *'Forever remembered by her loving family'*

Next to it was an even smaller headstone:

> *Rebecca May Hardcastle*
>
> *Born January 5, 1899*
>
> *Died May 23, 1899*
>
> *'In God's care'*

'It's the children who upset me the most. Poor little things, they didn't even have a chance to grow up.'

'Last time we were here you said you couldn't find the graves of your great-grandparents. Any luck since?'

'Not yet, but when I get the chance I'll go through the local parish records. They might turn up something. I've an idea they were married in this church, and their names should be on the register. But it's only a feeling. Something my father once said.'

'One last photo,' said Mike. 'Stand alongside one of those headstones. Any one, it doesn't matter. I'll get the church in the background. Then we'll call it a day.'

Noelene did as he asked, but looked uncomfortable.

'Do you believe in ghosts?' she asked. 'Do you believe the souls of people stay around long after they've died?'

'Don't ask me,' grinned Mike, packing away his camera. 'I'm agnostic. I don't believe in heaven or hell or any of that religious shit. So far as I'm concerned, when I finally kick the bucket that's the end of it. Goodbye, nice knowing you.'

'So you don't believe there's a God?'

'No.'

'And you've never prayed?'

'Not since my parents made me go to Sunday School.'

They were now getting into deep philosophic territory. Mike's words reminded Noelene that Charlie had also been agnostic. But in his last months he'd gone back to the religion in which he'd been baptised. He never explained why, just said he'd had 'a change of mind.' At his funeral she'd asked a minister to officiate rather than a civil celebrant. She'd made the decision at the last moment, and had hoped it was what Charlie would have wanted.

Someone once said that people who converted back to religion when about to die were having a two way bet on the hereafter. Well she supposed it was true, but she'd felt comfortable with it at the time. But she didn't tell Mike any of this. There were still parts of her life that were special to her, private, hidden away like the things in that little tin box.

They had dinner together at the city hotel where both were staying. Next morning Mike caught the first plane back to Sydney, while Noelene stayed on to talk again with her architect. They arranged to meet for drinks on Wednesday, when Mike would go over some of the material with her. All being well, the documentary should be finished in a month.

'By the way, make it late Wednesday. I've just remembered I'm going to be tied up most of the day. The Opera Trust has asked me to be a judge for their Young Singers program, and I've more or less said yes. We're going to talk about it over lunch, but these things tend to drag on a bit.'

'Suits me. How's five?'

'Perfect.' They shook hands on it.

As soon as she'd returned to Sydney and her apartment Noelene removed the contents of Lily's little tin box and spread them out on a table. There was an old-fashioned brooch and a length of narrow ribbon that could have come from a baby's bootee. And there was a rose, brittle and brown with age. Jammed right at the bottom of the box where she hadn't noticed it before, Noelene found a folded piece of paper.

She picked it up and examined it. The handwriting had faded but she could still make out the words. It was enough to tell her why Lily had locked it away for safe keeping. How sweet, she thought. How romantic. A love letter from some long-ago admirer. He must have meant a lot to her grandmother if she'd gone to all the trouble to keep it. It was like a whiff from the past, the scent of memories from a bygone era.

Noelene replaced everything in Lily's tin box and stored it on the top shelf of her wardrobe along with some hats and a couple of photo albums.

And promptly forgot all about it.

24

Mike was right. It was crazy time, beginning to get out of hand. Every newspaper and magazine was running a 'name the president' competition; every radio station and television channel had a program aimed at finding Australia's next Head of State. The prizes ranged all the way from cars and computers to an income for life. One smart entrepreneur announced a lottery, the winner to be flown to Canberra for a private dinner at Yarralumla … although how that could be arranged was hard to see. But it was all good publicity fodder.

There were guessing games and discussion panels. TV reporters invaded the city and suburbs to canvass the opinions of passers-by; the man in the street had never been more popular. Editorials editorialised. Politicians pontificated. There seemed no end to it, and the Prime Minister was starting to get worried.

'It's turned into a bloody circus,' he complained to his breakfast cabinet. 'Undignified. Un-presidential. The whole thing's becoming a joke.'

'Well, what else did you expect?' said his wife tartly, pulling apart (not slicing) her English muffin. She knew her table manners. 'It was your idea to include a public vote. Democracy at work, you said. Listening to the voice of the people. You should know by now that the public are a bunch of idiots.'

The PM conceded that yes, it had been his idea and he took full personal responsibility for it. It wasn't easy being the man at the top, by God it wasn't. But, as he reminded his wife, it had also been backed by Cabinet.

He'd felt he was on to a sure political winner in asking the public to help choose its own president. But now with all this hoopla and razzamatazz he wasn't so confident the decision had been the right one. Choosing a Governor-General had been simple, uncomplicated – just a matter of thinking of a name and picking up the phone. Choosing a president was turning into a disaster.

Money was the key to it. Too much marketing; too much media manipulation; too many smart operatives each with a barrow to push. Advertising campaigns, posters, billboards, press releases, commercials, T-shirts, naming rights, websites, sponsors, personal appearances, product placements, talkback radio. It was becoming increasingly clear, said the PM, that this was turning into a presidential election that could be bought.

And there was his final nightmare, the one that was giving him bad dreams when he went to bed. What if there was no one on the short list worth considering? What if his wife was right and his only choice was between three idiots? Of course there were still the official State and Territory nominations to rely on. But if he ignored the public vote, the whole thing could turn nasty.

He made a mental note to have a quiet word with Slippery Dick as soon as possible, away from the rest of the committee members. Slippery owed him a few favours, and this could be the right time to pay them back.

If there was one thing the PM disliked it was something getting out of his control. And this was not only out of control – it was bolting away like a frightened horse.

25

Lily was walking along a corridor and still thinking about the Prince when she ran into Nifty. She smiled politely and tried to pass, but he blocked her way. 'Not so fast, sweetheart,' he said. She thought she could smell brandy on his breath. 'It's time you and I had a little talk.'

He pulled her into a small room with shelves on both sides, so small it could have doubled as a storage closet. It smelled musty and unused. When he closed the door and she heard a loud click, Lily realised they were locked in.

'What were you doing out in the garden last night?' he demanded. 'And don't come all innocent with me, young lady. I was looking through my window and saw you there with a man. I couldn't get a good look, but I know you weren't alone. Come on now … who was he?'

Lily breathed a sigh of relief. So he hadn't identified the Prince or his companion. But she realised she was in a spot, and would have to think fast to get herself out of it and avoid a scandal.

'It was nobody,' she said. 'Nobody I knew, that is. I couldn't sleep and was going for a stroll when I ran into some stranger. I don't know who he was, maybe one of the other servants. I couldn't see him clearly in the dark.

'All he did was nod and walk past, then I went back to the house and went to bed. That's all there is to it. Now please let me out.'

But Nifty wasn't to be so easily fobbed off. He pressed closer, until she felt the sharp edge of a wooden shelf cutting into her back. It was painful, but with her mind focussed on the danger of Nifty discovering the truth she was barely aware of it.

'I don't believe you,' he said. 'You're lying.' He held her even tighter. Lily struggled to break free, but she knew she was trapped. All she could do was desperately play for time.

'Please, Nifty,' she said. 'If I don't get back to my work someone will come looking for me. I'm supposed to be doing the guest rooms, and if I'm not there I'll get into trouble. Unlock the door and let me out.' But Nifty, now breathing heavily, took no notice and just pressed closer.

'You played the sweet little country innocent, when all the time you were on with someone else. Come on now, stop playing games and tell me his name. If you don't, I'll put you in to Mrs Druitt and see where that gets you. She doesn't take kindly to the staff carrying on with each other, especially those hired as temps. It'll be my word against yours, and I can tell you now which one of us she'll believe.'

Lily thought desperately, still trying to talk her way out of it.

She knew what Nifty said was probably right, and she'd be fired on the spot if he reported she'd been out in the garden at night with a man. Above all, she had to protect the Prince.

'It was nobody,' she said. 'No one I know, honest. I'd never seen him before, and I don't want to get anyone into trouble. If you'll say nothing about it, I'd be ever so grateful.'

In an instant Nifty's mood changed. Instead of threatening Lily, he smiled down at her. The smell of alcohol on his breath was now unmistakable. She tried to wriggle free, but he pressed even closer, so she could barely breathe.

'Grateful, eh? I might be persuaded to forget the whole thing if you're very nice to me,' he said. 'Come on luv, how's about a little kiss?'

Lily turned away, but Nifty forced her head back and next thing his lips were on hers. They were wet and sloppy and she could feel his tongue inside her mouth. She felt sick with disgust, but he was so strong she couldn't do anything about it. Then she felt his hand pressed on her breast, as he began to unbutton her dress with the other.

Just then she heard footsteps along the corridor. Nifty heard them too, and paused. It was the thing that saved her.

'If you don't let me go, I'll scream for help,' she said. The threat caused Nifty to release his hold on her, long enough for Lily to unlock the door and escape outside. A passing maid smiled as she recognised her, while Nifty remained out of sight in the storage room.

'What's wrong, Lily?' she asked. 'You look a bit flushed and bothered. They been working you too hard? I know it can get you down at times, but don't worry. It'll soon be over.'

She began to move on, then paused. 'By the way, your top button's undone.'

Lily thanked her, then did up the top button and straightened her dress as the maid, with another smile and a friendly nod, walked out of sight. Moments later Nifty emerged from the storage room, smiling and unrepentant, as though nothing had happened.

'Better luck next time,' he said.

She couldn't be sure if it was a threat or a promise.

26

It was finally over. The hoopla and the voting had reached their use-by-date, the campaign was declared officially closed, the yellow and green boxes were removed from all the post offices, and the nominations from the States and Territories had been locked away in a security safe until an official announcement was made.

As expected, some of the States had doubled up on their choices. Noelene Jones had been nominated by both NSW and South Australia, and was the only woman on the list. The distinguished scientist Professor Sir Ernest McWilliam was the choice of the ACT and Victoria. Others among the official nominations were cricketing legend Bill Bunning, retired High Court judge Rufus Evans, novelist (twice Booker winner) Glyn Russell, and a former Australian of the Year, Aboriginal community leader Jack Minamurra. All that needed to be done was to add the two wild cards, the people's choices, and the final names would be submitted to the Australian people for the June 30 election.

It was Brawn-Davies who came up with the idea of doing a survey of the people's choice candidates. She pointed out this was an important time in the history of the nation, and they might as well make use of it. Separating the nominees into categories would give a valuable insight into the kind of person the Australian public favoured for first president.

'Could be useful for the future.' she said in the clipped no-nonsense voice she used when delivering a lecture to first year students. 'Doctoral theses, research papers, gender bias, projecting economic targets, applying practical measures to sociological theories, that sort of thing.'

Slippery Dick frowned. He wasn't keen on academics; they talked a language all their own. But he also didn't want to be seen as yesterday's man, holding back history. He decided on a delaying tactic.

'Won't it mean we'll have to put in a lot of extra time?' he asked, thinking nostalgically of the cosy retirement nest waiting for him on the Gold Coast.

'It shouldn't take that long,' said Brawn-Davies briskly. 'After all, the computer software will do the work for us.' The rest of the committee, bowing to her intellectual superiority, agreed. Despite Slippery Dick's misgivings, the vote was carried unanimously.

In the end, the results of the survey were predictable; the overwhelming number of nominations were for sports and pop stars. Cricketers, swimmers and tennis players headed the sports categories, with soccer and AFL the most popular of the football codes. Rugby rated low.

A whopping 24 per cent were from the entertainment industry: theatre, movies, television, and radio. Talk show hosts headed the list, followed by actors (male) and pop stars (female). Minor categories were ministers of religion (9%), the armed services (7%), fashion models (6%), jockeys and horse trainers (4%). Journalists rated poorly (1.5%), but they were still more popular than retired politicians who scraped in at the bottom of the barrel with 0.5%.

Danno's name was prominent among those from the entertainment industry. Like a turd rising to the surface, he was slowly moving to the top. Breathing down his neck was soccer superstar Jason, a close runner-up. But the surprise was number three, Harry Winston. Harry's dollars had done their work well.

'Bloody hell,' said Alf Bristow, public servant, as he surveyed the list. 'How did that bastard get there? If Harry gets the nod, I'm leaving the country.'

Someone pointed out that it wouldn't be a bad thing as Harry had been a very generous benefactor to all the major parties. Another commented that his rags-to-riches background would go down well with all the migrant communities. 'A good public persona,' was how he put it.

But it was his private persona that finally brought Harry to grief and caused him to come crashing down. Brawn-Davies said she'd heard from her literary agent that Harry's first wife had written a book about their marriage, and it would be released on the market in time for Christmas.

'What kind of book?' asked Slippery Dick nervously.

'Hot and steamy', said Brawn-Davies. 'Lashings of sex. All the reasons why he dumped her … or she dumped him, I've forgotten which it was. My agent says it'll walk off the shelves.'

A vote was taken to check the accuracy of the information. The reply came back in less than 30 minutes. Yes, there was a book in the pipeline, written by Harry's ex-wife. It was Madelina's revenge for being dumped for a younger woman. The book was titled *In Bed with Harry* and would retail for $49.95. Clearly Harry between the sheets would not be a suitable candidate for first president.

After a brief discussion and yet another vote, Harry – who had been busy practising: 'Would youse care to join us for drinks at Admiralty House?' – bit the dust.

27

'Take a look at this,' said the Press Secretary, handing a newspaper to the Prime Minister. It was an article by the political writer Magnus Holtermann, listing the three tipped to be frontrunners at the June 30 election. The Prime Minister was outraged. No names had yet been released by the Selections Committee. So far as he knew they were still safely locked away. Clearly this was a major breach of security.

'Bloody hell. Where'd he get it?'

The Press Secretary shrugged; in a place like Canberra secrets leaked like a sieve.

THE FIELD FOR THE PRESIDENCY

In just over a month the nation will know who has been chosen to be the first president, but already bets are being placed. Sources close to the Government indicate these are the ones to watch:

Professor Ernest McWilliam, scientist, 74. Has made major contributions to research on AIDS, especially in African countries, which have reported a 30 per cent decrease in cases since using the vaccine he helped to develop. *Author of AIDS: The World Crisis.* Recipient of numerous awards and honours, including the 2012 Rutherford Medal and the 2013 Harvard Award for Scientific Excellence. Married to paediatrician Dr Edith Knowles (retired). Four children, six grandchildren. No known political affiliations. Frontrunner, widely regarded as the one to beat.

Odds: 5 to 4 on.

Noelene Jones, 55, opera singer/philanthropist. Companion of the Order of Australia. Honorary doctorates from Harvard, Oxford, and ANU. Twice named Australian of the Year. Recently announced her retirement after a distinguished career spanning more than 30 years. No known political affiliations. Generous benefactor to the arts. Widow of industrialist Sir Charles Barrington. No children. Strong contender.

Odds: 2 to 1.

Jason Lazlo, 45, Australian sports icon and international soccer star. Divorced, no children. Popularity has boomed since the release of the movie *Superstar* based on his life. However, his relative youth for such an important and critically sensitive position might work against him. Rank outsider but could prove a last minute surprise going into the straight.

Odds: 10 to 1.

The Prime Minister, looking even more irritated, put down the paper. 'Frontrunner. Rank outsider. Going into the straight. What's he think we're running … a bloody horse race?'

'It's only speculation,' said the Press Secretary, going into damage control. 'Pure guesswork, nothing to worry about.'

'I still don't like it,' said the PM. 'It lowers the tone of the whole thing. Undermines the dignity of the office.'

'I agree, Prime Minister. It's unfortunate.'

'And how the hell did he get those names? That's what I want to know.'

'Didn't come from me,' said the Press Secretary, sensing his job starting to move from under him. 'Maybe someone's talked out of turn?'

'That'll be Slippery Dick,' said the Prime Minister. 'Couldn't keep his trap shut if you paid him.'

'What d'you want to say if I get any calls about it?' asked the Press Secretary, relieved the blame had now moved to someone else.

'Tell them it's just another media beat-up. A fishing expedition by the yellow gutter press to sell more papers.' He paused for a rethink, remembering a certain newspaper proprietor was one of his major political supporters. 'Maybe not in those exact words. Point out the election for president is still to be held, and until then my government is not committed to any one candidate.'

The Press Secretary looked up from the notes he was making. 'Not committed?'

The PM shifted uncomfortably. 'Well in the manner of speaking.'

'But you've got someone in mind?'

'Bloody oath. And I'll tell you who I haven't got in mind – that goddamn soccer player. What's he going to do when he fronts up at official functions … sign autographs? Anyway, 45's too young for a Head of State.'

'Mary Robinson was 46 when she was elected President of Ireland.'

'Yeah well, that's the Irish for you. Women can get away with anything if they're easy on the eye.' He paused, remembering. 'Y'know I tried to get that bottom age limit pushed up to 50. But no one'd listen.'

'He's very popular, especially with young people.'

'Well he's not popular with me. Wasn't he involved in some drug scandal?'

'Different code. So far as I know, Jason's squeaky clean.' The Press Secretary had a sudden thought.

'How about a TV spot to pull it all into perspective? A word from your Prime Minister … a nation finally coming of age. Cutting old ties. Moving on. Looking to the country's future … that sort of thing. It might take the heat off.'

'Good idea,' said the PM, brightening.

He was busy next morning working on his TV talk when the breakfast cabinet entered, wearing a satin dressing gown embossed with a large red Chinese dragon. The PM looked up, surprised she wasn't in her usual powerwoman suit.

'Not going into the office today?'

'I'm taking the day off for some body maintenance.'

The PM was about to crack a joke involving government cars but quickly thought better of it. 'What kind of maintenance?'

The breakfast cabinet ticked off a list on her fingers. 'Spa, massage, facial, manicure, pedicure, lash and brow tint, aromatherapy, skin peel, and a wax.'

The PM had never heard of a skin peel and wasn't sure which parts of his wife's body she planned to have waxed, but both sounded painful so he decided not to ask. Instead, he pointed to the newspaper alongside him.

'Look at this,' he said. 'They're at it again, trying to trick us into releasing confidential government information. Well they've picked the wrong person this time. They can guess all they want but I'm one step ahead of them.'

The breakfast cabinet glanced at the article. 'Glad to see Noelene Jones still in there,' she said. 'We could do with a woman to run the country.'

The PM looked distinctly miffed. 'A Head of State does not run the country,' he said. 'He's just a figurehead.'

'Or she.'

'Anyway, women don't make good politicians. They're too emotional.' The breakfast cabinet stopped buttering her toast.

'What d'you mean, emotional?'

'Of course it's all hormonal so you can't really blame them. They're trapped by their bodies, poor dears. Having babies. PMT once a month. Then when they're over all that, the menopause. Men don't have to worry about those things, thank God. That's what makes us natural born leaders.'

An eyebrow raised. 'Really?' But the PM was now in full stride.

'Men are more far-sighted and forceful. They make the major decisions, they know where they're going. They see the sweep of the broad canvas. The big picture. Women waste time on trivia. They love to gossip, everyone knows that. Then when it comes to criticism, they're so bloody touchy and sensitive. Can't tell them a thing or they burst into tears.' He paused, thinking. 'Anyway women have the wrong kind of voice for politics.'

'Wrong?'

'They don't talk, they screech.'

He should have read the warning signs but didn't. He'd also forgotten the breakfast cabinet was a woman.

'Anything else?'

'Not at the moment.'

'Then you might ask the housekeeper to make up the bed in the guest room for tonight.'

The PM looked surprised.

'I didn't know we had anyone coming to stay with us. Who's sleeping in the guest room?'

'You are, my dear.'

28

Lily put the encounter with Nifty out of her mind, and as she got ready for bed, turned her thoughts once more to the Prince. The night seemed to last forever. The hands on her bedside clock moved on to eleven, eleven-thirty, then midnight. It was almost one in the morning when she heard once again that familiar sound of someone whistling *Lily of Laguna*.

She parted the curtains and looked out. This time there was only one person in the gardens, and she recognised the Prince immediately. Emma was fast asleep, snoring softly, as Lily quietly opened and shut the door and hurried down the corridor. The whole house seemed to be sleeping. There was not a sound from any of the rooms, either upstairs or downstairs, as she quickly made her way to the servants' entrance near the scullery and let herself out by the side door.

He was waiting there by the rose garden, still dressed in white tie and tails from the Lord Mayor's ball at the Town Hall. He looked so elegant, so handsome, that her heart lurched at the sight of him.

He took both her hands in his. 'I was afraid you mightn't come.'

She was too choked with emotion to answer and could only look into his face, trying to read his thoughts. Why did he want to meet her again? Unbelievable as it seemed, did he also feel this attraction between them? Could a prince love a commoner?

They walked through the gardens and she felt once again a warmth and closeness as though they'd known each other all their lives. Somehow it seemed the most natural thing in the world to be here by his side. She closed her eyes, praying the night would never end.

They talked of inconsequential things, the people he'd met, the places he'd seen, his impressions of her country. He told her about the train accident in Western Australia when the carriage in which he was travelling had run off the rails and overturned on its side. 'No one hurt, fortunately,' he said. 'Had to climb out of the windows. Could've been worse, of course, if we'd been travelling faster. It gave us a bit of a fright at the time.' Lily listened to the Prince talk, occasionally making a polite comment. But hovering over it all like a dark cloud was the thought that in another day he'd be gone.

She kept calling him 'Sir', still aware of the vast social gulf that lay between them. When he again asked her to call him 'David' she hesitated, then took her courage in her hands and said she felt it wasn't proper, seeing he was a royal.

He paused suddenly, under an oak tree. 'My darling Lily,' he said, tilting her face with one hand so she looked up at him. 'If I could wave a magic wand and be an ordinary person, believe me, I'd do it. Have you any idea what it's like to be born a royal?' Lily shook her head.

'It means you have absolutely no control over your

destiny. Other men can have any career they want, marry anyone they choose, live like normal people. But what's ahead for me? Just waiting around until my father dies, so I can take over his job. And to tell the truth, Lily, I'm not even sure I want to do it.

'It's like being given a prison sentence, except that even a prisoner has some rights, some hope of eventually being free. But there's no escape for me. Absolutely none.' Suddenly his outburst subsided as quickly as it had appeared, and he seemed to regret what he'd said.

'I'm sorry, I shouldn't worry you with my personal problems. Please forgive me, it was thoughtless. I have to accept I'm not an ordinary person, and never can be.'

'But what would you do, Sir, if you were an ordinary person?' Lily asked.

The Prince thought for a long moment.

'What would I do? Let's play a game of make believe, shall we? I'm walking in a garden, just like this one, and I meet this ordinary young woman. Except she's not ordinary at all, she's very special … a beautiful young woman with a sweet, kind, and loving nature. And as this is make believe, let's pretend, Lily, that this young woman is you.

'She's different from anyone I've met before and I don't want to lose her. So I decide to woo and win her, and I give her a red rose as a sign of my love. Then I ask her out … and wonder of wonders, she agrees.

'We go to a dance or a concert, or perhaps have tea in a cafe. We sit and talk and get to know each other … just two ordinary people. After a while I ask if she'll be my sweetheart, and she smiles at me and says "yes". So we start walking out together.

'Then one day I pluck up the courage to put my arms around my little sweetheart and kiss her, just like this.' The Prince's arms were around Lily and his lips pressed briefly, but tenderly, on hers.

'And this ordinary man knows he has finally found the woman of his dreams, the one he wants to spend the rest of his life with. So what d'you suppose happens next?'

Lily shook her head, unable to speak.

'He goes down on his knees and begs her to be his wife. He promises to love and look after her for the rest of her life. Then if she says yes, they get married, have a family, and live happily ever after.' The Prince looked down at her, suddenly serious.

'So how'd you think this ordinary man's sweetheart would answer? Could she possibly find it in her heart to love him?'

'Yes … oh yes,' breathed Lily.

Just at that moment it started to rain. And not just a light sprinkle, but a torrential downpour. Even with the shelter of the tree, Lily could feel her clothes becoming soaked. The Prince took off his jacket and placed it protectively over her.

'No sense getting wet,' he said. 'Let's go inside.'

She was suddenly reckless. She didn't care what might happen, she didn't worry about the consequences. Scandal, gossip, disgrace, dismissal – it all flew out of Lily's head. There was only one thought, that they would soon be parted, and she wanted to be with him more than she'd wanted anything else in her life.

With the rain still pelting down and the Prince's arm around Lily's shoulders, they hurried back towards the house.

29

As Noelene had predicted to Mike, the Opera Trust lunch had dragged on. It was close to four by the time she left and began to make her way home. It was a clear sunny day with cloudless blue skies, the kind of Sydney day that sometimes comes along to brighten the winter gloom. She decided to stroll along Macquarie Street before catching a taxi back to her apartment.

It was a mistake. She knew it was a wrong move as soon as she saw the crowds gathered outside Parliament House. It was a demonstration of some kind, and as she drew nearer she saw the reason for it. The monarchists hadn't given up the battle, although the referendum and most of the Australian people were against them. Like the Eureka diggers, they were determined to make one last stand.

Most of the demonstrators were middle-aged to elderly. Walking sticks abounded. There was one protester she particularly noticed, a grey-haired woman in her mid-seventies. She was in a fawn skirt and hand-knitted twin set, with a string of pearls. But it was her footwear that caught Noelene's attention – sensible brown lace-up shoes, the kind older women wear when their feet finally give up the battle to corns and bunions.

She looked like everyone's grandmother, but her voice was strident, carrying clearly over all the others. 'Down with the republic,' she was shouting. 'Save the monarchy. Protect our Queen.'

Poor old duck, was Noelene's first thought. Poor old misguided duck. She should be home baking scones or nursing grandchildren on her lap, not out here in the middle of a wild demonstration.

There was also a sprinkling of late teens and twenties, which surprised Noelene. Students? Children slavishly following in their parents' footsteps? Why on earth would a young person want to support a system that was so archaic, so out of step with modern life? A system that blatantly discriminated on the grounds of sex, race and religion? Did they know what they were doing?

As she came closer she could read the placards and name tags. LEAGUE OF MONARCHISTS. SAVE OUR CONSTITUTION. IF IT AIN'T BROKE DON'T FIX IT. DON'T TURN AUSTRALIA INTO ANOTHER BANANA REPUBLIC. All the tired, worn out slogans that had been trotted out during the referendum campaign. What did it take to convince them that this was the end of it?

One of the demonstrators was arguing with a uniformed official, demanding to be allowed inside. Someone else began to rattle the locked front gate. The shouting grew louder. Things started to turn ugly.

Noelene was about to cross to the other side to avoid the crowd when the situation abruptly changed. From the other end of Macquarie Street a group of republic supporters began to arrive. Clearly they'd been tipped off about the demonstration and were determined to break it up. There were counter signs: ADVANCE AUSTRALIA and GOODBYE QUEEN LIZ. It was like a battlefield, with two opposing armies advancing in formation.

Someone – it was never clearly established afterwards if it was a monarchist or a republican – threw a punch. A fatal mistake. Someone on the other side responded. In a matter of minutes it was a wild melee in which walking sticks and poster boards became lethal weapons.

Noelene found herself in the middle of it all. She felt herself pushed and shoved and jostled, trying to escape, but she was like the ham in the middle of a sandwich.

It was an accident. No one could blame either side for what happened. Noelene lost her balance and fell heavily to the ground, hitting her head on a slab of concrete. She felt something warm and sticky oozing into her hair.

The last thing she remembered was a voice saying: 'For God's sake someone call an ambulance' before she fell into a black void of nothingness.

30

Noelene recovered consciousness to find a concerned Mike looking down at her. Her head throbbed as she struggled to fit it all into place. She had a hazy memory of voices, being lifted on to a stretcher and into an ambulance, and then it had been blackness again.

'What happened?' she asked. 'Where am I?'

'You're in hospital. Suspected concussion. It appears you had a nasty fall and hit your head on something. Knocked out cold.'

'So how did you find out?'

'The news,' Mike said. 'I happened to be listening on my car radio. You're not exactly a nobody, you know. "Opera star caught up in wild demonstration outside Parliament House. Presidential candidate injured while supporting republican cause."'

'Rubbish,' said Noelene. She winced as she felt her head, the hair still matted with blood. 'I wasn't supporting anything. I was just walking along minding my own business and somehow got caught up in it.'

'Well that's not the way it's being reported. The press is having a field day.'

Noelene touched her head again gingerly, just as a nurse came to wheel her into a curtained cubicle. 'The doctor'll be along in a moment,' she said. When Mike tried to follow, he was waved back with a peremptory: 'I'm sorry. Unless you're a close relative, you'll have to wait outside.'

Mike waited, fortifying himself from a coin-operated machine with a drink of brown sludge from a tap marked Coffee. An hour later he was told he could visit Miss Jones in Room 72B, where she was to be kept overnight for observation. Well at least she'd been spared from sharing a ward, where there'd be more questions. One bonus, he supposed, of being famous.

Mike took a lift to the second floor, and found 72B at the end of a long corridor. Noelene was now in a white hospital gown, with a sign at the foot of her bed that said: DR LILIENTHAL. Who was Dr Lilienthal?

Noelene shrugged. 'No idea. One of the residents, I guess.' She tapped her head, 'Maybe the one who gave me these stitches.' The phone alongside her bed rang, and she picked it up. She listened for few moments, and Mike heard her say: 'Yes I agree. Thanks a lot. That's a good idea. I appreciate it.'

'Who was that?'

'The hospital's public relations officer. She's been getting some phone calls from the media, and wanted to let me know she's not giving out any information other than confirming I'm here. She's coming shortly to talk over a press release … that's if I want one.'

'Do you?'

'God, no. I feel enough of a fool without making a big song and dance about it. Less said the better. Anyway, what's there to tell? I hit my head, had a few stitches, and now I feel fine. It's a nothing story.' Noelene glanced at her watch. 'She said fifteen minutes.'

Mike got to his feet. 'In that case I'd better get going.

Anything you want me to bring you? I can come back later.'

'A dry martini?'

Mike laughed. 'I'd almost forgotten. We were supposed to be having drinks, weren't we?'

'Man proposes, God disposes.'

'Something like that.'

He looked down at Noelene, who seemed to have shrunk since he last saw her. She looked somehow small and vulnerable, swallowed up in the white hospital bed.

'Well give me a call if you think of anything you need. And let me know what time you'll be discharged.'

'I can take a taxi.'

'Nonsense. I'll come and collect you.'

'Thanks,' said Noelene. She closed her eyes, and he took it as a cue for his departure.

'By the way, did you find anything interesting in that tin trunk of your grandmother's?'

'Depends on what you call interesting. Nothing valuable, if that's what you mean. I'll show it to you some time when you're around.'

At the admissions desk on the ground floor he noticed two people, one with a camera, arguing vehemently with a blonde woman around 30 years old. The woman wasn't in hospital uniform, but she wore an ID badge with her photo and carried a clipboard.

As he passed he heard her saying: 'I'm sorry, but I can't let you up there. Definitely no visitors. Doctors orders. But if you'd just wait a while, I'll talk to Miss Jones and see what I can do.'

So this was the PR person. Mike had a feeling that in spite of Noelene's optimism it was going to be harder to keep a lid on the nothing story than she thought.

It was on all the news programs that evening, complete with pictures. An amateur cameraman had filmed Noelene as she was lying in the gutter and sold it to one of the television channels. There were also scenes of the demonstration and the pitched battle that followed. Mike called her shortly afterwards, to check her reaction.

'Not the most flattering picture I've ever had taken,' said Noelene. 'But what can I do about it?'

'Nothing. Just grin and bear it.'

Noelene told Mike that Dr Lilienthal wanted to keep her in another day, to be on the safe side, but she would be out on Friday.

'Just let me know what time, and I'll be there. And I promise I won't bring a camera.' She could almost see his smile at the other end of the phone.

The newspapers had a field day the next morning. There was a cartoon of a fierce-looking Noelene in shorts and boxing gloves, shaping up to an opponent wearing a crown. The same paper had an editorial headlined: A DIVIDED COUNTRY? It made the point that although the 'yes' vote had been carried by a clear majority, public opinion polls showed there was still a sizeable number not happy with the country becoming a republic.

Of these, roughly half said they would support the monarchy so long as Queen Elizabeth II remained on the throne, but once she died, their position could change. The underlying message seemed to be that the prospect of King Charles III as Australia's next Head of State was not a popular one.

'Yesterday's fracas outside Parliament House,' the editorial concluded, 'reveals there are still strong feelings in the community for both sides of the argument. Fortunately no one was hurt other than the well-known singer Noelene Jones, tipped as a possible first president. But who knows what might happen next time? Lives could be put at risk, or even lost, for the sake of holding on to a principle.

'It is time both those who support the new republic, and those who wish to retain the monarchy, bury their differences and unite for the good of the country. We must now look to the future.'

'D'you know why they chose the kangaroo and the emu for Australia's coat of arms?' asked Mike when he arrived at the hospital to take Noelene home.

'Is there a prize for the right answer?'

'Because they can't travel backwards.'

Noelene laughed, then winced. 'Ouch. My head still hurts. What brought that on?'

Mike pointed to the newspaper he was carrying. 'Today's editorial.' He grinned. 'But you look good in boxer shorts.'

'That's what's worrying me. People are going to get the idea I was somehow part of the demonstration, when all I did was walk into it.'

'Don't worry,' said Mike. 'It'll be wrapping up garbage tomorrow. One day wonder. Just forget it.'

The Prime Minister had read the same editorial and was also concerned, but for a different reason. He'd thought the monarchy business was dead and buried and here it was raising its nasty little head again, causing all kinds of mayhem and controversy. And he didn't much like that headline A DIVIDED COUNTRY? It put Australia on the same level as those South American places always in the middle of a civil war or toppling some dictator or other.

A few of his own ministers had voted 'no' at the referendum. He knew that, and it didn't worry him. He'd taken what he liked to think was a broad statesmanlike approach and urged his Cabinet members to vote any way they wished.

He'd even been undecided himself, right up to the last minute. He still had a soft spot for the monarchy, and had to admit he enjoyed the pomp and ceremony that went with it. You can't beat the Poms when it comes to putting on a good show.

He had warm memories of how he and his wife had been invited to a private luncheon with Her Majesty during one of their visits to London. Prince Philip was absent because of ill health, but Prince Charles had stood in for him. There'd also been a couple of younger royals whose names he couldn't remember.

It had been a very happy occasion, he'd told the press on his return to Canberra. The Queen had told him how much she enjoyed her visits to Australia, and how touched she had been by the many displays of affection and loyalty. She'd drawn his attention to the diamond wattle brooch she was wearing, a gift from the Australian government on her first visit in 1954. After lunch he'd had the privilege of meeting the royal Corgis.

'What else did you talk about?' one journalist had asked, hoping for some crumbs of information, a brief snippet that might make the early morning trek to the airport worthwhile.

'I'm sorry, but what Her Majesty and I discussed is a private matter,' said the PM, cleverly disguising the fact that most of the conversation had been about absolutely nothing.

'Why are you touching your forelock?' asked the PM's wife, breaking into the royal reverie.

'I am not,' said the PM indignantly, quickly bringing his hand down.

'Yes you were. You looked ridiculous.'

From experience, the PM found that when his wife was in one of these moods it was better to ignore it. He pointed to the editorial.

'It's this piece on Noelene Jones. I've been wondering if I should make some sort of gesture on behalf of the government and send her flowers. But if I did, would it look as though I'm taking sides? And whose side would I appear to be on?' He sighed. 'It's a tricky situation.

'The problem is I don't want to antagonise either the republicans or the monarchists. When you get down to it, they're all voters. I know the republicans feel they have a watertight case and that they proved it in the referendum. On the other hand I concede the monarchists have a point, although I'm not entirely sure what the point is.

'So I ask myself the question, should we stifle all argument and dissent? Should we gag the voice of the little man?' He caught the start of a frown and quickly took pre-emptive action. 'And little woman. This is still a free country, thank God. We pride ourselves on being a democracy. People are entitled to have their views.'

The PM heaved another sigh. 'It's not easy being a prime minister. People think it's a piece of cake, but it's not all it's cracked up to be. Uneasy is the head that wears the crown … although maybe that's not the right expression under the circumstances. Noblesse oblige. Well that's not quite it either. One tries to be fair. One tries to be even handed.'

He was dithering and he knew it.

'Send flowers,' said his wife briskly.

'Exactly what I'd decided,' said the PM, proud once again for having a wife who could always make up his mind.

31

The flowers were delivered to Noelene's apartment the day after she came home from hospital. Pink and white carnations and a signed note on the Prime Minister's personal stationery: 'My wife joins me in wishing you a speedy recovery from your unfortunate accident. Warmest regards.' In the end the PM had decided it was better not to make it an official government gesture. Be on the safe side. When in doubt, don't. Steer a middle course. Don't rock the boat. Leave well alone. He knew every cliche in the book.

After the flowers, the letters and cards started pouring in. They were from every part of the country, the writers ranging from the elderly to young children. Sorry to hear you've been hurt. Hope you soon get better. Thank you for supporting the cause. Stay firm to your beliefs. Australia needs you. Don't let us down.

Then the dirty work started.

It began with a small trickle of mail pointing out if she hadn't involved herself with the republican cause, then she wouldn't have landed herself in hospital with a split skull and concussion. 'Stay out of politics,' said one. 'Stick to singing, lady,' said another. The unspoken message was that Noelene had only herself to blame for what happened. Some of the language was disgusting, unprintable. Many of the notes were unsigned. She tossed them all into the wastepaper basket.

But then came a handful in which the warnings were not only explicit, but more sinister. One in particular stirred her to a white hot fury she hadn't realised she was capable of feeling.

'Republican bitch,' it said. 'You've got it coming to you.'

Noelene was angry. Very angry.

It was just after nine in the morning when Noelene's front doorbell rang. Still in her dressing gown she answered it, to find a woman standing there with a bunch of flowers and a face that was vaguely familiar.

'Miss Jones?' the woman said. 'I've come to apologise.'

'Apologise for what?'

'For our rude behaviour the day you were hurt. It was unforgivable.'

For a moment Noelene was puzzled. Who was this woman?

The shoes did it. The penny dropped when Noelene looked at the woman's feet. Those sensible brown lace-ups. It was the grandmother with the raucous voice who had distracted Noelene's attention on the day of the demonstration.

Although Noelene wasn't pleased at the unexpected visit (how did a stranger get her address?) she could see the woman was upset and anxious. So she asked her inside and calmed her down with a cup of tea.

'I can't say how sorry I was to hear you were in hospital,' the woman said. 'I rang to see how you were, but they wouldn't tell me anything. By the way, the name's Gwen McIlraith,' adding with emphasis: '*Mrs* Gwen McIlraith.'

Funny how women her age saw marriage as a badge of honour, thought Noelene. She'd never used Charlie's name. In all their years together, she'd always been Noelene Jones. The title 'Lady Barrington' didn't sit comfortably with her; much as she loved her husband, it had been important to keep her own identity.

Aloud, she was asking why Gwen had felt it so important to seek her out. There was absolutely no need for apologies, said Noelene. None at all. It had been an accident, pure and simple.

If she'd been more careful and looked where she was going, she might have managed to stay on her feet. No blame was attached to anyone. The police had investigated and made that quite clear.

But apologies were not the only reason for the woman coming. 'I wanted to explain,' she said. 'To help you understand. So you wouldn't think we were just a lot of bad losers stirring up trouble.

'Back way before you were born, my dear, the Queen paid a visit to this country. Well, it was historic – the first time a reigning British monarch had ever been here. I was still at school but I can remember as if it was yesterday. We had the day off, and lined the road where her car was passing, wearing our uniforms and waving Union Jacks.

'It was a very hot day, high nineties in the old temperature, and one of my friends fainted. They carried her off and revived her under a tree in someone's front garden.

'The Queen was very young then, still in her twenties, and I remember she was wearing this pale green dress and hat with a diamond brooch and white gloves, and she waved to us as she went by. Prince Philip was sitting alongside her.

'She looked so beautiful, just like in her pictures. Radiant. That's the word all the newspapers used. Radiant. And she was, too. Just like a movie star.

'I remember our Prime Minister at the time saying he'd love her till the day he died. Well he was quoting from some poem, but the words were beautiful. I suppose some might say it was all a bit sentimental, but that's the way everyone felt. We loved her.

'We were sorry she'd had to leave her children behind, but that's what royalty does. They put duty before pleasure.

I remember when she was in South Africa for her 21st birthday, how she promised she'd devote the rest of her life to her people and her empire. It was very moving.'

'Of course if she wanted to hand over the crown she could abdicate, like her uncle the Duke of Windsor. But it isn't in her character. She'll go on doing her duty, when other women her age have their feet up, taking it easy. She'll work until she drops dead. That's the kind of person she is.' She paused for breath, her face flushed with the intensity of her feelings. Noelene offered her another cup of tea, but she waved it politely away.

'So that's why I admire her. She's a good woman – a wonderful woman. Absolutely dedicated to her job. You've only got to look and listen to her to know that. And that's why I feel so bad this country is dumping her, like we're saying good riddance, we don't want you any more. It's rude. It's unforgivable.'

Gwen McIlraith stood up, clutching her handbag, backing off like a startled animal caught in the headlights of an approaching car.

'I'm sorry to have intruded. I don't normally just drop in on people without an invitation, especially someone like you.

But I just wanted you to know why I was at that demonstration, so you'd understand.' They shook hands at the door, and she disappeared down the corridor.

Noelene found herself strangely moved by the confrontation. 1954 – six years before she'd been born. Royal motorcades. Cheering school children. A radiant queen. A poetry-spouting prime minister. It was like looking back through snapshots of history. The woman's ideas were light years removed from Noelene's, but she could understand her point of view.

But later when she told Mike about it, he was unsympathetic.

'Ratbags … the world's full of them.'

'She wasn't a ratbag,' insisted Noelene. 'She truly believes in the monarchy.'

'The point is, do you?'

'Of course not.'

'Then stick to your principles. Don't give the buggers an inch. Once you start seeing the other side's point of view, you're gone. It's been a tough fight to get this far, and there's no room for compromise. Whether people like it or not we're now a republic, and that's the way it's going to stay.'

He was right, of course.

32

She never saw him again. All the next day was a flurry of comings and goings, doors opening and closing, cars pulling up and then leaving. She strained to catch a glimpse of him, to know what was happening, but Miss Patchett had given her duties that kept her trapped in the kitchen from early morning.

She knew the Prince's itinerary included a display by school children, and that later in the morning he would be given an honorary degree at Adelaide University. Then he'd catch a train to Port Adelaide and on to Outer Harbour to board his ship.

It was heartbreaking to listen to her colleagues discussing her beloved like some alien landed in their midst from another planet, soon to be out of their lives and forgotten. It hurt like a physical pain when a fellow housemaid confessed she was 'glad to be finished with all that bowing and scraping to those snooty Poms'.

The day moved slowly. Word filtered back that the Mayor of Port Adelaide, carried away by the importance of the occasion, had rambled on far too long with his speech of welcome and had to be reminded of the royal timetable.

Orders were given that the Governor and Lady Weigall, now the royal visit was over, would dine privately tonight. Beds were stripped, towels collected, dead flowers removed, and windows thrown open as house guests moved out and rooms went back to their original functions. The royal visit was fast becoming just a memory.

Emma noticed that Lily was quieter than usual. 'Not feeling well?' she asked, concerned at Lily's pale complexion. 'I can fill in for you if you want to go to your room and have a lay down and a bit of a rest.' But Lily insisted she was fine.

The Prince's suite was given special attention, with a senior housemaid assigned to it. Lily couldn't resist pausing a moment to glance through the open door as she walked past on her way to the laundry with an armful of linen.

A small antique desk that had been moved into the Prince's rooms for his use during his stay stood near the entrance, alongside two chairs borrowed from the Governor's study. Towels were piled in a heap in the middle of the carpet, and the silver vases that had once held flowers from the Government House gardens now lay empty.

Lily felt empty herself, as if part of her life had been taken from her. Someone close and dear to her had been in this room only hours before. She could feel his presence, so real she could almost reach out and touch him. Now he was gone and she would never see him again. It was like a death.

It was more than poor Lily could bear, and try as she might she couldn't stop the tears flowing. She dabbed at her eyes with a corner of her apron as the housemaid assigned to the Prince's rooms came into view, carrying some bedsheets. 'Can I help you?'

She recognised the housemaid as Florence, one of the more senior servants, grey haired and in her late-fifties. Lily stood there, choked by her feelings and unable for a moment to speak. Then with the personal discipline she'd been taught over the years by her father ('always keep a stiff upper lip, Lily') she pulled herself together.

'Sorry, ma'am,' she said. 'Just curious, that's all.'

'Curiosity killed the cat,' said Florence, but there was a smile in her voice. 'No harm in a quick look. There's no one here.'

Lily thanked her, but said she was already running late with her duties and wouldn't delay any longer. If you only knew, she thought, as she turned away and walked along the corridor. If you only knew. It was strangely comforting to hug her secret.

At the laundry she ran into Emma, who was all agog with news. Eddie had been given a gold sovereign as a tip from the royal party for his services, and been promoted. He was taking her out this Sunday to celebrate. And the housekeeper Mrs Druitt had asked for all the domestic staff hired especially for the royal visit to assemble in the dining room at four o'clock sharp.

'It's to give the temps their marching orders,' said Emma. 'I'm sorry you're going, Lily. I'll miss you.'

The rest of the day went by in a blur, as Lily did her work and then reported to the dining room at four. There were a dozen others already there, men and women who'd been hircd as cleaners, messengers, drivers, waiters, and kitchen staff. Lily was the youngest.

Mrs Druitt had a list of their names and ticked them

off as she checked they were all there. Then she made a short speech, thanking them 'for the excellent dedication to duties you have all shown.' She said she was sure it was something they would remember for the rest of their lives, and pass on to their children and grandchildren.

As a memento of such an historic occasion, said Mrs Druitt, the Governor has graciously signed a personal letter of thanks to everyone who had served at Government House during the royal visit. These would be handed out by his aide-de-camp as each person left.

There was a subdued mood in the staff dining room as everyone ate their evening meal. Some had stories to relate about the royal visit, interesting or funny things that had happened to them. Everyone had their personal likes and dislikes of those in the royal entourage, but all agreed the Prince was 'a decent enough bloke, not stuck up like some of the others in his party. He'll make a good king when his old man dies.'

The general feeling was that while such a close and personal contact with royalty had been an interesting experience, it was a relief now it was over and they could all get back to their normal lives.

As they were leaving, Emma tried again to persuade her to stay. 'You're a good worker,' she said. 'I'm sure if you asked, they'd find a place for you.' Lily said sorry, she was homesick and wanted to get back to her family; they needed her. But Emma was determined not to give up.

'You're a sly one, you've never told me who you were sneaking out to meet that night I caught you. Well if you don't want to say, I won't press you. That's your business. But if you're still keen and he works here, there's an extra reason to stay a bit longer. Come on, Lily, you'n me are pals. Another couple of days won't hurt you.'

Lily paused to think it through. She had been hired only until tomorrow, but Mrs Druitt had said any staff who needed to travel some distance out of town could have the use of their rooms for as long as necessary. And just before she'd left, her father had said he'd have no objection to her staying on for a bit, provided she could find decent accommodation.

'This is an opportunity for you to see something of life in a big city,' he'd said. 'It mightn't come your way again for a long time. I know how hard you work looking after us, and you deserve some reward. Just remember we all love you, and don't stay away too long.' So she gave in and told Emma she'd remain for the weekend and go back on the first train Monday morning.

It was a decision she'd regret.

Lily was getting ready for bed when the package arrived. It was delivered by one of the Government House messengers – just a plain cream envelope with her name on it. Even before she opened it, she knew who it was from. The note was brief, in a firm handwriting, and took less than a minute to read. By the time she'd finished she was weeping.

That night she went to sleep with the letter and the red rose clutched tightly to her breast.

The next day the morning newspaper had this:

A PRINCE'S FAREWELL

The Prince of Wales after his departure on Friday sent the following message to His Excellency the Governor:

I would like to express my appreciation for the warm welcome South Australia has given me, and to say how deeply sorry I am that I could not have stayed longer and seen more of your country districts and their communities.

I was deeply touched by all the sentiments expressed, and leave Adelaide with sad feelings.

Please convey my personal thanks to your Premier and the Government, and all who helped make my visit run so smoothly.

33

June 30, 2016

It was finally here. The election that would decide the frontrunner for president. The ground rules were simple: first three past the post, with no preferences.

The candidates nominated by the States and Territories were:

Professor Sir Ernest McWilliam, scientist

Noelene Jones, singer

Rupert Evans, retired High Court judge

Bill Bunning, cricketing legend

Glyn Russell, prize-winning novelist

Jack Minnamurra, Aboriginal activist

and for the 'people's choice':

Daniel (Danno) Littleworth, TV presenter

Jason Lazlo, soccer superstar

There were no surprises or shocks, except for the shock felt by Harry Winston when he read the results in the papers. He immediately cancelled all branch bonuses and booked a long holiday on the French Riviera.

There had been one unexpected hiccup in the run-up to

the election. An enterprising journalist had uncovered a letter written by the Prime Minister at the time of the 2013 Harvard award, in which he had lavishly praised Professor McWilliam and hinted at a vice-regal appointment. It had been written the day after a small intimate dinner party in the professor's honour held at The Lodge in Canberra. The letter read:

> *Your academic brilliance and dedication to the cause of science has been justly rewarded. Your importance to the nation cannot be under-estimated. As one of your warmest admirers, please accept this as a personal tribute to your well-deserved success.*
>
> *Following our private conversation last night, I am delighted to know you would be willing to serve this great country of ours in the capacity discussed. You appreciate, of course, the need for absolute confidentiality at this early stage.*

It was the words 'private conversation' and 'in the capacity discussed' that caught the attention of the journos, especially as the Prime Minister kept claiming he had no favourites for the short list. But if Sir Ernest had been the PM's first choice for Governor-General, didn't it follow he was also first choice for Head of State? And if so, it would seem to make nonsense of the PM's support for 'a people's president'. There were claims of partisanship, skulduggery and vote rigging. The press were starting to make a meal of it.

At first the Prime Minister fell back on the standard response of those unwilling to incriminate themselves in the witness box: 'I don't recall'. Prodded into an improvement of memory, he then blamed it on 'a media beat-up'. Further challenged, he said he had been quoted out of context. And finally he admitted to writing the letter, but denied the words had any hidden meaning.

'How many of you can remember what you talked about three years ago?' he said testily, when questioned about it at a press conference. 'Sir Ernest is a distinguished Australian, and it was natural we should chat during the evening. It was a good dinner party, I can remember that much.'

'Good wines?' asked one of cheekier members of the Fourth Estate. The PM bristled. 'If you're suggesting I had too much to drink and that's the reason for my poor memory, let me say categorically that wasn't the case and I strongly resent the inference.'

The reporter decided on a strategic withdrawal. Whenever the PM used words like 'categorically' it was always safer to drop the subject.

—⧟—

The polling booths opened at nine and closed at six. But unlike a political election, no one pressed How-to-Vote cards on voters as they arrived. There were no party campaigners with ribbons and name tags, no billboards, no posters, no sausage sizzles, no razzamatazz. It was all very quiet and orderly. Almost boring, as someone commented. Who would have thought that Australians were about to choose the new head of their nation?

When Noelene arrived at her local polling centre she couldn't help contrasting it with that wild demonstration she'd walked into only a few weeks ago. People smiled and nodded their heads as she walked into the hall. Maybe the monarchists had now bowed to the inevitable and accepted that whether they liked it or not, the country was going to change.

A photographer took her picture as she slid her folded vote into the box. 'Good luck,' he said.

'Thanks.' Her vote had gone to Jack Minamurra.

All the TV networks were covering the election, but with Western Australia two hours behind results weren't expected until late in the evening. Noelene had invited Mike to sit in with her to watch the election cover on television. He arrived with a bottle of champagne.

'To celebrate,' he said.

Noelene frowned. 'Celebrate what?'

'You winning.'

She was in an odd mood tonight. She seemed thoughtful, preoccupied. 'Aren't you jumping the gun? The votes have only just started to come in.'

'No contest,' said Mike confidently. 'You're a shoo-in. From tomorrow, the working title for the documentary is *Noelene: First President.*'

'Now you're making me nervous.'

'Anyway, it doesn't matter,' said Mike. 'It'll stand on its own, whichever way the votes go. I can always change the name.'

'To what … *Noelene: The Almost Ran*?'

Mike laughed. 'It'll be fine, believe me.'

Noelene had prepared a light meal of chicken and salad and they ate it from trays on their laps as they watched television, sipping wine and exchanging the occasional comment as fresh results came up on the screen.

Just like Charlie and I used to do.

The thought gave her a pang of nostalgia that was like physical pain. She forced herself to bring her mind back to the present and the election.

By seven o'clock the numbers were leaning towards Sir Ernest McWilliam and Judge Evans, but two hours later there was a sudden spurt of South Australian votes for Noelene. The two people's choice candidates were all over the place.

'What's your gut feeling at this stage?' the ABC man asked the political analyst sitting alongside him. 'Willing to go out on a limb and make an early prediction?'

'My feeling is McWilliam will top the votes at the end of the night, with either Jones or Evans in second place,' said the analyst. 'Bunning, as you can see, is trailing badly, so I think you can safely rule him out. And I don't think any of the other nominees have the numbers … it'd take a miracle for them to catch up now.'

'How about the people's choice?'

'Well that's the interesting thing. They're polling much better than I'd have expected, especially in NSW and Victoria. So you'd have to say they're definitely still in contention.'

It was close to midnight when the final results were declared.

As predicted by the political analyst, Sir Ernest McWilliam had easily topped the votes. Noelene had nudged out Judge Evans to run a close second. But soccer superstar Jason Lazlo had failed to score a winning goal.

The third candidate to be shortlisted for the highest office in the country – first president of the republic of Australia – was none other than the hennaed, coiffed and surgically enhanced king of daytime television, Danno.

'Well that's a surprise,' said Mike. 'How on earth did that dickhead make it?'

'Power of the people. He's got a lot of fans.'

'Power of the people be buggered. Like I said, the whole thing's crazy. They should've stuck to the old system instead of trying to please everyone.'

'Look Mike, I don't like him any more than you do, but he's won fair and square. It's a democracy. We all had a chance to vote, so there's no point in complaining about the result.'

Mike suddenly jumped to his feet and grabbed the bottle of champagne. 'Hey, why am I complaining? We should be celebrating. You've just made the top three and that's all that bloody well counts.'

He'd popped the cork and was already filling their glasses, lifting his in a toast. 'Congratulations, champ. How d'you feel?'

'Numb. Still in shock.'

'I don't know why. You've done well all through the campaign. You're a national treasure, it's no wonder people voted for you. If the PM doesn't choose you, he needs his head read.'

Noelene smiled but didn't respond. Mike was suddenly alert.

'You are going to accept, aren't you? I know you've said all along you didn't want to run, but surely you're not going to knock it back now?'

Still no response. Mike could contain himself no longer and exploded.

'Noelene, I voted for you. So did a lot of others. If you don't want the job why the hell don't you just say 'no' and be done with it?' It was a mark of their relationship that he could talk to her like this and get away with it.

Noelene put down her glass. 'Mike, you've been a good friend, so I feel I owe you an honest answer. And you're right. After that business when I finished up in hospital, I decided nothing would ever persuade me to run for president.

'I thought about what it would cost me. Giving up my retirement. Always being on display. Never having a private life of my own. Becoming public property. I hated the whole idea. It was the last thing in the world I wanted.

'But last night just before I went to bed I started to think about what Charlie would say if he were alive today. He always had such faith in me. When no one else thought I could make it as an opera singer, he never stopped believing I could do it. Charlie kept on encouraging me. He was that kind of guy. "Aim for the stars", he'd say. "If you don't aim for the top you'll never get there. Just go for it, girl." That was one of his favourite expressions. "Go for it".'

'So?' Mike knew the answer before she'd even spoken.

'I'm going for it.'

34

The next morning the election with its three winners was front page news. In a matter of hours Danno had asked his agent to check his contract for a 'get out' clause. Jason Lazlo took up an invitation from a wealthy Miami widow who'd long lusted after him to move to Florida and teach the Yanks how to play soccer. Judge Evans accepted a teaching post at the same University as Brawn-Davies. Glyn Russell turned on his computer to begin his next book. Cricketing legend Bill Bunning started work on his memoirs. Jack Minnamurra went bush. Sir Ernest told his wife to buy herself a new wardrobe. And Noelene took her phone off the hook.

A short time later she was opening the front door to Mike. 'Couldn't get through so I decided to come around,' he said. 'Just to check how you're coping.'

'I'm getting used to it. Come in.'

'I gather you took the phone off the hook.'

'You gathered right. The damn thing hasn't stopped ringing.'

'Get a silent number. It's not going to stop, y'know.'

'I know.'

'Anyway you won't have to put up with it much longer. The PM's promised to make an announcement within a month.'

'How's the documentary coming along?' she asked.

'That's another reason I came around. I thought you might like to hear what your old school mates had to say about you.'

Noelene pulled a face. 'Not sure I do. But go ahead.' Mike reached into his briefcase and pulled out a batch of notes.

'Melanie Boswell. Remember her?'

'Vaguely. Red hair and freckles. Fat.'

'She's not fat any more. And she's no longer a redhead.' He studied his notes. 'She says you were brilliant. She says everyone knew you were going to make it big some day.'

'Hindsight's a wonderful thing.'

'Don't be so cynical. How about this one? "Noelene was always the first to put up her hand when the teacher called for volunteers to pick up papers in the yard, or stay after school to help. She had a lot of energy, just seemed to like doing things. Always into everything, it didn't matter what it was. When Noelene was around, no one else could get a look in."'

Noelene was amused. 'In a word – pushy.'

'Don't put yourself down. Everyone said nice things about you. In fact, I had trouble finding one who didn't think you were the perfect student destined for fame and fortune.'

'So did you?'

'How about this: "I never liked Noelene, although I must admit she didn't have a bad voice. We just didn't click. She was such a goody two shoes, always hogging the limelight and playing up to the teachers. Of course they made sure she was the star turn in all the school concerts. No one else got a look in. I know she's been very successful, but we were never close."'

'Who on earth was that?'

Mike consulted his notes again.

'Sally-Ann Nicholson.'

'Don't remember her.'

'Well she remembers you. She said a lot more, but it'd be defamatory.' He checked his notes again.

'Correction. She was Sally-Ann Bannister. Nicholson's her married name.'

'That rings a bell. She wasn't one of the names I gave you.'

'No. Someone else suggested it might be worth talking to her, so I tracked her down. A bit of a contrast to the other stuff. I don't want this documentary to be all sweetness and light.'

'God, nor do I.'

'Change of subject. As I'm here, can I have a look at what's in that box you discovered behind the bricks at your grandmother's house? It might be useful, something to add to the family history.'

Noelene had to think for a few moments to remember where she'd put it. She went into her bedroom, reached up into the top shelf of the wardrobe, and came back.

'There was a letter in it,' she said. 'Jammed right down at the bottom, which is why I didn't notice it at first.' She took all the bits and pieces out and handed them to Mike. He glanced briefly at the ribbon, the brooch and the dead flower and began reading the letter, frowning.

'Imagine a rose lasting all this time,' said Noelene. 'In those days women kept them as a sentimental keepsake. Pressed them between the pages of a book, that sort of thing. No one bothers now, more's the pity.'

But Mike wasn't listening, too busy studying the piece of paper.

'Have you had a really good look at this?' he asked.

'Not particularly. Why?'

He handed it back to her.

'Read it again.'

My darling Lily:

I am sorry I could not see you once more before I left. Whatever the future brings us both I want you to know I will never forget you.

God bless my little sweetheart. May He protect and look after you always.

Yours,

David

'It's just a love letter. What's so special about it?'

'Did you notice what's printed at the top?'

Noelene looked again.

'*HMS Renown*. That's a ship, isn't it? Does that mean David was a sailor?'

'In the manner of speaking. Mind if I borrow it? I promise I'll take good care and bring it back again.'

Noelene was astonished. 'Keep it as long as you like. I'm sure Lily won't mind. But what on earth for? It's just an old letter written nearly a hundred years ago. Look at the date on it – 1920.'

'That's exactly why I'm interested in it.'

Noelene's curiosity was sparked even more.

'Come on, Mike, don't act all mysterious. I know you better than that. There must be a good reason why you want it.'

But Mike wasn't giving anything away other than to say he had a hunch and needed time to follow it up.

'What kind of hunch? Give me a clue.'

'I could but I won't. I want to be sure before I tell you anything. I might be wrong and I don't want to finish up with egg on my face.'

Wrong about what? But try as she may, Noelene couldn't get anything more out of him. It was downright exasperating.

As soon as he left Noelene's apartment, Mike drove to the State Library on Macquarie Street. He parked his car and went straight to the information desk.

'I'd like to look through some old newspaper files,' he said.

'Certainly, Sir. Which ones?

'*The Advertiser*, Adelaide 1920.'

35

Lily's last days at Government House went in a haze of joy and sorrow – joy that she'd met the love of her life, and a deep aching sorrow knowing she'd never see him again.

Emma noticed her moodiness and tried to jolly her out of it, thinking she was worried about her future. 'Come on, Lily,' she said. 'It's not the end of the world, there're plenty of others who'll take you on when you leave here. You're a good worker, you'll get another job without any trouble, mark my words.' But Lily, desperately trying to hide the real reason for her sadness, assured Emma it wasn't the fear of being unemployed that worried her, it was leaving behind the friends she'd made here.

'Everyone's been so kind and helpful,' she said. 'I'm going to miss you all.'

'Never mind,' said Emma. 'When me and Eddie get married, you can come and visit us.'

Nifty had been keeping his distance since their last encounter. At meal times she made a point of never looking directly at him, keeping her gaze steadfastly on her plate, although she could feel his eyes burning into her.

She had never mentioned the incident in the storage

room to Emma, knowing Nifty was Eddie's friend and not wanting to cause trouble. Sometimes it was better to keep one's mouth shut. But if Lily had reckoned on leaving Government House without running into Nifty again, she was badly mistaken.

As it was a weekend, some of the staff had been given a half day off. Lily had thought to spend it packing her things and quietly reading in her room, but Emma had other ideas.

'Put on your best dress and doll yourself up. If you think you're going to spend the day moping here on your own, then you've got another thing coming. Me and Eddie've planned a farewell surprise for you. We're all going out.'

Lily, with a warm glow at Emma's thoughtfulness, quickly put down her book and changed into the one good dress she'd brought with her. She checked herself in the mirror, smoothing down the curls, as Emma waited impatiently.

'Come on Lily, you look lovely. Stop fussing. We don't want to keep them waiting.'

Them? As they walked out the rear staff door and into the grounds, Lily realised with a sickening feeling that the surprise outing included Nifty. But it was too late to turn back.

And it was a transformed Nifty who stood there alongside Eddie. Gone was the junior footman's uniform and in its place was a smart navy suit with shirt and flowered tie. A white initialled handkerchief peeped out from the top of the breast pocket. P? She'd forgotten his name was Peregrine.

His leather shoes had been shone to a mirror-like

polish, and on his head he wore a jaunty felt hat with a feather tucked into the band. As Lily and Emma emerged he doffed his hat, and the waves of his hair, heavy with brilliantine, gleamed in the sun. Not for nothing had he earned the nickname Nifty.

'Eddie's organised a special treat for us,' said Emma. 'Tea and cakes at Balfours.'

They walked to the popular eating place, where Eddie had booked for four in one of the cosy alcoves. As Nifty slid in alongside Lily she could feel the pressure of his thigh against hers. But the more she tried to move away, the closer he came, until she was hard against the wall and could go no further.

Emma, oblivious to Lily's discomfort, studied the menu as a waitress approached to take their orders. 'I'm having one of those yummy cakes that look like a green frog.' Balfours was famous for its frog cakes. 'How about you, Lily?'

Lily, her mind distracted by Nifty, made an effort to look at the menu. 'I'm not very hungry,' she said. 'Maybe just a sausage roll. And tea.'

The tea came in a large pot with a jug for the milk and a bowl of sugar cubes with little silver tongs to lift them out. 'Shall I be mother?' asked Emma, starting to pour. Nifty offered Lily the sugar bowl, but she declined.

'Sweet enough, eh?' said Nifty, with a grin. His thigh pressed even firmer against hers.

'When d'you go back, Lily?' asked Eddie, demolishing a large slice of fruit cake.

'Early train Monday morning. I've had a lovely time here, but I'll be glad to get home.'

'We'll miss you, won't we Nifty?' said Eddie, with a

wink and a grin at his friend sitting opposite. Nifty nodded and put an arm around Lily's shoulders.

'That we will, luv,' he said.

Lily, starting to panic, wondered how she could remove Nifty's arm without making too much of it. But no one else seemed to take any notice or think it strange, so she decided the best tactic was to ignore it and get on with afternoon tea. It would soon all be over.

Finally the last cup had been poured and the last cake crumb cleaned from the plates. But if Lily hoped to return to the security of her room at Government House, she was badly mistaken.

'Eddie says there's a band playing in the Botanic Gardens,' announced Emma. 'Let's go and have a listen. It's not far to walk.'

So they set out along North Terrace, and as they drew nearer they could hear the steady oom-pah-pah of the brass. Sure enough there was a band playing in the rotunda, with a small crowd gathered around it.

Eddie bought them threepenny ice-cream cones from the kiosk, and they sat on the lawns to listen to the music. Again Nifty edged closer, but this time Lily had more room to manoeuvre and made sure she put some distance between them.

When the concert finished they strolled through the gardens, admiring the flowers and the ducks on the pond. Eddie and Emma were a short distance ahead, walking together arm in arm. But when Nifty tried to put his arm through hers, Lily pulled away. He gave her a look, but said nothing. He seemed withdrawn, almost moody.

They'd been walking for several minutes when Lily

noticed Emma look back, then pause to whisper in Eddie's ear. Eddie smiled and nodded in agreement. As Nifty and Lily drew level, the two in front stopped for a chat. But if Lily was hoping for a rescue by Emma, she soon found out she was mistaken. Her roommate was still intent on match-making.

'Eddie and I are going to take a bit of a breather,' she told Lily. 'We've got a few things to talk about, so we'll sit on that park bench for a while. You and Nifty go on, and we'll all meet back here in half an hour.' There was nothing Lily could do. She was trapped like a fly in a web spun by Emma. And the spider waiting for her was Nifty.

They'd walked for another ten minutes when Nifty paused and turned towards her. 'We've gone far enough,' he said. 'Let's you'n me have a little talk. Somewhere private.' He steered her towards a shelter shed for picnickers, with wooden table and bench seats. There was no one in it.

'I've been thinking a lot about the last time we were together,' said Nifty. 'Seems like we got off on the wrong foot.'

'Please,' said Lily. 'It's done and forgotten. I don't want to talk any more about it.' But of course it wasn't forgotten. And Nifty wasn't to be silenced.

'I'm sorry if I had the wrong idea about you,' he said. 'You can't blame me ... nicking out the way you did. I jumped to the wrong conclusion, that's all. Anyone would. Decent girls don't go wandering around at night. But I'm willing to take your word there was nothing in it.'

He paused, looking at Lily for her reaction. She was silent.

'I like you, Lily. I like you a lot, more'n just about any

other girl I've ever met. And I know you're dead set on going home Monday. Em told me she tried to talk you into staying and didn't get anywhere. So if she couldn't do it, I reckon I'd be wasting my breath. The thing is, Lily … I don't want you to leave thinking badly of me.' She could see small beads of perspiration starting to appear on his forehead.

'I don't,' said Lily. 'You gave me a scare, that's all.'

'I know, and I'm very sorry for it. I got carried away, that's all.' He held out a hand. 'So, can we be friends?'

Lily thought carefully about her response. If she said 'no' was she being un-Christian, not obeying the command to turn the other cheek? And when it came down to it, what was there to forgive? Just a clumsy sexual advance with no real harm done. On the other hand, 'yes' could give Nifty false encouragement. All her instincts told her he was the kind of person who wouldn't give up easily.

'Friends, Lily?' Nifty still had his hand out, waiting for her answer.

She thought of her mother and father. She remembered the words of the Good Book, read each Sunday as they sat with bowed heads around the kitchen table. Goodness and evil. Sin and redemption. Forgive thy enemy.

So Lily took the outstretched hand in hers.

'Yes, Nifty,' she said. 'I'll be your friend.'

It was a mistake. All her instincts had been right. The touch of her hand acted like a trigger, releasing a floodgate of emotion in Nifty. He held on to it tightly, then took her in his arms and began to shower her with wet, passionate kisses. His lips were on her mouth, her face, the curve of her neck. And this time there was no one around to rescue her.

When he finally released her she was shaking, not from fear but from anger. She felt her whole body had been violated. Nifty was talking but she barely heard what he said.

'Em reckons the two of us could make it a go of it, like her and Eddie. She reckons we've got a future. I won't be a footman all my life. I've got contacts, know a few people. With a bit of luck I'll set myself up in my own business some day. Stick with me and you'll never want for anything, Lily.' Then came the words that shocked her. 'So what d'you say we get married?'

It was so totally unexpected, so out of the blue, that for a moment Lily couldn't speak. Nifty read her silence for assent and again took her in his arms. But this time she struggled free.

'It's impossible,' she said. 'I could never marry you.'

Nifty's mood changed once more. He was like a chameleon.

His face darkened and he grasped her shoulders so tightly that she flinched from the pain. 'Come on Lily, I want a better answer than that. Not good enough for you? Reckon you could do better?' She shook her head.

'It's that bloke in the garden, isn't it? Do you love him?'

When Lily remained silent he repeated the question. 'Do you?'

She'd never said the words out loud before. Saying it now was like a commitment, a vow as solemn and sacred as any made between two people standing before a church altar. For better, for worse; till death us do part.

There was no going back. Her voice was clear and firm as she spoke up.

'Yes,' she said. 'I love him.'

Nifty knew when he was defeated. Without another word he walked out from the shelter and out of her life. It was all over.

She never saw him again.

36

The shortlist had been given to the Prime Minister. All three candidates had expressed their willingness to accept the presidency, if offered to them.

Danno had been particularly effusive. 'Great honour,' he puffed. 'Delighted to serve my country in any capacity. Thank you, Prime Minister.' Privately he was hoping it would send his ratings skyrocketing through the roof.

What no one knew was that the PM had already made his choice and it was Sir Ernest McWilliam. However, if he was expecting a pat on the back from the breakfast cabinet, he was sorely disappointed.

'That boring old fart? Are you out of your flipping mind?' The PM's wife pulled a face like she'd just swallowed a lemon.

But the PM held his ground, even though he knew there could be some chilly nights ahead in the matrimonial bed. There were times when the national interest had to take precedence over domestic comfort, and this was one of them.

The PM thought long and carefully about his next moves, and in which order to make them. He was determined the machinery of choosing the first president would be a blueprint for all future governments, with him as chief architect.

But first of all he had to give at least the appearance of carefully scrutinising all three candidates for a final decision. It would look bad to make a quick judgment. So he held off on the announcement for another week. Then he made a number of phone calls, the first to his deputy, and then to the leaders of the other major political parties. All of them agreed Sir Ernest would be excellent, and congratulated the PM on his choice. He told his press secretary to prepare a statement to be released to all media.

The last call was to Sir Ernest to give him the good news. He added that the appointment still had to be ratified by Parliament, but he was confident it would be passed.

The PM said there were still some technical details to be ironed out to ensure a smooth and seamless changeover from Governor-General to president. Sir Ernest would of course, be moving his residence from Melbourne to Canberra, but he assumed this would pose no great problems for him and his good lady wife. He offered the services of the Prime Minister's department for any help Sir Ernest might need.

Finally he passed on his warmest congratulations, 'with the hope this will signal the start of a bright new era for our nation.'

Sir Ernest listened, and after some polite words of thanks, put down the phone and smilingly turned to his good lady wife to pass on the news. But his smile turned to a look of agony as a crushing pain seized his chest. He groaned and collapsed on the floor … stone dead.

He had been President of the Republic of Australia for exactly two minutes.

37

The next day the papers were full of the sad news. PRESIDENTIAL CANDIDATE DIES said one headline. SHOCK COLLAPSE OF TOP SCIENTIST was another. There were full page obituaries as well as tributes from science organisations, community groups and universities. The government expressed its regrets at Australia losing such a great man.

A State funeral was briefly considered, but finally decided against. And not one person, not even the well-informed Magnus Holterman, twigged the fact that the country's first president had quietly come and gone.

But the Prime Minister was now presented with a personal dilemma. It was going to take considerably more time than the thirty seconds or so he'd given to choosing Sir Ernest, to select his replacement. There were options, of course. He could go back to the Selections Committee and ask them to come up with a new shortlist. But that seemed pointless and time wasting and mightn't please the mums and dads who'd voted. He could flip a coin. Again, not a good idea.

He agonised over it for days until he could put it off no longer. It was a very painful decision to have to make. What would be the lesser of two evils – a preening TV celebrity or a hormonal woman? The gloating face of the breakfast cabinet didn't help.

'Frankly, my dear, you have no choice,' she said. 'Noelene Jones will make an excellent president. So take it like a man.'

Noelene took the call at seven in the morning. 'The Prime Minister wishes to speak to you,' said a public servant-type voice at the other end of the line. It had the feel of a royal summons.

The PM apologised for the early hour, but explained it was a matter of urgency. He said that after carefully considering all the candidates presented to him, Noelene was his choice as president. 'A clear choice, I might add. I will have no hesitation whatever in recommending it to Parliament.'

Of course Noelene said yes. She said all the right words, such as being highly honoured by the Prime Minister choosing her, adding that she looked forward to carrying out her duties and would try to fulfil them to the best of her ability. She was already starting to sound presidential.

The PM said he'd appreciate it if she kept the appointment confidential until he had the opportunity to make a public announcement. There would, of course, be the usual press conference, 'but with your long years of experience in dealing with the media, I'm sure that won't be a problem'.

There was one more thing to clear up. The PM said he had November 8 in mind for the inauguration ceremony, and needed to confirm it so he could advise Her Majesty as soon as possible. Would the date be suitable?

Noelene said that would be fine; she had no commitments beyond September. With that the PM concluded the conversation, congratulating her again and saying one of his staff would be in touch. As soon as he'd hung up, he called in his private secretary to advise him of developments. As the secretary was about to leave a sudden thought occurred to the PM.

'Find out the funeral arrangements for Sir Ernest and send some flowers on behalf of the government, along with a letter of sympathy to his widow. You know the kind of thing … sincere condolences, great loss to this nation, distinguished citizen, will not be forgotten, etcetera etcetera.'

The Prime Minister was nothing if not adaptable, and poor old Sir Ernest was soon forgotten. In less than a day he was completely erased from the Prime Minister's mind, as though he'd never existed. There was not even a passing thought given to the fact that the distinguished citizen, so recently deceased, had been his one and only choice for the top job in the country. Instead, his mind was occupied elsewhere, concentrating all his thoughts and energy on the November inauguration.

One door closes, another opens, was the PM's philosophy. Win some, lose some. At least they now had a president who could sing the national anthem in tune.

38

In late August she suspected something was wrong. By September Lily knew for certain she was pregnant.

Her father blamed himself for placing her in the way of temptation by allowing her to go to the wicked city. He held her in his arms, saying over and over again: 'My poor little Lily. My poor little motherless child.'

Of course he wanted to know who was responsible. So did all her brothers. They lined up in a four-man squad, Samuel, Horace, Arthur and Thomas, and vowed to confront the black-guard, the cad and scoundrel who had seduced their innocent little sister. They said they would demand he do the right thing and make Lily an honest woman by marrying her.

But Lily steadfastly refused to name the father of her child, adding that a marriage was 'impossible'. All she would say was that he was an honourable and decent man, and she loved him. She wasn't ashamed of her condition, and was proud to be carrying his child.

The four brothers discussed it in private together, to spare Lily's feelings. And of course their first suspicion fell on the staff of Government House. Was the culprit one of her workmates?

Thomas, however, had a different theory. He reckoned any Aussie bloke would have done the decent thing by her. In his opinion it was more likely to be 'one of them snooty-nosed Poms' out here for the Prince's tour. An innocent trusting little colonial girl, Thomas argued, would be easy prey for a man of the world. He could then duck his responsibilities by escaping home to England with no questions asked.

Samuel put forward an idea even more startling than that of Thomas. Could Lily have been pregnant before she went to the city? It seemed unbelievable, but he reminded his brothers of the many times she'd worked at wealthy Hills homes helping out at dinner parties. Perhaps a houseguest was responsible, or even a son of one of the families? And if her mystery seducer already had a wife, then that would explain why Lily had said marriage was out of the question.

They had no precise dates to guide them, and knew little or nothing about women's biology. And when questioned, Lily was very vague about when the baby was due.

In the end they gave up and decided to make the best of a bad job. Unmasking the guilty party could wait; right now their only concern was to take care of Lily and her unborn child, shield her from unkind gossip, and make sure she was happy.

So Samuel, Horace, Arthur and Thomas made a solemn pact on the family Bible that from now on, Lily's baby would have not one, but four fathers. No matter what happened in their own lives, whether they married or remained single, Lily's child would never lack a male guardian and protector.

They would take the place of that unknown man who had so cruelly abandoned their little sister to her fate.

39

Parliament met in a joint late night sitting of both Houses, and the motion was put that 'Noelene Jones be appointed President of the Republic of Australia'. It was carried by an overwhelming majority, well over the two thirds needed.

Of course there were some noisy interjections from a small number of diehard monarchists. The Honourable Member for Warragumbilly shouted out 'God Save the Queen' in the middle of the Prime Minister's speech, and was named by the Speaker. When he tried it again, this time with 'Rule Britannia', he was warned he would be thrown out of the Chamber if he persisted with his disruptive behaviour.

There were also some questions on the new president's salary and terms of employment, which the PM said would be worked out shortly by a special committee and put to Parliament for approval before the inauguration.

An independent from the wheatbelts of Western Australia raised a query about what would happen to paintings of the Queen now hanging on the walls of both Houses. Were they to be consigned to the scrap heap? It was a tricky one but the PM neatly deflected it by saying the appropriate place might be the National Portrait Gallery.

The general mood, however, was one of elation that a president had finally been chosen without any bloodshed. 'Thank God we live in a democracy and not a dictatorship,' observed the Honourable Member for Port Adelaide. 'Hear, hear,' chorused his colleagues.

The joint sitting ended with a vote to extend Parliament's congratulations to the country's new Head of State, and wish her well for the future.

The news was announced in all the papers, with a photo of Noelene splashed over the front pages and the words: OUR FIRST PRESIDENT! The Prime Minister held a press conference, with Noelene by his side. She noted Mike was among those present.

'First of all,' said the PM in his most statesmanlike voice, 'Let me say how delighted I am to be able to introduce to you our first president.' He turned and made a short bow to Noelene, who was unsure how to respond. Should she bow back, or just smile her acknowledgement? She decided on a smile.

'I am particularly pleased by the fact that the public were able to take part in this historic process. We, the government, have listened and taken note of what you have told us.' He paused, for a brief round of applause.

'Miss Jones has graciously consented to take on the role of Head of State for our new republic. I am also pleased to announce that His Royal Highness Prince Charles will be attending the inauguration ceremony to represent his mother the Queen. The ceremony has been scheduled for November 8.'

'If the Queen's not coming, does this indicate royal disapproval?' The voice came from the back of the media scrum.

Tricky one. A bouncer. The PM thought carefully about it before he answered.

'As you all know, Her Majesty turned 90 in April this year. Although her health is remarkably good for her age, and her medical advisers assure there is no cause for alarm, it was still thought wise not to subject her to the stress of a long plane journey. That was explained when I contacted Buckingham Palace to invite Her Majesty to attend. She has indicated that Prince Charles will bring a personal message from her, to be read at the inauguration.'

The attention now turned to Noelene. How did she feel about becoming president? 'Honoured and delighted.' When did she hear the news? 'Yesterday morning, when the Prime Minister phoned me.' What was her reaction? 'Total surprise. I hadn't expected it.' Where would she live? She glanced at the PM, who answered this one for her.

Yarralumla, presently occupied by the Governor-General, would be retained as the official Canberra home of the new president. The same applied to Admiralty House in Sydney. His government could see no reason for any change. Domestic arrangements would remain substantially the same, although naturally the new president would have some choice with her personal staff.

'So if Yarralumla's out, where will the royals stay … if they ever visit us again?'

'Put 'em up at a pub,' called a voice from the back. It was the same cheeky journalist, clearly intent on trying to provoke. The PM frowned. He didn't like levity on an occasion such as this. But he kept his cool. He said that would be a matter for arrangement between the government and the persons concerned, but he had no doubt the former hospitality extended to the royal family would be continued as a matter of courtesy 'as with any visiting VIP'.

The mention of VIPs brought up a question about Kirribilli House, once a Prime Ministerial residence and now a resource centre for cultural and heritage studies. The PM said he understood Kirribilli House had enough private rooms to house visiting dignitaries if needed, but he would look into the matter.

He glanced at his watch, feeling the press conference was getting away from him, and decided to cut it short.

'Time for a few more questions, but please keep them brief.'

The next was for Noelene, from a female member of the press corps.

'Madam President ...' She paused. 'Is that the correct way to address you?'

'I'll answer to anything,' said Noelene.

'Your Excellency,' corrected the PM.

'Thank you. My question is this. All previous Governors-General have been married, with spouses to help them carry out their duties. You're a single woman. Do you see this as a problem?'

Another curly one. But Noelene handled it with aplomb.

'I don't see that being single has anything to do with it,' she said. 'I can think of a number of women in positions of authority who didn't have a husband to support them.' She smiled. 'Queen Elizabeth the first, for a start.'

Mike felt the press corps starting to warm to her. Good one, Noelene.

'I readily acknowledge that being without a partner can be a lonely life. I'd be the first to admit it, having been on my own now for a good many years. But I'm sure if the occasion arises and I want help with hosting an official function, there will be someone available.' She paused. 'What I definitely don't need is a male handbag.'

There was laughter and loud applause. She's got 'em, thought the PM with a sense of personal satisfaction. Look at their faces. They're bloody well eating out of her hand.

And it's all due to me. I'm the one who did it. By combining my political skills with keeping a finger on the public pulse, knowing what the mums and dads want, I finally picked the right one. The perfect first president.

Thank God that boring old fart dropped dead when he did.

40

It was time to change the public face of Australia. And first in line to be tackled was that tricky word 'royal'.

The Sydney and Melbourne telephone directories alone had a staggering 268 entries. There was 'royal' used as a business name (Royal Car Repairs, Royal Drycleaners, Royal Insurance) and any number of Royal hotels. There was even a listing for a brothel curiously named Royal Choice (had any royal actually used it?).

And then, of course, there were those who were entitled to use the word by royal appointment, such as the Royal Society for the Prevention of Cruelty to Animals, the Royal Flying Doctor Service, Royal Life Saving Society, Royal Hospital for Women, and the Royal Sydney Yacht Squadron. The PM said he recognised the granting of the title was a privilege with historical significance, and it was understandable that many would want to keep it. His government could see no problem with this.

But whatever the origin, it was very clear that events and the republic had now overtaken the word, and some would have to go. The Prime Minister called a special press conference to clarify his government's policy on the issue.

First casualties were the armed services. The Royal Australian Air Force would in future be known simply as AAF (Australian

Air Force). The same would apply to the Navy (AN) and Army (AA). The Queen had been advised as a matter of courtesy, and had graciously given her approval to the change. References to the Crown, such as Crown Solicitor and Crown Prosecutor, would no longer be part of the legal language.

There were other changes that would flow on as a natural consequence of the country becoming a republic. At some stage the Queen would be removed from Australian coins.

'Chop chop. I thought Charles the first was the only British monarch to lose his head,' said a voice from the back of the room. The PM frowned, recognising it as the same clown who'd earlier suggested putting up visiting royals at a pub. He decided to ignore the remark.

'Any questions?'

'How about the Queen's Christmas message?'

'That's a programming decision for the TV networks to decide. The government has no view on the matter.'

'Queen's Birthday?'

'My personal view is that the Queen's Birthday may no longer be relevant. It's never on the right day, anyway, it's all over the place. When is it again, Larry?'

He turned to his press secretary standing just behind him.

'June most States. Last year Western Australia had it in October.'

'Right. Next question?'

'Queen's Cup at Flemington?'

'One for the racing authorities.'

'Queen pudding?' The smart alec again. The PM could sense things getting away from him.

'I think we might wrap this up now. Any more questions?'

There were a couple of minor queries such as gold crowns on

uniforms (no change for the present) and the cost of removing O.H.M.S. from official stationery (to be phased in), and then the PM wound up the press conference with a short speech.

'My fellow Australians,' he said, exactly as though addressing a political rally. 'We recognise the need to give time for some of these changes to come into effect. Long standing traditions and customs cannot be tossed aside lightly … and frankly, my government would not want them to.

'It is in the interests of the public to proceed slowly and carefully in the new direction to which we are committed.

'I am sure you would all agree that's the only sensible course to take, and it's the one we intend to follow. Nothing will be rushed; nothing done without long and careful consideration.'

But he was wrong; he hadn't read the mood of the nation. Australia was now a republic on the move. And it was in a hurry.

41

Noelene had been invited to inspect Yarralumla, a rambling mansion that looked exactly like the country homestead it had once been. One of the reasons for the visit was to give her a chance to put her own stamp on it once she moved in. A grant had been set aside by the government for redecoration and renovations.

'Of course it's completely liveable as it is,' explained the public service official on the phone. 'As an official residence, a certain standard naturally has to be kept up. But there are personal touches you might like to change. Furnishings, curtains, pictures, that kind of thing. The present incumbents, as you know, have been there for some time and have a style that might seem a bit, well … old fashioned.' He hesitated on the word as if afraid he was saying too much, then quickly added: 'Not that there's anything wrong with it, of course. It's just that it may not appeal to someone like yourself.'

Reading between the lines, Noelene understood he was referring to her age. At 55, she had a good 20 years on the Governor-General and his wife. He was a former ambassador, not long retired from the diplomatic service when the Prime Minister had appointed him. Initially he'd filled the role reasonably well, but of late had made so few public appearances as to become almost invisible. His wife's ill health had been given as the reason. Republic or not, he wouldn't have remained much longer in the job. Or so the scuttlebutt said.

Mike wanted to come along and film, but had been refused on the grounds of security.

'Do I look like a terrorist?' he asked, when Noelene relayed the news. Then he added: 'It's okay. I've plenty of material without it. I'll spend the day editing. Enjoy yourself.'

A black government limousine with chauffeur arrived right on nine, and Noelene was driven from her Sydney apartment to Canberra. Although almost spring it was still chilly, but inside the car it was warm and she had time to sit back, relax, and enjoy the scenery as they sped smoothly along.

When they arrived at Yarralumla, a policeman at the front gate saluted her. It gave Noelene a strange feeling, but she knew it was something she'd have to get used to. The Governor-General and his wife weren't in residence, and an official in a dark suit with striped tie greeted her at the door. He introduced himself as Neil Matheson from the Prime Minister's department.

'Welcome to your new home,' he said. Home? Another strange feeling. This presidential business would take some getting used to.

Neil led the way through the entrance foyer. 'I'll just walk you through and give you an idea of where everything is first, so you can get a general impression,' he said. 'Then if you've any particular comments, I'll make a note of them. First time here?'

Noelene said no, it wasn't her first visit. But the others had been in very different circumstances, and she hadn't seen any further than the public rooms. Certainly not the private quarters. One visit had been a reception for the visiting head of another country; and then there'd been the time she received the Order of Australia. There might also have been a fundraising function for Opera Australia, when the Governor-General had graciously made his home available. But it was all now a bit of a blur in her memory.

'We'll do it room by room,' said Neil, pulling out a notebook. 'Take your time, there's no hurry. I've ordered lunch for one o'clock. Chicken salad okay?'

The public rooms were magnificent, all gilt and velvet with crystal chandeliers and ornately framed pictures. Period furniture, of course. Persian carpets on polished floors. She didn't really feel there was anything she should do to change them.

The private rooms were another matter. As soon as they reached them, she could see what the official had been hinting at. There was no getting around it – old fashioned was the right word. And it most definitely was not her style.

For a start it was very chintzy. 'Overdone Victoriana' would be another way of describing it. The main bedroom with its massive four-poster bed had acres of lace, ruffled cushions, and a pink velvet love seat with matching footstool. Alongside the vice-regal toilet stood a pink-cheeked Dresden shepherdess, her wide-skirted, tiered satin gown disguising a toilet roll.

Neil caught her look. 'We've got one of those at home. Wife's idea, she loves it. Picked it up at a church fete'. He up-ended the shepherdess and looked under her skirt, exactly like a dirty old man. 'Personally I can't see why you have to hide the damn things. What's wrong with a bit of loo paper?' He grinned. 'But Leonie'll be chuffed when I tell her the vice-royals have one as well.'

The pictures on the wall were mostly English garden scenes, and a print of a fox hunt with hounds. Neil explained the

Governor-General had spent some years in 'the old country' during his time as a diplomat, and was a committed Anglophile. He had a vague idea he'd met his wife over there. Anyway, she was English-born – somewhere in the Cotswalds, he thought. A nice lady.

Noelene winced at the phrase 'the old country'. Were people still talking like that, with Australia on the brink of becoming a republic? She made a mental note to replace the garden scenes with some Australian art. Maybe a Drysdale or a Whitely. On the other hand, they were probably personal possessions that would be gone once the GG and his nice lady moved out.

That reminded her of something she needed to find out. How much of the space was government property, and how many of her own things would she be allowed to move in? She had some pieces she was particularly attached to, including a writing desk that had belonged to Charlie.

Neil reassured her. Of course she could have any of her own furniture in the private apartments. The same went for pictures and ornaments. This was the whole purpose of today's exercise, he said, to get some idea of her needs. The government was very sympathetic to the fact this would be her home, and was more than willing to go along with any reasonable requests.

The public areas didn't lend themselves to much change, he added. There was a committee in charge of the furnishing of official houses, and many of the paintings on the walls were on loan from the National Gallery. But even here, there would be room for Noelene to express her personal taste. The wife of a previous incumbent had been very keen on Aboriginal art, and had hung it in some of the corridors and the dining room.

'Not quite my taste,' he said 'All those dots and swirly bits. But it went down well with our overseas visitors, particularly the

Americans. I understand several pieces were later given by their Excellencies as gifts and finished up in Washington. I believe there's one in the White House.'

Noelene was beginning to get a surreal feeling she didn't exist as a person any more, just as a figurehead. The incumbent. The president. Head of State. Excellency. Still, she was starting to look forward to the future more than she'd at first thought. Now that she'd taken on the job, she was determined to give it all her strength and energy, to prove that the decision to become a republic had been the right one.

After all, this is what it was all about, wasn't it? It had taken 113 years for Australia to unite as a Commonwealth; and more than a century longer to cut the ties with the monarchy. There was now no Queen of Australia. The Union Jack had gone, and the house in which she was standing was no longer a vice-regal residence.

So like the young princess all those years ago (strange it had taken an ageing monarchist in brown laceup shoes to remind her of that) Noelene made a silent vow to dedicate herself to the new republic.

Neil was busy making notes as they moved along. 'Would you like me to put together an inventory of what's in the private rooms once they become vacant?' he asked. 'Just to give you some idea, so you can decide what you want to keep and what you'd like to change once you're installed?'

Installed. It made her feel like a bathroom fitting. Noelene said an inventory would be fine, very helpful, thank you. She added that she might keep on her apartment in Sydney as a city base. Neil looked surprised. 'I think you'd find Admiralty House more appropriate,' he said. 'It's a magnificent mansion. And of course, there's the matter of security.'

Security. Another word to get used to.

The inspection and lunch finally over, there was a short break for refreshments. Silver teapot, cakes and finger sandwiches on Royal Doulton china. It followed introductions to the housekeeper, butler and chief gardener. The housekeeper looked like Mrs Bail from the English television series *As Time Goes By*. Noelene was half expecting her to say: 'Afternoon tea will be served in precisely six and a half minutes'.

Neil then escorted Noelene back to the car and shook her hand: 'It's been an honour, a pleasure.' He said it several times.

The driver took a different route back to Sydney. The road hugged the coastline, and Noelene relaxed in the back seat, catching glimpses of the Pacific ocean as it kept appearing and then disappearing from sight. She felt tired yet at the same time exhilarated.

It had been a long day, but a good one.

42

It was some days before Noelene heard from Mike again. When he rang, he sounded excited. 'Got some news that's going to knock you off your presidential feet,' he said. 'It's a shocker.'

'Mike, I've had all the shocks I can handle for a while,' she said. 'Nothing you can tell me will make any difference.'

'This will,' said Mike mysteriously. 'I guarantee it.'

'So what's the big news?' Noelene asked as Mike arrived at the door. 'Win the lottery?'

'Better than the lottery. You'll never believe what I've discovered about that letter you showed me.'

Lily's letter. The little tin box. In all the hullabaloo of becoming president Noelene had forgotten about it.

'So what did you find out?' she asked as they wandered into the lounge room.

'I think you'd better be sitting down when I tell you this.'

She threw him a look, amused at his seriousness.

'Noelene, I'm almost certain that the person who wrote that letter to your grandmother was none other than the heir to the

British throne, the Prince of Wales.'

A stunned Noelene immediately sat down. 'Impossible'.

'Is it? Come on, Noelene, look at the facts. He did a tour of Australia in 1920 and the ship he came out on was the HMS Renown.

'He had a string of names like all the royals do, starting with Albert Edward – but his family and friends always called him David. It's Welsh, y'know. Prince of Wales. Get it?'

'How do you know all this?'

'History was my best subject at school. Some things just stick in the mind.'

'But how on earth could Lily have known him? According to Dad, she was just a quiet little country girl who never went anywhere.'

'That's the piece of puzzle I still need to find out … how they met.'

'*If* they met,' amended Noelene quickly. The name's not that unusual. There could've been another David on the ship.'

'Maybe. But would a sailor be writing on fancy notepaper like this? Not very likely. And look at the wording: "Whatever the future brings us both." It's not the way ordinary people talk. Why would anyone say something like that? Unless …' The words hung in the air.

'Unless what?'

'Unless he knew for some reason there was no hope of them ever meeting again. Something that would always keep them apart. No, Noelene, it's all too much of a coincidence.'

'Anyway what difference does it make? It was a long time ago.'

It was then that Mike dropped his bombshell.

'When was your father born?'

'April 12, 1921.'

'Exactly nine months after this letter was written.'

Noelene was shocked. 'I know what you're thinking. But it's out of the question.'

'Why? It wouldn't be the first time someone's been born on the wrong side of the royal blanket. Nor the last, probably.'

'It's still all just guesswork.'

'Crazier things have happened. And how's this for a crazy thought? If what I'm thinking is right, as the granddaughter of Edward VIII, that puts you in direct line of succession. You could push Liz off the throne. How does Queen Noelene sound?'

It was so audacious, so totally off-the-planet, she had to smile. 'No thanks. I'm having enough trouble coping with the idea of being president. Anyway, as I understand it, illegitimates don't count.' He noticed she carefully avoided the word bastard.

'All right, granted you mightn't have a legal claim – although I think there's still a moral issue here. But aren't you the least bit curious about your family tree? You told me there was some mystery about your father's birth. This could solve it.'

'What's the point? Everyone's dead. There's no way after all these years of finding out anything.'

'There might be. Look, if I could prove beyond doubt that the David of that letter was the Prince of Wales, would you be convinced then?'

'I don't know. Maybe. But how're you going to do it?'

Mike turned mysterious again. 'I've got an idea but I need more time to work on it. Do I have your permission?'

Noelene was torn. The idea of a royal prince falling in love with her grandmother was too incredible to believe. The stuff of fairytales. Lily had taken the name of her lover with her to the grave, kept it a secret all these years. Would she now want it to be revealed? On the other hand, maybe she owed it to her father to finally find out the truth about his birth.

She took a deep breath.

'All right. Go ahead,' she said. 'And good luck.'

That night she dreamed of Lily again. But this time there was no baby in Lily's arms, just a small smiling figure in a flowered dress holding out her hands as if in welcome.

Noelene started walking down the pathway towards her. There were so many questions she wanted to ask, so many answers she needed to know.

But as she got closer Lily began to fade away like the Cheshire cat in Alice in Wonderland, until all that was left was not even a smile — just a deserted garden and the shell of an empty house.

43

Now the real business of becoming first president began in earnest.

First the government asked two artists, both Archibald Prize winners, to paint Noelene's official portrait. One would be displayed in Parliament House and the other in the National Portrait Gallery, with framed prints to be made available at a nominal charge to schools, government offices, councils, clubs, and any organisations that might wish to display them. Pictures of the Queen – gracious and matronly in tiara, floor-length gown, and long white gloves, hands clasped sedately in front of her – started coming off walls.

Head and shoulder shots of Noelene were to be taken for a new issue of postage stamps scheduled for November, in time to be mailed out on Christmas cards. An official biography had also been commissioned.

Then there were the souvenirs, most of them bad taste money-making exercises. Tea towels. Coffee mugs. Plates. Cup and saucer sets. Placemats. Drink coasters. Colouring books. Stickers. Badges. Pencil cases. Scarves. Children's backpacks. Fridge magnets. The President Jones Rose (pink touched with mauve). Also a lethal-tasting cocktail.

A company developing a housing estate announced one of its streets would be named 'Noelene Jones Boulevard'. A newspaper survey showed that 'Noelene' was now the most popular name for newborn babies, displacing Sophie, Madison and Chelsea.

One enterprising wine company had even brought out a range called REPUBLICAN RED, with a smiling Noelene on the label. After talk of legal action they removed the picture but kept the name. An advertising agency offered $50,000 to endorse a new chocolate bar called PRESIDENT'S CHOICE ('first in the nation'). She turned them all down. She didn't want to be turned into a product. She didn't want the appointment of the first Australian as Head of State to be tainted by crass commercialism.

Everywhere Noelene looked she saw her face staring back at her from billboards and posters. She tried protesting, but was told she was now public property. Besides, said the government official she consulted, it was all good publicity for the inauguration on November 8. No real harm done. Keeps people's minds focussed.

Noelene talked on the phone to Mike about it. To her surprise he was of the same opinion as the official.

'Look, it comes with the territory,' he said. 'You'd better start getting used to it. But a word of warning – be careful and keep your wits about you.'

The documentary was almost complete, apart from footage of the inaugural ceremony. Mike had been assigned to the official press group covering the event. The documentary screening was programmed for mid-November, with a repeat screening on Australia Day, January 26. The title had been shortened to *First President*. It would run for 90 minutes, with all channels agreeing to show it commercial free.

'By the way, how's the detective work coming along?'

'On Lily? I might have some news shortly.' And that's all she could get out of him.

By the end of the next week Noelene had met both artists for a preliminary discussion of what form the portraits would take. And the two proved very different. Septimus Mortimer, a white-haired man in his late sixties, planned to paint her standing alongside a grand piano wearing one of her more elaborate opera gowns. Elanora Dewhurst, a plumpish smiling woman with orange hair and a frazzled look, said she preferred a more casual pose, maybe in a garden setting. Did Noelene have any kind of household pet such as a small dog? She'd found dogs added a touch of informality to a portrait session. A King Charles Spaniel, for instance, would be perfect. Noelene was sorry she couldn't oblige, she had neither garden nor spaniel. But she liked the artist's approach.

There was also a meeting with the official biographer, a neat-looking little man with a wispy nicotine-stained moustache. He'd been given six months leave from some government department or other to complete the work, and asked Noelene for photos. Anything from her childhood, such as family snapshots? She promised to look through her albums.

There was a conference with government officials to discuss what form the inauguration would take. The PM said it would be based on the ceremony for installing a Governor-General, but 'in view of its historic importance, and the fact His Royal Highness the Prince of Wales will be present, a little more formally structured'. Stuff and nonsense, thought Noelene privately. Aloud she said that sounded fine. To her surprise she was starting already to fit snugly into a presidential mould.

In addition to all the official demands, there was also the media. There were so many requests for interviews and photographs that the government decided to assign Noelene an office and a personal assistant – a bouncy young blonde by the name of Margaret-Lea Davenport ('call me Mags'). Solid background in television and newspapers, Noelene was told, seconded from the Department of Communication and Information Technology. Noelene warmed to her immediately, which was lucky, as for the next couple of months they would be living in each other's pockets.

Every request was channelled first through Mags, who made a quick judgment on its worth and then passed on her recommendations to Noelene. Mags worked fast, kept her cool, and was clearly efficient at her job. Noelene made a mental note to see if she could hold on to her when she officially became president.

In a week they worked their way through 32 interviews, half a dozen photo sessions, eight appearances on talkback radio, and eleven on TV current affairs shows, plus two 'exclusives' for magazines. There was also a call in the small hours from a plummy-voiced British broadcaster wanting to know how Australians felt about dumping the Queen and the monarchy. Any regrets?

'Don't they realise there's a time difference?' an exasperated Noelene complained the next day.

'Sounds like the same guy who rang me,' said Mags. 'He rang back twice and I thought I'd managed to put him off. But he must've found your number somehow. We'd better look at getting you a silent line.'

When Noelene got home there was a message from Mike waiting for her.

'Eureka!' Mike said. 'I've found the missing pieces to the puzzle of your grandmother's letter.'

44

Mike arrived half an hour later, looking elated. Over drinks he explained what his research had uncovered. 'You thought there could be more than one David. Well, I've authenticated the signature. It's definitely that of the Prince of Wales.'

'How'd you do that?'

'I remembered there'd been some books published, letters written by the Prince to a couple of close friends. Wallis Simpson was one of them. There was another, letters to a married woman rumoured to have been his lover. So I looked them up at the library and compared the handwriting.' He held out Lily's letter. 'Look at the way that "s" is written. The same way he wrote it in all those other letters. It's a perfect match.'

But Noelene was still unconvinced. 'Maybe you're reading too much into it. It could be wishful thinking. Anyway, who'd believe you?'

'I knew you'd say that. So just to be on the safe side I asked a mate of mine, a retired detective who's a handwriting expert, to take a look at it. And guess what? He confirmed it.'

Noelene was stunned. 'So what does that prove?'

'Well it proves the letter was genuine, but it still doesn't explain how they met. That part of the story puzzled me. So

I started browsing through old newspaper files. Here's what I found in one of the Adelaide papers.' He reached into his briefcase and handed Noelene a photocopied page.

'Look there, that story in the right-hand corner. It was written a month before the Prince arrived, and was mainly on preparations for the visit … school children practising their displays, street decorations, the best places to view the Prince, that kind of thing. But see here, this last line. It says Government House would be employing additional staff for the duration of the Royal visit.

'Then I put on my thinking cap, and asked myself this question: where would a place like Government House go to find additional staff? I did another search and found this.' He pulled out another piece of paper.

'Tucked away in a corner among the employment notices. It's so small, I almost missed it.'

Noelene was impressed. 'You've really been doing your homework, haven't you?'

It was an advertisement for casual domestic workers to be employed in 'a superior establishment' between the dates of July 10 and 17, 1920. 'Only highly experienced staff need apply', it said. 'References essential. Country applicants welcome.'

'Didn't you say Lily was a country girl?'

'That's right.'

Mike was jubilant.

'I checked the address and phone number in the advertisement and it belonged to a business that called itself the Elite Employment Agency. Established 1911. It apparently specialised in placing domestic staff in some of the wealthier Adelaide homes. Its motto was 'Discretion and Client Satisfaction Our Policy.'

'Those dates correspond to the time the Prince of Wales was

in Adelaide. So my theory is 'the superior establishment' was Government House, and Lily was hired to work there. If that's right, then it solves how they met.'

'I know what you're saying. But it's still circumstantial. It wouldn't hold up in a court of law.'

'You're a tough nut to convince, Noelene. So take a look at this.'

Mike took out another photocopy from his briefcase, a record of the Prince of Wales' visit. It had begun on Monday, July 12 with his arrival by train from Western Australia, to be greeted by the governor Sir Archibald Weigall.

The following four days had been filled with official dinners, meetings with returned servicemen, nurses and war workers; a couple of balls, a display by schoolchildren, and a march through the streets by navy personnel. He'd unveiled a statue of his grandfather Edward VII, and gone to the races (none of his bets won).

'Look at those dates', said Mike. 'The last day the Prince was in Adelaide. It says he boarded the HMS Renown at Outer Harbour and then set sail for Tasmania. Friday, July 16 – the exact same date as that letter. My guess is he must've sat down and written to Lily almost as soon as he went aboard. He'd want to get the letter away before the ship sailed so she'd receive it the same day. Probably gave it to one of his staff to deliver, or maybe some local official. Anyway, that's my theory. So – what do you think?'

'I'm starting to believe it. Question is, where do we go from here?'

'There's one thing that might finally solve the puzzle of who got Lily pregnant,' said Mike. 'I kick myself I didn't think of it before.'

'What's that?'

'Your father's birth certificate.'

45

Lily was in the front garden pruning the roses when her labour started. First it was just a faint flutter, like a small bird stirring its wings. Then the flutter became a dull muscular ache like the ones during her menstrual period. Here it comes again. Hold tight. There it goes. Relax, breathe deeply. She was surprised there was almost no pain.

She kept on pruning, unwilling to alarm her father inside the house, puffing on his pipe and reading the newspaper. There was nothing he could do for her anyway, except send for the midwife. And she knew it was too early for that. Her four brothers were all at work, but would be home in a few hours.

The thought of her brothers coming home made her think about dinner. She'd better prepare something for them, just in case. She walked into the house, and her father looked up from his paper. 'Everything all right, Lily?' he asked. She said yes, everything was fine. He went back to his reading.

In the covered back verandah which served as a kitchen, she checked the cool safe for the remains of a leg of lamb which could be eaten with a salad. Then she went out to the garden to pick a lettuce and tomatoes. The day before she'd boiled and pickled beetroot, its glossy red globules now sitting in a glass bowl.

There was also freshly baked bread and cheese from the local dairy.

Satisfied they would have plenty to eat, Lily then retired to her room. The small muscular movements, now more like sharp twinges, were still coming and going. But they were irregular, so she wasn't sure if this was the real thing or not. It might be a false alarm.

Lily lay down on her bed and closed her eyes. As soon as she did so, the movements stopped. She wished she had a mother she could talk to, someone she could ask if things were going normally or not. A sister. Even an aunt. Giving birth was woman stuff. But all she had was a houseful of men.

Lily lay alone in her room, waiting for something to happen. And as she lay there she prayed. Please God, make me brave. Please give me the strength not to let down my dearly beloved who has given me this miracle of life.

46

Noelene and Mike caught the first plane next day to Adelaide. When they walked into the Registry of Births, Deaths and Marriages, the clerk behind the desk recognised Noelene immediately. Noelene explained what she wanted, giving her father's name and date of birth, and asked how long it would take. The clerk said in view of the 'special circumstances' he'd expedite the search for the certificate. It usually took 48 hours, but if she cared to call back after lunch he should have it for her. He suggested filling in time at the nearby River Torrens, where there was a very fine restaurant that had enjoyed good reviews from all the food critics.

'And congratulations,' he added. 'My wife and I both voted for you.'

'Special circumstances, eh? Pulling royal rank already,' Mike teased as they walked out into the sunshine. But he could sense Noelene was feeling edgy and not in the mood to be amused. He decided to sidetrack the issue, try to get her mind off it. They were walking along King William Road towards the river. He nodded towards a street sign.

'William the Fourth,' he said. 'His wife Queen Adelaide gave this city its name.'

Noelene was surprised. 'How do you know all this?'

Mike grinned. 'It's just that I've been doing a lot of digging around in royal files lately. You'd be surprised at some of the things I found out.'

They were at the river now and the clerk's suggestion to kill time proved a good one. The weather was warm and sunny, the gardens surrounding the Torrens delightful … and yes, there was a very smart restaurant as well as a kiosk for takeaway food. But it was too late for breakfast and too early for lunch, so they decided to go for a stroll along the riverbank.

It was an idyllic day. Lovers lay on the grass clasped in each other's arms. Small boys in team jerseys kicked around a ball (AFL territory here, Mike noted). Black swans sailed by majestically while a young girl with her mother threw them scraps of bread. Two boatloads of schoolboy rowers slid lazily by on the water, pulling on oars as their coxes issued commands.

'Fancy a coffee?' Mike asked after they'd been walking for nearly an hour. They went across to the kiosk and bought cappuccinos in styrofoam cups and sweet sugary doughnuts. As they sat on a park bench Mike asked Noelene how she was feeling.

'I don't know,' she said. 'Stunned. Confused. Anxious. I wish I'd never found that damned letter. I wish it'd stayed where Lily hid it. I'm not sure I want to know the truth.'

'Did your dad ever talk about it? Did he ever discuss who might be his father?'

'Never. He knew he'd been born illegitimate and just left it at that. It never seemed to bother him. He said once he felt he'd been luckier than most because being brought up by his uncles was like having four fathers instead of just one.

'Anyway, even if he'd asked, no one knew anything. No one

ever found out who was responsible for Lily's child. When Lily died, her secret died with her.'

They sat on the bench for a long time watching the passing parade. The little girl and her mother had long gone home. The small boys with the football had also disappeared. Some office workers on a lunch break were eating sandwiches. It was like another world, isolated from reality. The sun disappeared behind clouds, and Noelene shivered in the sudden chill. Mike looked at his watch.

'It's been three hours. Let's see if anything's turned up.'

They threw their food scraps in a bin and started walking back to the Registry office.

47

The labour continued through dinner and well into the early evening. She had eaten almost nothing, and excused herself to retire to her room soon after the meal was finished. The pains had given way once more to a nagging backache.

Her brothers and father were still sitting around the table talking among themselves when her waters broke. The midwife, who lived only a short distance away was immediately sent for. After examining Lily she said she was almost fully dilated, and the baby could be born within the hour.

The backache had given way to long painful contractions, more intense than anything Lily had ever experienced. She bit her lip, trying not to scream. In the middle of the contractions there was now an uncontrollable urge to push down, and she felt as if she was about to split in two.

She tried to stay silent, to be as brave and as uncomplaining as she'd vowed she would. But in spite of the promises to herself, she groaned aloud each time another push inched the unseen child within her a little further along the birth canal. It was as though she no longer had any control over her body and it was functioning in an independent life of its own.

'Not long now,' said the midwife encouragingly. 'You're doing fine, Lily. The head should crown any moment. Just hold on to the bed post and push again when I tell you.'

So Lily held on tightly, shut her eyes, and prayed for strength.

48

The clerk at the Registrar's office had a smile on his face when they returned.

'Well it was a bit tricky,' he said. 'A couple of things didn't quite add up when I started searching. But I finally managed to track it down.'

He handed Noelene the certificate. She looked at it and frowned.

'What's it say?' asked Mike impatiently. 'Did Lily name the father of her child?'

'No,' said Noelene. 'In the space for the father's name it just says: "Not stated".'

'So we're back to square one.'

'Not quite,' said Noelene. She was still frowning. 'Are you ready for a surprise?'

'Try me.'

'All my life I've believed Dad's name was Jack, after his grandfather Jackson. I've never known him as anything else, although a couple of his mates used to call him Jacko.

'Jack Jones is the name he used when he married my mother. It's there on their marriage certificate, I've seen it. Jack Jones is the way he signed all his cheques. When he died, he was cremated as Jack Jones. There's an urn in the Memorial Rose Garden with his ashes and his name on it. Jack Jones 1921–1977. But it seems I've been wrong all these years.'

Mike was growing more impatient.

'If it wasn't Jack, then what was it?

She handed him the piece of paper. The name of the baby, male, born at Bisley on April 12, 1921 to Lily Annabel Jones, was David.

49

Finally it was all over. The head slipped through, and then the shoulders, arms and legs. A wet, slippery, bloodied mass of humanity. The cry told her it was alive. After cleaning and wrapping, the midwife placed the tiny bundle in her arms.

'A boy, Lily,' she said. 'You have a son.'

50

Back in Sydney, Noelene and Mike discussed the puzzle of the two names. Why had her father been known all his life as Jack if he was David? Who changed it and when?

'It had to be Lily,' said Noelene. 'I think she decided to bring up her baby as Jack to protect her lover's identity. If she'd called him David, there'd have been too many questions asked. And if there happened to be another David in the neighbourhood, then the wrong man could've been blamed. I can understand why she did it.'

'But that still doesn't get away from the fact the person who wrote her that love letter was the Prince of Wales ... and your father was born nine months later. Come on Noelene. It all adds up.'

Noelene frowned. 'Maybe. So where do we go from here?'

'That's the million dollar question. Where the hell do we go?'

'What about a DNA test?'

'I thought about that. Which do you want, the good news or the bad?'

'I could stand with a bit of cheering up. Give me the good news.'

'When I was researching at the library I found out that as

the Duke of Windsor, he was twice hospitalised for surgery. The first time was 1964 in Texas. Something to do with his heart, I gather. Maybe a bypass. Then next year he was admitted to the London Clinic for eye surgery.'

'So?'

'Well there could still be medical records that might help. You know – tissue matches and so on.'

'You mean leftover bits and pieces, after more than 50 years? Mike, I don't think so. What's the bad news?'

'To get any kind of a DNA match you'd have to get permission from the Royal family. And that's the problem. Do you honestly think they'd do that just so some brash colonial could come over from the other side of the world to claim the throne?'

Noelene had to agree he was right. But she was worried about the 'not stated' on the birth certificate. She felt it left a question mark hanging over her father's birth, and she wasn't happy about it.

'Look at it from Lily's point of view,' said Mike. 'What d'you think would have happened if she'd put HRH the Prince of Wales on that birth certificate? It would never have been accepted. They'd have called in the cops. She'd have been put away as a loony.'

'I still think she was trying to protect him,' said Noelene. 'A love affair between a royal Prince and a servant girl … it would've been shocking, a scandal.'

'Y'know, there's a bit of irony here, when you think about it,' said Mike. 'When the Prince became Duke of Windsor he married a woman with two husbands still living. How's that for a scandal?'

'Yes, but it cost him the throne.'

They were getting nowhere. It seemed plain that under

English law Noelene had no legal right to the monarchy. But was there another issue? Would she be letting down both Lily and her father if she remained silent? Questions, questions. And still no answers.

'I keep thinking of my Dad. Do I owe it to him to prove who his real father was? And then there's Lily. Would I be hurting her if the truth came out?' Mike noticed Noelene was beginning to talk about Lily as if she were still alive. Curious, that.

'Well I can tell you one thing,' said Mike. 'If you decide to bring it out in the open, the British press will have a field day with it. They'll make mincemeat of you. Have you thought of that?'

'Yes,' said Noelene soberly. 'And it'll also be goodbye to the presidency. I know I can't have it both ways.'

Mike put a hand on hers.

'Whatever you decide, mate, I want you to know I'm here for you.'

Mate. She liked that.

'I know, Mike … and believe me I'm grateful. I don't know how I'd cope with all this without you. But it still doesn't help me make up my mind'.

Mike was thoughtful for a long time. Then he looked up.

'So realistically, how much time do we have?'

'Realistically, five days.'

'How do you work that out?'

'I've an appointment with the Prime Minister on Friday to discuss the program for the inauguration. I can't with any decency postpone it longer than that – it wouldn't be fair to him or the country. I've got to decide one way or the other.'

It was clear to both that time was running out.

51

The first president had gone missing. Disappeared. Vanished into thin air.

The Prime Minister found out when he phoned Noelene's personal assistant to change the time of their Friday meeting. 'What d'you mean, you don't know where she is?' he demanded, when Mags told him. 'This is ridiculous. She's got to be somewhere. Didn't she tell you where she was going?'

But all Mags had been told was her boss needed some time out, and to hold all phone calls and appointments for two days. She'd taken her mobile but wasn't answering it. Even Mike had no idea where she was.

'Sorry,' he said, when Mags passed on the PM's concern. 'I know she has a lot of things on her mind right now, so she's probably gone somewhere quiet to clear her thoughts. If she gets in touch with me, I'll tell you. I'm sure she's fine and will turn up eventually.'

But 'turn up eventually' wasn't good enough for the Prime Minister, as he told his wife.

'What if Buckingham House calls to firm up arrangements for the visit of Prince Charles? What if the press get on to it? How will it look if I tell them I've lost my Head of State? I'll be a laughing stock.'

His wife said she was sure it would turn out all right. There were times in a woman's life when she needed her own space, and this was could be one of them.

'You mean she's going through one of those female things? At her age I thought she'd be bloody well past it.'

The PM's wife sighed. 'I mean, she could be feeling pressured by the dominance of the male hierarchy and needs to sort out her gender priorities.'

The PM hadn't the faintest what his wife was talking about; it sounded like typical feminist stuff and nonsense. But he agreed to a delay before pushing the panic button and calling in Federal police.

Although Mike had seemed unconcerned when talking to Noelene's assistant he was also starting to worry. Why hadn't she told him if she'd wanted to get away for a while to think through the problem of Lily's love letter? He'd have understood. And where had she gone?

The PM's wife was right. Noelene needed space, a quiet time to be alone with her thoughts. So she'd caught a plane and booked herself into a motel not far from her grandmother's cottage. And now here she was, in the front parlour, staring at the empty space in the wall where the little tin box had been hidden. So many things to decide. Which was the right path to take?

Last night she'd dreamt of Lily again. And like all the other dreams, as soon as she started to walk towards that small figure, it faded away and disappeared. Was Lily trying to tell her something?

Noelene suddenly realised she'd had nothing to eat since yesterday. She decided to walk to the nearby village, find a place with takeaway food, then go for a long walk to clear her head.

She found a shop doubling as a general store and post office and ordered coffee and a blueberry muffin. No one recognised her. No one asked what the president of Australia was doing here in the middle of nowhere. The woman behind the counter had a thick middle European accent.

Noelene sat in the sun outside the shop, sipping her coffee and trying to get her brain cells working. She took long deep breaths to recharge her energy; she'd forgotten how clean and fresh country air could be.

After she'd tossed her empty cup into a bin, she noticed a well-trodden path leading off to the left of the store's parking area and into the bush. It looked interesting. She decided to take it.

She followed the track, walking briskly, confident that when the time came she could find her way out again. In the distance she could still hear the faint noise of traffic.

Around her were all the sounds of the bush: the mournful cry of a magpie, the screech of a cockatoo, the crackle of small animals as they scuttled out of her way. Something slithered into the grass before she could step on it. Snake or lizard? A sharp twig jutting from a branch brushed her face and drew drops of blood, but she barely felt it.

Was this the same bush Lily had roamed through as a young girl? Was she walking in her grandmother's footsteps? It was a nice thought.

After a while (an hour? two? she'd lost all track of time) Noelene sat down to rest on a fallen log. The eucalyptus smelled like the oil her mother used to rub on her chest when she was a small girl and had a cold. She breathed it in, intoxicated. She could understand why Aussies abroad felt homesick just from the scent of a leaf crushed between the fingers.

Funny how the bush can bring back all those well-worn clichés of what it means to be an Australian. Waltzing Matilda and the swagman at the billabong. Cuddly koalas. Blue skies and red earth and brilliant sunshine.

It was early afternoon by the time Noelene returned to the motel. She kicked off her shoes and lay on the bed, exhausted. And she still hadn't made up her mind what to do.

If she said nothing and went on with the presidency, no one would be the wiser. Life would go on as usual. On the other hand, there was that recurring dream of Lily. Should she tell the world a prince had once loved her grandmother? Was it her duty to claim her father's birthright?

Incapable of making a decision, she decided to clear her mind with a bit of escapism. She turned on the TV. There were the usual afternoon offerings. An American soap opera, a cooking demonstration, an ancient movie. As she absentmindedly flicked through channels, something caught her eye – a replay of a Test match in Sydney last summer. Not a sport she followed, although Charlie had been a lifelong fan.

And there they were, the Barmy Army. Boisterous and out for a bit of fun. They were decked out in their war paint, waving beer cans and loudly chanting their national anthem. But it was the way they were singing the anthem that caught Noelene's attention. It was a deliberate attempt to needle the Aussie crowd.

All those Poms with their pink faces and their fish-and-chip paunches and their silly hats and red, white and blue body paint, waving Union Jacks and singing 'God save *your* Queen' – rubbing it in that Queen Elizabeth II on the other side of the world was also this country's monarch.

Your Queen? For God's sake, she thought, as she angrily switched it off. Where the hell are we going as a nation? What's happening to us? And at that precise moment she knew what she had to do.

Being the granddaughter of a king didn't matter any more. Crowns and thrones and princes? Just sentimental baggage from the past to be left where it belonged. A storybook fairytale that had no place in her life.

What was real was the future of this country. This was her patch of ground, her heritage. She had been given a unique opportunity to serve it, and it was an opportunity she mustn't turn down.

Noelene picked up her mobile and called Mike.

52

The inauguration ceremony was held in the Great Hall of Parliament House, on a day of blue skies and brilliant sunshine. It had been meticulously planned by an events organiser, with giant screens positioned inside the building and outside on the lawns, so that those not on the official guest list could still watch the ceremony. Thousands of sightseers jammed the area, causing headaches for security and police.

It was the same right across the country. Australians watched the inauguration of their new Head of State, on televisions in shopping centres, pubs, clubs, bars, and public squares. At Circular Quay in Sydney, people were jammed shoulder to shoulder to see it on a screen two stories tall, suspended above the Cahill Expressway. It was like the 2000 Olympics all over again.

Before the actual inauguration, the big screens ran a documentary (put together by ScreenSound and the National Archives) showing two previous landmarks in Australian history: the 1901 opening of the first Federal Parliament in Melbourne and the 1927 opening of Parliament when the seat of government had been moved to its new home in Canberra.

The 1901 ceremony had been held in Melbourne's Exhibition

Building in the presence of the Duke and Duchess of York and Cornwall, cheekily dubbed 'pork and corned beef' by some local wags.

According to contemporary press reports, it had been a formal affair of much pomp and ceremony, with hymns sung and prayers said for the Duke's father Edward VII, who had come to the throne just a few months earlier on the death of his mother Queen Victoria. The Union Jack was unfurled and onlookers enthusiastically joined in singing *Rule Britannia*.

In the evening, the Duke and Duchess had attended a concert at which Nellie Stewart, fresh from Drury Lane, sang *Australia*, an ode specially written for her. The royal couple sat through it appearing (reported an onlooker) totally bored by the proceedings.

The 1927 event was a shade more lively. This time it was another Duke and Duchess of York – Bertie, second in line to the throne, and his Scottish-born young wife Elizabeth. Dame Nellie Melba sang the national anthem, and newspapers waxed lyrical about the sweet-faced Duchess and her charming smile. The ceremony was held in the newly-completed Parliament House, on land that a short time before had been sheep farms and cow paddocks.

The business of swearing in the country's first republican president now began. Mike had a special place in the media contingent, filming what would be the final sequence to wrap up his documentary. It was scheduled to go to air on all channels within the week. There was serious talk of moving Australia Day from January 26 to November 8, to commemorate today's event. January had never been an ideal date for a public holiday, coming so soon after Christmas and slap bang in the middle of the summer holidays. And there was also the sensitive matter of the Aboriginal community, who saw it as a day of mourning for invasion of their country rather than a cause for celebration. So a change might be welcomed.

Noelene, hatless and wearing a simple blue suit, stood on the dais alongside the Prime Minister. Just behind Noelene was her recently appointed aide-de-camp, Captain Josephine Phillips. The new flag of the Republic of Australia hung proudly as a backdrop.

A grey-haired Prince Charles in dark double-breasted suit, sprig of yellow wattle in his buttonhole, made a short speech on behalf of Her Majesty the Queen, paying tribute to the long tradition and history the two countries shared. He likened the constitutional change to a child growing up and leaving home, adding with a smile: 'I speak from personal experience as one who many years ago did that myself. Now with my two sons both adults and living their own lives I, too, join the ranks of the empty nesters'.

He paused a moment, fiddling with his cufflinks, as a ripple of laughter followed his remark.

'Breaking away from parental bonds', the Prince continued, 'does not mean any lessening of loyalty or affection. Rather, it should strengthen the ties that bind us together as friends … or as you Aussies might put it, in mateship.' The PM smiled approvingly at the use of his favourite word. And in spite of her feelings on the monarchy, Noelene had to admire HRH as a skilled professional who knew how to work a room. In another life he could have made a decent living as an actor. Or a stand-up comic.

'I am happy to convey to your government and people this message from Her Majesty the Queen on this historic occasion. She has asked me to express her regret at not being here in person, and to pass on her warmest good wishes and the hope that the close ties between our two countries will continue to grow and flourish.

'One hundred and fifteen years ago, just after the turn of a new century, this country formed itself into the Commonwealth of Australia. As we have just seen, my great-grandparents were here to open your first Parliament in Melbourne. My grandparents, following that royal tradition, were present in 1927 for the opening of Parliament in its new Canberra venue, in a building not far from where we stand today.

'We from the mother country will watch your progress in the sure knowledge that those things which have bound us together in the past will continue to form close and lasting links in the future.

'I would like to extend my personal congratulations to the first President of the Republic of Australia, and to express the hope that this day signals the start of a bright and prosperous new era for you all.' He sat down, to loud applause.

The usual royal twaddle, was Mike's first reaction. Meaningless words strung together by some nameless hack, chain-smoking in a back room of the Palace. But almost immediately he dismissed the thought as ungenerous. He's probably a decent enough man, born to a life he didn't ask for or want, trying to fill a difficult role to the best of his abilities. When his turn finally comes to take over from his mother, my hunch is he'll make a much better king than a lot of people now think.

The Prime Minister made a brief speech, thanking His Royal Highness for his gracious remarks. And then Noelene stepped forward to take the Oath of Office administered by the Chief Justice.

I, Noelene Jones, do swear that I will faithfully fulfil the role of President of the Republic of Australia according to the laws and usages of the Commonwealth, without fear or favour, affection or ill will, to the best of my ability.
So help me God.

A choir of schoolchildren sang *Advance Australia Fair*, and Noelene was presented with a bouquet of wildflowers. Someone in the crowd called out 'Hip hip hooray' and the cry was taken up and echoed outside. For a brief moment Prince Charles looked as though he was about to kiss her on both cheeks, continental-style, but at the last moment seemed to change his mind. Instead he shook her hand with murmured words of congratulation.

It was now the new president's turn to make a speech, and she kept it brief and to the point. She emphasised that her role was largely symbolic, and she would have no part to play in everyday politics. At the same time she did not plan to be just an empty figurehead.

'I am very conscious that this is a country made up of people from many different backgrounds in race, religion and culture. But although we may be different, we are united in a common purpose – dignity, justice and freedom for all.

'Those are the principles on which this republic has been established, and I intend to do everything within my power to make sure they are upheld. Thank you, my fellow Australians, for putting your faith in me. I give you my promise I will not let you down.'

There was a standing ovation, and cheers could be heard from outside Parliament House. As Noelene made her exit from the official dais past the crowded press group, she gave Mike a brief fleeting smile.

She'll make a good president, he thought. She'll fill the role with dignity and distinction. It's going to be all right.

53

Lily had left her small son sleeping in his cot, and was crossing the road to post a letter when the car hit her. It was coming around a corner. It didn't see her and she wasn't used to motor vehicles on a country road.

She never had a chance.

The driver got out and rushed to the limp figure of the woman lying on the road. Her eyes were wide open, staring vacantly into space, and her face had a startled look as if still trying to work out what had happened.

Blood trickled from a corner of her mouth. But it was too late to do anything for her. Lily was dead.

54

Mike's documentary had been well received, topping the ratings for the week. It included footage of Noelene exploring the old house in the Adelaide hills, but there was no mention of Lily or her letter. Noelene had offered him a job on her personal staff but Mike turned it down, saying 'it would destroy a beautiful friendship'. She understood perfectly.

In the meantime, life went on much as usual. She had sorted out which of her things to put into storage and which to move to Canberra. With the help of a secretary, she had answered most of the messages of goodwill that had flowed from the inauguration.

A start had been made on the official biography. There had been one more sitting for each of the two artists. The packers had begun to move in.

Prince Charles was now back in London, having planted a tree grown from the acorn of an English oak ('symbolic of the strong ties between our two countries'). The spade that the royal hands had used to dig the hole was now behind a glass case in Parliament House.

Messages poured in from all parts of the world including one from the president of the United States.

'Congratulations and best wishes for the continuing close

and friendly alliance between our two countries,' it said. 'I look forward to us working together towards a future world that is both peaceful and prosperous.'

Now Noelene's first priority was a 'getting to know you' visit to all States and Territories. The Prime Minister felt particularly pleased that the idea had been his and not that of his breakfast cabinet.

He was anxious to promote the new Head of State as the People's President and not just some political stooge of his government. Noelene put in a special request for South Australia to be the first State she visited, as it would tie in with a long-standing engagement to open a new arts centre in Adelaide. The request was granted.

On previous trips Noelene had always booked into a hotel, but now protocol required she stay at Government House. The white building on the corner of North Terrace and King William Road was familiar to her, as she'd been to official receptions there during her musical career. But this time it would be different.

Shortly after the referendum that had made Australia a republic, the government announced it recommended three choices on the future role of State governors: (1) retain both the post and name, but drop its former role as personal representative of the reigning monarch; (2) retain the post but change the name; and (3) abolish it altogether.

South Australia was the first cab off the rank. It decided to continue with the title of Governor, with the duties to be largely ceremonial. Government House would remain the official residence and would not be restyled, as it was felt the name had historical significance. Most of the other States followed South Australia's lead, with Western Australia still to decide its Governor's future.

The changeover from monarchy to republic had been

achieved seamlessly and painlessly. Most people hardly noticed the difference.

By the third week of November Noelene had vacated her Sydney apartment and was settling in to her new life in Canberra. And the move had been less traumatic than she'd feared. Charlie's desk was happily in its new place in her study, along with her books and personal files. The foxes and hounds and the English gardens had gone from the bedroom walls, replaced with modern prints. The Dresden shepherdess had moved house with the nice lady.

Noelene had kept on all the domestic staff, and Mags was more than happy to carry on as assistant to the new president. A young man by the name of Barry Drinkwater, highly recommended by the PM's department, had been appointed to handle the press. He had a nice wacky sense of humour and they got along well together.

Now Noelene was ready for the first stage of her long tour around Australia. In her luggage when she boarded the plane to Adelaide was Lily's little tin box.

Noelene was greeted warmly on her arrival at Government House, and ushered to her suite. As there would be no official functions until tomorrow, the Governor suggested a quiet relaxed dinner with just himself and his wife, leaving the rest of her evening free.

'The gardens are looking particularly beautiful right now,'

he said. 'I can recommend a walk through them while there's still some light. Of course, if you'd prefer to retire early, that's perfectly all right. Just let us know what you'd like to do.'

Noelene thanked him for his suggestion, and took a stroll in the gardens after dinner. He was right, they were beautiful. Tall conifers. Lawns as immaculate and smooth as a bowling green. She caught the heady perfume of roses, mixed with lavender and jasmine.

A gardener working on a flower border tipped his hat as she passed. Did he know who she was? Or was it just a polite gesture to an anonymous visitor?

Later still at the Governor's invitation she shared a quiet nightcap in their private sitting room. They were a charming and intelligent couple, and she liked them. He had been Vice-Chancellor of Adelaide University before his appointment, and his wife was a distinguished academic in her own right. She'd gained her doctorate with a history of women in South Australia, later published as a book: *The Politics of Being Female*. 'Did you know we were the first in the world to give women the vote?' she asked. Noelene made a mental note to make reading it a priority when she returned to Sydney.

'We feel very honoured you chose to come here as the first stop of your tour,' said the Governor. 'If we can be of any assistance to you, please don't hesitate to let us know. We are at your service.'

At your service? Was this the kind of officialese she'd have to get used to from now on? But just as quickly she dismissed the thought as mean-spirited. She was sure that behind the words was a genuinely warm and hospitable man who, like her, was trying to adjust to his new role in public life.

'Please look on this as your home while you're here. We

trust your stay with us will be a happy one.'

'I'm sure it will,' said Noelene.

'Would you like me to walk you to your room?' It was the Governor's wife speaking. 'It's just along the corridor from us.'

She had the faintest of accents, which made Noelene think she could have been born in another country. Her name was Antoinette. French, perhaps?

'Thanks, but I'm sure I can find my way,' said Noelene.

After a short briefing on tomorrow's official functions, Noelene excused herself and headed for her room. As she walked along the corridor, hung with framed landscapes and portraits of past governors, a strange thing happened.

The air had been warm and humid, clammy to the point of being uncomfortable. Suddenly without any warning there was a chill, and a force of energy like an electricity charge seemed to pulse through her. It was so strong it was almost tangible; she felt if she reached out her hand she could touch it. Yet there was nothing to touch. Nothing to see. But the feeling persisted.

Someone else was walking with her along that corridor. She caught the heady perfume of a rose. But there were no flowers in sight.

It was at this moment she realised she was working side by side with Lily.

55

Noelene knew what she had to do and she did it quickly.

The winding road to the Hills. The walk down the same path her grandmother had walked long ago. A key in the rusty lock, and the front door swinging open. And there it was, that gaping hole in the wall that had hidden Lily's secret all these years.

Noelene carefully replaced the old tin box in the cavity and hid it once more with the loose bricks. Some time later she would tell the builders to plaster over it. But for today it would be safe in its resting place – the final chapter in a story that would never be told.

'*Whoever he was who loved you ... whatever the truth ... may you now both rest in peace*,' she whispered.

Noelene stood for a long moment thinking of the young woman who had given birth to a lovechild, and in so doing had also given life to herself. She thought of the links between mother and son, father and daughter. The continuity of being. And suddenly the room no longer felt empty.

'Goodbye Lily,' said the first president, and walked out of the house.

56

December 31, 2016

The Lodge, Canberra

The Prime Minister was feeling in a particularly jovial mood as he breakfasted with his wife on the last day of the last month of the year. It had been a good year, one of change and innovation, the opening of a new chapter in the country's history. The country was now a republic with an Australian as Head of State.

The portraits of the Queen hanging on countless walls, relics of another era, had gone. The Union Jack had gone. *God Save the Queen* had gone. The monarchists hadn't completely disappeared, but had either gone underground or had the good sense to stay silent.

He'd kept a cool head, chosen a candidate who seemed to make everyone happy, and emerged a clear winner. Someone had to make the tough decisions; someone had to bite the bullet. And he'd done it all. Without fear or favour, without political pressure. Although he had an audience of only one, he decided a short speech was called for.

'I don't mind admitting it took a bit of doing to get us there. The plebiscite followed by the referendum. The inclusion of

States and Territories in the selection process. Inviting public nominations for a people's choice – now that was a stroke of sheer genius!

'The ballot boxes in the post offices. The committees. Yes, the whole business was a masterpiece of planning, if I do say so myself. Mind you, it didn't come without cost. That's the heavy burden of being a prime minister. I don't mind admitting there've been nights when I've stayed awake, wondering if I was going along the right path. But we got there. By God, we finally got there.

'As that bloke who walked on the moon put it: "One small step for man, one giant leap for mankind."'

'Womankind.'

The PM frowned but continued.

'By a combination of the democratic process and some astute decision-making on the part of yours truly, we now have a president of whom this country can be justly proud. A worthy occupant of this high office.'

'Next time just stick a pin in a piece of paper.'

She always had the last word.

Epilogue

*So the country prospered and grew,
as the woman who might have
been queen took her place as the
chosen head of her people.
And lived happily ever after.*